The Shortest Way Home

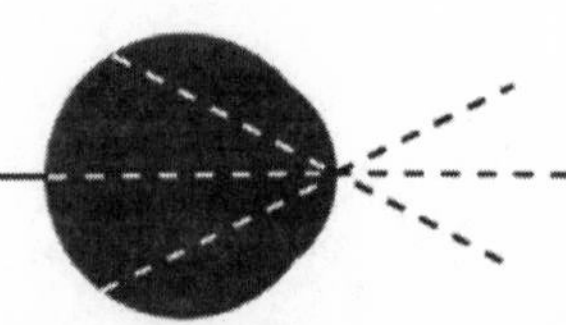

The Shortest Way Home

MIRIAM PARKER

CENTER POINT LARGE PRINT
THORNDIKE, MAINE

This Center Point Large Print edition
is published in the year 2019 by arrangement with
Dutton, an imprint of Penguin Publishing Group,
a division of Penguin Random House LLC.

The text of this Large Print edition is unabridged.
In other aspects, this book may vary
from the original edition.
Printed in the United States of America
on permanent paper.
Set in 16-point Times New Roman type.

ISBN: 978-1-64358-058-6

Library of Congress Cataloging-in-Publication Data

Names: Parker, Miriam (Miriam Rebecca), author.
Title: The shortest way home / Miriam Parker.
Description: Center Point Large Print edition. | Center Point Large Print : Thorndike, Maine, 2019.
Identifiers: LCCN 2018046102 | ISBN 9781643580586 (hardcover : alk. paper)
Subjects: LCSH: Women graduate students—Fiction. | Wineries—Fiction. | Man-woman relationships—Fiction. | Self-actualization (Psychology) in women—Fiction. | Sonoma (Calif.)— Fiction. | Psychological fiction. | Large type books.
Classification: LCC PS3616.A74546 S56 2019 | DDC 813/.6—dc23
LC record available at https://lccn.loc.gov/2018046102

For my parents,
who have always believed in me

Think you're escaping and run into yourself.
Longest way round is the shortest way home.

—James Joyce, *Ulysses*

I choose me.

—Kelly Taylor, *Beverly Hills 90210*

Part I

APPETIZER

Grilled peach and mint salad, served over a bed of cilantro pesto

PAIRING

Highway 12 Sauvignon Blanc 2015
(Sonoma, California)
Crisp aromas of green apple, pear, and melon

Chapter 1

I would have never predicted that a winery could change my life. But when I walked into the empty tasting room at Bellosguardo on the first weekend in May of my thirtieth year, a feeling came over me. The kind you get when you taste a new food for the first time and you know it will be your favorite, or when you see a guy across the bookstore and you know he'll be your new boyfriend. It was like inspiration. Never before had an empty room made me feel like I belonged in it, but this room had that quality.

The tasting room, whitewashed stucco with exposed beams, was infused with the soothing, earthy smell of a room that had seen a lot. A room that knew things. A huge brick fireplace was embedded in the wall on one side and a floor-to-ceiling diamond-shaped wine rack filled the back of the room. An ornate oak bar was to the right, with nobody behind it, but two glasses were placed right in the middle, an open bottle of wine with a black label on it between them. A perfect photo. A brown-and-white Cavalier King Charles spaniel lounged in a patch of light from a window in the back corner. The dog lifted his head slightly to acknowledge me and I nodded in his direction. He lazily put his head back on the floor, thumped his tail a few times, and closed his eyes. Clearly, he approved of me.

My boyfriend, Ethan, and I had spent the day driving up from San Francisco to Sonoma, taking more than three hours to do a one-hour drive. We had wound around the twists and turns of Highway 1, stopping to get out and appreciate the view based on Ethan's pretrip evaluation of the best lookout spots on our route—we held hands, gritted our teeth, and dipped our toes into the cold water of Muir Beach and gasped at the view from the cliffs in Point Reyes. My iPhone photographs didn't come out nearly as good as Ethan's DSLR photos, but I took the time to imprint the vista on my brain. In the age of Instagram and Snapchat, I think a memory is the most private thing. When things are important, I make a point of closing my eyes and taking a mental photo.

We were about to go back to New York to start our real lives, leaving the beauty of the Pacific coast behind us. We were both in California for graduate school at Berkeley's Haas School and we were still awed by its resplendence—on days that weren't foggy (of course). We lived for the fog-free days. It seemed almost criminal to be returning to the East Coast after just two years in the West. But jobs beckoned.

Our last stand would be a weekend in wine country. We had arrived in Sonoma at around eleven and had dropped our bags at the front desk of the El Dorado Hotel. Our room wasn't ready yet, so we were advised to walk to Bellosguardo. "It's Sonoma's oldest and most beautiful winery," the woman behind the desk wearing a name tag that read BETTY had told us. She drew us a map of the town and showed us how to get there. "And when you've worked up an appetite, come back here and go to the Girl and the Fig across the street. Get the lavender crème brûlée no matter how full you are. It's the best." The winery hadn't been on Ethan's carefully planned itinerary (although the restaurant had). He preferred to plan trips down to the hour, with attractions, restaurants, and hotels that he carefully selected based on an amalgam of travel websites and message boards he visited. But, since we had arrived an hour early, his itinerary hadn't kicked in yet.

"It sounds amazing," I said.

Ethan silently acquiesced to the change in plan, although I could tell that he was irritated. But he smiled and took my hand, and we walked together following the hand-drawn map rather than the blue dot on our iPhones.

"I feel so lucky to be here with you," he said.

I felt lucky to be with him, or at the very least I felt lucky to be with anyone after many years as a single woman in New York City. Plus, it felt good to be away from the pressure cooker of the past few months of school. The competition for jobs had been fierce and many of my friendships had frayed, especially with my best friend, Tyra. We'd both interned at Goldman the summer before and I had beat her out for the job in Global Investment Research in New York. It was a perfect job for me because it was focused more on research and writing than on straight data analysis. Math hadn't always been my strong suit, although I had made it through accounting and macroeconomics relatively unscathed. Tyra had been offered the same job in Singapore, which she had grudgingly accepted. But I knew she still didn't think it was fair. "I'm worried about graduation. Packing. Moving back. I'm going to miss California. And I still feel bad about Tyra."

"Two days off. Away from all of that garbage," he said. "You'll be fine. You have plenty of time to pack, and if you don't, you'll just hire someone to do it. You're going to be rich soon."

"I don't know," I said, unconvinced.

I loved Ethan, but he and I were pretty different. His pragmatic side both attracted and irritated me. Since I didn't think everything through as much as he did, we often butted horns. I wanted to do things right away; he wanted to consider them deeply for extended periods of time. He made me feel like my neuroticness was a mind-set I could stop indulging in, rather than a character trait. Take our respective travel styles—he was a planner; I liked to ask the locals what to do.

We strolled through beautiful downtown Sonoma, past brightly painted bungalows and lush trees. "Those people have an entire citrus salad in their front yard," Ethan pointed out as we passed a blue-and-pink house with a hammock strung between two trees and a real parrot sitting on the porch rail. "Another glass of wine?" the parrot yelled at us, making me smile. Of course parrots in Sonoma knew to ask for glasses of wine rather than crackers. We turned onto Old Winery Road and the oak trees exploded around us. They were tall and shaded the entire street. The sidewalks were littered with acorn shells and we crunched along, going over the points that we'd need to address in our ethics final. It was an essay test that we assumed would present some sort of ethical business dilemma (products made in sweatshops? carbon offsets? workplace integrity outside of the office?) and that we would take two hours to solve in essay form. We worked well together on the business school projects that we overlapped on: He was the practical one; I brought the creative energy.

We crossed a little bridge over a delightful stream and walked into the parking lot of Bellosguardo, a large stone building embedded into the side of a hill. It was covered in ivy, and a wooden door peeked out, inviting me inside. I left Ethan in the parking lot examining the cornerstone and the foundation. He was a recovering civil engineer and still felt obligated to evaluate the structural integrity of old buildings as he encountered them. I pulled open the huge wooden door to enter the tasting room. I couldn't help but notice that next to the door was a small FOR RENT BY OWNER sign. But I almost forgot about it after I entered the tasting room—the whitewashed walls, the stone fireplace, the beams, the earthy smell. I had found my heaven.

As I stood in the middle of the room, awe-struck, a tall, slim young man walked through a doorway behind the bar and gestured toward the wineglasses on the bar and the leather-topped stool right in front of it. His blond-streaked hair was long on top but a little spiky, and he had a hint of a beard growing—not like he really wanted to grow a beard, but that he was just lazy enough to let things get to this point. The room was dark, aside from the dog's small patch of sun, and cool. Natural air-conditioning, I assumed, provided by stone and the hill behind.

"Good morning," he said warmly, pushing a piece of paper across the bar. "Here's what we're tasting today." I approached and examined the list. It had a shorter menu on one side featuring more recent vintages and a longer list on the other with a variety of years and wine names. "Would you like to do the reserve tasting or the standard tasting? The reserve includes our Syrah

Port, which I think is one of the most unique wines being made in America. It also includes a 2012 Pinot Noir that won the Double Gold medal at the Sonoma County Harvest Fair. The Pinot is only available here at the vineyard."

Ethan and I had planned to visit three or four wineries during the course of the day, most of which involved driving. The reserve list here included twelve wines, including the dessert wine, and doing it meant we were committing to this place for the first half of the day, but I already knew that I didn't want to leave here so quickly. I settled myself on the barstool. As I did, the dog stood up, yawned, did a yoga stretch, making himself long and lean, and trotted to greet me. He approached the barstool, stood on his back legs, and rested his front paws on my leg, his tongue hanging out a little, which made it seem like he was smiling, although it also might have meant that he didn't have a lot of teeth. He licked my bare leg and I patted his head. The dog let out a contented sigh and stayed standing on his back legs, tail wagging as I scratched behind his ears. "The reserve, please," I said, still scratching. "He's a good sales dog."

The bartender smiled. "We've trained him well. You won't be sorry about the reserve tasting. We make some of the best wines in California. And I'm not just saying that because I grew up here."

"You grew up in California?"

"In this very winery," he said, gesturing to the room.

"That's amazing," I exclaimed. "What a cool childhood."

He shrugged and opened the first bottle. "It's the only one I know. Ready?"

"My boyfriend is on his way as well. He's just outside looking at the building. I can't imagine what's taking him so long."

"He probably met my dad," he said. "He loves to talk history. The place was founded in the 1870s, but was basically abandoned during Prohibition. Everett's father revived the vines and started making wine again. We've only recently reopened this space. Up until then, we just sold to local restaurants, a few stores in the area. My mom would do the deliveries and the bookkeeping."

"That's a lot of work," I said.

"She still handles most of the business stuff around here. My dad handles the wine making. Anyway, since we opened the tasting room and started a wine club, things are getting better. We're up to three thousand cases per year."

"Is that a lot?" I asked.

"It's okay, but it could be better. The Francis Ford Coppola Winery makes ten thousand a day."

"That's insane," I said.

"Completely," he said, and flashed me a little grin.

He poured a hearty taste of white wine into the glass in front of me. Tiny bubbles appeared clear against the pale lemon of the wine. "It's beautiful," I said, swirling the glass of citrusy sparkle before sipping. It felt bright, effervescent. "Amazing. It tastes like . . . I don't know, like really good ginger ale or something. I can't believe people aren't lining up outside your door."

He suppressed his laugh at my comparison of the sparkling wine to ginger ale. I remembered from our wine-tasting class at school that you were supposed to remark upon what you tasted. The instructor recommended that we taste things like "leather" or "currant" in red wines, but I didn't know what leather tasted like. I'm just a girl from Iowa; I didn't know the first thing about how to describe wine, and in that class every time I tried to say something, someone snorted. But I knew I should say something and I did know what ginger ale tasted like and it was delicious. "We're not as exciting as some of the other places around here, but we do have good wines, if I do say so myself."

"This place should be overflowing," I said.

"What could we do?" he said.

"Lots," I said.

"I wouldn't even know where to begin," he said.

My hands otherwise engaged with a wineglass,

the dog returned to all four feet and settled under my seat. He emitted a contented sigh.

"Oh, Tannin," the bartender said. "So dramatic."

"Tannin? That's a good name for a winery dog."

"He has the best life in the world."

"I'm jealous," I said.

"Me too," he said, his eyes twinkling.

A few months earlier, we had come up to Sonoma with a group of friends from school, in the midst of all the job drama, and ended up in a tasting room that had felt like Disney World—everyone assigned a tasting time in fifteen-minute increments using little register receipts like you were at a deli. While you waited for your appointed time, they screened a video about the history of the winery—founded in 2008—and after you were done with your fifteen-minute tasting, you exited through a gift shop selling wine and grape-themed hand towels and kitchen aprons and wall hangings with sayings like I COOK WITH WINE. SOMETIMES I EVEN ADD IT TO THE FOOD. I have a few rules about home décor—they include no "clever" signs, no faux vintage posters, no photo collages, no figurine collections, no themed rooms. Ethan often teased me about my taste, although I was pretty sure he secretly supported my rules in his heart.

Tyra, of course, bought one just to make me mad and put it up on the front of her apartment door (across the hall from ours). It read, GIVE ME COFFEE TO CHANGE THE THINGS I CAN. GIVE ME WINE TO ACCEPT THE THINGS I CAN'T. I took to putting Post-it notes on the sign to slowly cover it up, square by square, as I left the apartment each day. In the evening, I would return home to find one or more of the Post-its removed and placed on my door with yet another wine platitude written in Sharpie. It was like a subtle, maddening culture war that got more aggressive as our friendship shifted.

Aside from both of us not having a lot of clever signage, Ethan's and my New York experiences could not have been more different. Ethan had grown up on Park Avenue and I had lived in a studio apartment in Ditmas Park. He had grown up with a cook, a housekeeper, and a private bath with marble shower that could turn into a steam room. (But the part I found most shocking about his childhood home was the interior staircase. Who has a staircase *in* an apartment?) My Ditmas kitchen was so small that it didn't have a drawer for silverware, and my refrigerator was only slightly bigger than the one I had had in my dorm room in college. There was enough room in the internal freezer for one pint of ice cream, but only if I kept the thing defrosted. Often the frost encroached so much that there was room to freeze only a Snickers bar, which I kept in there just to prove that I could have dessert in my own apartment, even if it was paltry. Even after college Ethan had lived in his parents' apartment, because why not? They were more often than not in their houses in Southampton or Palm Beach. In Berkeley, we all lived in graduate student housing. Small, efficient apartments with slightly rickety kitchens and laminate floors that had seen better days. But for me, my place, which had an actual bedroom, not to mention a full-size refrigerator and a dishwasher, felt palatial. And something about the peeling kitchen linoleum and particleboard cabinets had reminded me of my youth in Iowa, in a small, unremarkable house. For Ethan, graduate school housing was a major step down. But he put up with it for the sake of appearances. Or he liked being down with the hoi polloi; I could never quite tell.

"This place is different," I said to the adorable spiky-haired bartender. "From the other places around here . . ."

"It isn't as popular with tourists," he said.

"Maybe tourists are stupid," I said.

"There have to be a few smart ones," he said. "Like you."

I blushed, and instead of saying anything that I would regret, I just smiled. Sometimes I said every word that came into my brain, which generally got me in trouble. So, I decided just to keep quiet and swirl the wine in front of me. The wine-tasting class we'd been required to attend during business school orientation had taught us to swirl, sniff, and then taste when trying wine. So, in lieu of something witty to say, I swirled. Sniffed and sipped. And smiled.

"I really do love the wine," I finally eked out, wondering, *Where the hell is Ethan?* If he didn't get in here fast, I would continue to flirt. This is not to say that I was very good at flirting. When I lived in New York, I had met guys mostly in bars, and my main mating technique was to figure out what they were interested in and argue with them about it. I felt strangely proud of the time that I spent hours arguing about recycling with a solar panel company vice president. We had dated for a few weeks as a result. It wasn't that I couldn't be charming; I just wasn't great at batting my eyes and saying, "Oh, you're interesting." Because most of them weren't. I preferred a challenge. My first encounter with Ethan was absolutely a challenge—we almost came to blows in the Berkeley bookstore. But nothing about the current situation indicated that getting in a fight was necessary or even possible. So I had to resort to my (minimal) feminine charms.

"Thanks," he said, smiling back.

I felt a little flushed from the wine and could feel little beads of sweat forming on the insides of my elbows and my cheeks warming. *Be calm,* I told myself. *Be cool.*

"Do you help make the wine? Help your dad, I mean."

"I know the basics," he said. "But mostly my dad makes it. And Felipe. He's our new expert winemaker from Chile. He's making things even better. But I'm moving to New York. To get an MFA in screenwriting."

"You want to run away from here?" I asked, incredulous. *You have a boyfriend,* I told myself, trying to relax the smile out of my cheeks. *A nice, stable, responsible boyfriend named Ethan.* "I don't get it," I said. "It's the most beautiful place on earth. Have you been to New York? It's gross. From mysterious puddles even on the sunniest days to stinky subway platforms and aggressive pigeons."

"I've lived here my whole life. Except when I went to LA for college. But LA's not real. And this place doesn't really feel real either. I want to see what the rest of the world is like. Even if it is, to use your word, gross."

I guessed that was a good enough excuse. I had wanted to get the hell out of Iowa when I was growing up there. But there wasn't any possibility of a future for me there, and there wasn't any reason to stay other than a few friends. If Iowa had been a place that other people wanted to visit and I had a skill like wine making, I couldn't imagine leaving. On the other hand, I had never felt settled anywhere I lived. When I was growing up in Iowa I dreamt of a glamorous life in New York City, but when I finally got to New York I found it exhausting, dirty, and remarkably unglamorous. I couldn't believe how far I had to live from work in order to pay the rent on my thirty-five-thousand-dollar-a-year assistant salary and how small my apartment was, even with an hour-plus commute. I hated how my feet were black at the end of a summer day wearing open-toed shoes just because of the essential filth of the city. And it was depressing that groceries were so expensive that it made more sense to eat takeout. After a year of feeling sad, dirty, and overwhelmed, I set my sights on business school and California. I wanted the life I saw in the pages of the magazines I obsessively read at the library when I was a child—*Town & Country*, *Architectural Digest*, and the back pages of the *New York Times Magazine*, which advertised the luxury homes and estates. I devoured those descriptions as a little girl and dreamt about the homes. I wondered: *What would it be like to live in one? How would I decorate it? Would I sleep in the same bedroom every night or rotate?* I still don't know why I wanted a life like the ones I saw in magazines. Maybe it was because my life felt so imperfect, I never felt like I belonged there.

I wanted to ask the bartender more questions: about his childhood in Sonoma, about his screenwriting, about how he got the stubble on his face to be just that length and not any longer. But as he poured the second taste, Ethan and an older man I assumed was the bartender's father walked into the room. The father's baritone laugh filled the large space and the dog popped up from under my stool and rushed to greet him. Tannin gave an excited bark and threw himself against the father's legs, his tongue coming wildly out of his mouth like a snake. The man picked up the dog. "Did you miss me, Tanny?" he asked. The dog licked his face and let out a squeaky bark. "I missed you too." He put the dog under his arm and turned to Ethan. "This is Tannin. He really runs this place."

Ethan patted the dog's head but pulled back when the dog tried to lick his fingers.

"Ethan!" I said, hopping off of my stool to give him a kiss on the cheek. "There you are! I'm one taste ahead of you. You have to catch up."

"Thanks for the history lesson, Everett," he said, shaking the hand that wasn't holding the dog. Then he put his hand on the small of my back.

"Thanks for coming to Bellosguardo. Enjoy your tasting. William, make sure to sneak that sparkling rosé into their flight. I think Ethan's wife will like that one." Everett put the dog on the ground and the two of them headed out the front door, the dog trotting behind like an adoring fan.

William, I thought. *That's a good name.*

"We're not married," Ethan said.

I bristled. I had an inkling that Ethan was going to propose to me this weekend, which I felt both excited and ambivalent about. I wasn't sure if we were ready, but who doesn't want to be asked?

"My dad loves that dog more than he loves humans," William said, ignoring the tension and the marriage comment.

"And the dog loves him right back," I said.

"Licks too much," Ethan said. He approached the bar and threw back the pour of wine like a shot of tequila, still standing, without even tasting it. William poured another white.

"We're moving to New York too," I said. "Although I wouldn't if I lived here." Ethan glared at me.

"What are you two doing there?" William asked. His smile sparkled and he looked directly into my eyes. My stomach felt at attention.

I took Ethan's hand, as if I needed to prove that we were together, even though at this very moment, I wished I could snap my fingers and make him disappear. "Jobs. We're at business school at Berkeley. Well, we were. We're about to graduate. I have a boring old job in New York.

Ethan is more ambitious than me and is starting a company."

"I'm not more ambitious," he said, staring at his glass and dropping my hand. "You have an amazing job in New York. One that everyone wants. It's the type of job people go to business school to get."

"It's okay," I said. All of a sudden, even though I had been so proud of getting the job at Goldman, at beating out my classmates for the coveted seat in New York, now I was embarrassed by it. I had come to terms with moving back to New York because Ethan wanted to, and also because it was prestigious. But my true ambivalence about the city was now coming through.

"We could use some business expertise here," William said. "My dad is great at making wine, but not at making money."

I swirled, sniffed, and tasted the second white. It was a bit sweeter, but still crisp. Maybe I tasted peaches? "He should be selling millions of bottles. What do you think, Ethan?"

Ethan carelessly threw back this taste as well. He was acting differently than he had on our drive up and walk over. He had been fun this morning, playing around with the camera during our drive, teasing me about how I would need to wear a suit every day to work instead of my vintage-inspired flowy grad school wardrobe, which he called "faux boho." Now he was cranky and rude. Maybe he was allergic to ivy?

I couldn't help but think about the local marketing workshop that I'd been to right before the semester ended—focusing on events and social media. "You should have so much fun here this summer," I said. "You could have a weekly music event with a local jazz band set up over in that corner." I pointed to the corner where the dog had been sitting when I walked in. "Call it something like Drink and Dance. Just get the local inn owners to promote it, like the El Dorado folks; they sent us here today. And tell some local residents. Maybe give locals free admission and charge the tourists or something. I would come to that, wouldn't you, Ethan?"

He shrugged. "Sure, if you wanted to go."

"That's a good idea," William said. "I'll tell my dad."

"And maybe you could do weekly or monthly tastings of special bottles—like your wine that wins awards," I said. "And wine-tasting classes. We took one of those at orientation. Maybe you could even go down to Berkeley and Stanford and run them."

"Sorry," Ethan said, putting his hand over my mouth the way he did when I was talking too much. Normally, it was playful, but today it felt aggressive. "She's in business school mode."

"No," William said, "I think it's cool. I mean,

I won't be here, but maybe my mom could do it. Although her hands are full—"

"And the dog! You could have a Dog and Wine Day! Oh, and you can give him an Instagram feed. Post his photos."

"Seriously, Hannah," Ethan said. "That's enough."

"What's gotten into you?" I whispered as William went to get the bottle of sparkling rosé. "You're *so* cranky."

"I just have a weird feeling about this place," he said.

"Well, I think it's beautiful," I retaliated. And it was. It looked like something straight out of one of the magazines I had loved as a kid. The whitewashed stucco walls, the high ceilings, the leather couches. I had a feeling that this room was going to be important to me. I had never lived anywhere beautiful before—not in Iowa, not in New York, not in Berkeley. But I had always craved it.

Ethan, on the other hand, wanted to get out of there. He stood up when we got to the light reds. "We've got to go," he said.

"But . . . ," I said.

"We have a lunch reservation," he said.

"We do?" I asked.

"It's on our itinerary. Sorry, man."

"But I want to buy some wine," I said, hating it when he called me "man."

"We have to go," he said, turning toward the door.

I shrugged my shoulders at William and gave him a mournful look. I didn't want to leave. There was something about this place. It felt like home.

Chapter 2

On the way back to town, I started chewing on the cuticles of my free hand. A nervous habit.

"You're doing it," Ethan said. He took my hand; usually that was a gentle gesture, but now it felt antagonistic. To be fair, my cuticle chewing drove Ethan crazy. I kept my hand in his for a few minutes, to appease him and also to quiet my mind, which was reeling.

"I know," I said.

"I'm just trying—"

"I know!"

"Hannah."

I gritted my teeth and walked in silence for a few minutes.

"Ugh," I said. "I'm starving."

"We might as well have lunch," he said. "We're a little late for our reservation, but I'm sure they'll seat us." It was after two P.M. We were both hungry. Maybe that was it.

By the time we got to the restaurant, we were not really speaking. And before they could offer us a table, Ethan sat at the bar. He always did that when we were fighting. He preferred having serious conversations at bars rather than across tables. Maybe because it seemed less confrontational.

A kind older bartender with gray hair to his shoulders came over to greet us.

"I'm Reed," he said. "I'll be at your service today." He gave us wet lavender-scented towels for our hands and put a big bowl of rolls in front of us.

"Hi, Reed," I said, grabbing a roll from the basket. It was already in my mouth when I thanked him.

"Nice to meet you," he said. "How do you like Sonoma?"

"We just had a wine tasting at Bellosguardo," I said, well into my second roll. "It was beautiful and the wine was perfect."

"So you're ready for some sustenance," he said. He presented us with menus. "I spent thirty years toiling away for the Chicago Public Schools, living in that frozen town, teaching children, and every night before I went to sleep, I told myself that one day I'd live in wine country and I would never use a snow shovel again. I used to come out here every summer and help out on farms and in restaurants. I even managed to buy a little piece of land that I would set up camp on for the summer. Solar shower and everything. Now I have a little cottage on that land that I built with my own two hands and I can walk to work. And that snow shovel? I turned it into a piece of art that hangs over my mantelpiece. Whenever I feel a little sad, I look at that shovel and think, 'I'm living the dream.' This is a special place; only a certain kind of person can live here."

"What does that mean?" Ethan asked.

"You know, it's just . . ." He gestured to the room. "It takes a certain kind of person." Reed winked at me.

"I'm jealous that you get to live here," I said. Ethan shot me a look.

We both glanced at the menu. I was too hungry to really make decisions. I was pretty sure Ethan had predecided what he was going to order based on TripAdvisor recommendations, but I hadn't.

"Reed," I said, "I'm going to need your help. What's your favorite thing on the menu?"

"Well, I'm sure you've heard about the crème brûlée, but my favorite thing right now is the pasta in brown butter sauce. The menu changes every week, based on what's available seasonally, but this is pretty special."

"Sold," I said. I looked at Ethan. "Do you want to share the pasta and something else? Maybe the duck breast?" Ethan hated sharing with me, but I always asked.

This time, he didn't even have the courtesy to say no. He just said, "I'll have the steak frites, medium well."

"Medium well? Are you sure?" Reed asked.

"Medium well," Ethan said.

Reed nodded and recorded the order. He then brought us each a glass of Pinot Noir and a bottle of water. We clinked glasses in silence. I wondered what Reed was thinking about us. It was a game that we played when we were in restaurants that I liked to call Unhappy Couple. We would judge each couple in the restaurant based on how they interacted with each other, if they smiled, if they talked (so many people didn't even talk to each other in restaurants, I wondered why they went out at all), if he stood up when she went to the bathroom or returned. If they were courteous to the waitstaff. It made us feel like our relationship was the good one. Now, all of a sudden, we were the bickering couple in the restaurant. If Reed played Unhappy Couple in his mind, he had a lot of material. Certainly, he was judging Ethan's steak order. Waiters always did.

Perhaps as a peace offering, perhaps as a house specialty, he brought us a dish of olives, the kind that melt in your mouth. I had never had olives this divine before. We sipped our wine in silence and devoured the olives. We each left a little pile of pits in our napkin.

"These olives are incredible," I said.

"Locally grown, in my backyard, in fact," Reed said.

"I wouldn't have it any other way," I said. I could tell that I was embarrassing Ethan. He hated it when I talked to strangers. He preferred to observe rather than interact. But I liked to get to know people; maybe it was because of my midwestern roots. "It's impressive," I said to Ethan when Reed had gone to check on our lunch order.

"The olives?" Ethan asked.

"They're amazing, but that's not what I mean," I said. "Reed. He's impressive. What he did. Following his dream."

"Hannah, you can't dream all the time. Sometimes you have to be practical. He had his career and then he's doing what he wants in his retirement. He's probably got a great pension from Chicago and this job just keeps him busy."

Reed came back and placed our meals in front of us and refilled our wine. I had a taste of pasta, which was sweet and salty and perfectly al dente. Ethan focused on cutting his meat into tiny pieces but ate only one French fry.

"Mine's good," I said. "Want a taste?"

He ate another fry and didn't respond.

"I seem to have lost my appetite," I said, slamming down my fork.

"Too much bread?" he asked.

"No," I said. Ethan did know that bread was my vice. More than ice cream or candy or wine or even French fries. I loved bread—all bread—from artisanal corn bread and focaccia to Wonder Bread. Especially Wonder Bread, actually. The way you can make it into little bread balls. The way it tastes with raspberry jam. It was the one food from my childhood that made me nostalgic and that I craved. When I was little, both of my parents worked crazy-long hours, my mom as a nurse and my dad as a truck driver. When they got home, all they would do was sleep and watch game shows on television. I remember sitting in the living room with them one night at around six o'clock, watching my dad nap on the recliner and my mom nap on the couch while I flipped through my library book, hoping someone would make me dinner, finally deciding on making myself a peanut butter and honey sandwich on Wonder Bread. Of course, after everything that happened, I would be nostalgic for those lazy days. "Well, I wouldn't want to waste my whole life waiting for a dream to come true when I could seize it right now. Why not have your life be your dream?" I felt tears come to my eyes. All of a sudden, I felt so passionate. I did want my life to be my dream. "Remember that song 'Working for the Weekend'? Why not work for the week?" My life in Iowa certainly was not varied and it definitely wasn't fun. I knew that there was more out there and I went after it.

"What about other dreams?" he asked. He put his hand over mine, probably trying to remind me of the house with the yard in Bedford where we would build a huge tree house like the one we'd seen on HGTV, so the kids could have sleepovers in it; the Tribeca apartment that I had leased, sight unseen, with a portion of my signing bonus, where we would live together when we got to New York after graduation.

"Everything happens for a reason," I said.

"You know I hate that 'fate' nonsense," he said. We had an ongoing debate about the concept of fate. I'd always believed in it, which annoyed him, because he was a firm atheist. It wasn't a religious thing for me, just kind of a sense.

"Well, I like to believe it's true," I said. "Don't you think it was meant for us to meet?"

"Not right now," he said. "I feel like we have nothing in common right now."

That was a punch in the gut. I stood up. "I'm going to the bathroom. Don't eat the crème brûlée without me."

Normally, we were totally in sync. We'd be judging the other diners and making up stories about people's lives—on a regular day, we'd be inventing an entire backstory for the people at the winery, the history-obsessed dad, the son trying to escape, the overworked mother. On a regular day, we'd even be into figuring out how to fix the place. We often spent hours riffing on marketing ideas for failing businesses. We'd done it in the car on the way up: How do you help the hotel with the crooked sign and one rusty minivan in the parking lot? What draws truckers in to truck stops? Is it a mistake to have a T.J. Maxx next to a Bed Bath & Beyond in a strip mall? Is it better to start your own sandwich shop or buy a Subway franchise? It was like our business school version of I Spy. But I didn't feel like inventing stories as I made my way back to the table.

"What is going on with you?" I asked as I cracked the brûlée with the back of my spoon.

"I don't know," he said. "I started to feel worried about our future."

"Why?" I asked. "We'll be in New York together. We can show each other the places we liked when we lived there before. Before we knew each other."

"I don't know," he said. "We'll both be busy working a million hours. It won't be like grad school. And I felt something weird at that winery. Like you liked it a little too much. Besides, I know how much you hate New York."

"I don't know what you're talking about," I said. Although we both knew that he was right.

We were quiet for a minute. Up until this moment, our prospects had felt pretty secure. We were both thirty, were about to finish graduate school, were about to embark on fruitful careers. Ethan was going to start a company with his two best friends from MIT. I had this amazing opportunity at Goldman. His company would be supersuccessful. I would move up at Goldman. We could live the American dream. I could have the life I dreamt of growing up—a house from the Luxury Homes and Estates section of the *New York Times Magazine* (which I later learned was just a real estate advertising section, but I had fallen for it, it seemed editorial to me), furniture from *Town & Country*, and two children who would never, ever eat Wonder Bread, unless I decided to make a from-scratch, organic modernist take on Wonder Bread and say things like "This is what Mama used to eat when she was a little girl." It was all rolled out in front of me: the most socially acceptable life I could possibly imagine. I just needed to consent to it.

"What were the other wineries you wanted to go to?" I asked, a little half-heartedly.

He shrugged and handed his credit card to Reed. "I think I'm going to go back to the hotel to take a nap. Why don't you go without me? There was that one we passed on our way back to town that you can walk to. Ravenswood?"

I guessed he was testing me, to see what I would do. We stood up and said good-bye to Reed, and Ethan kissed me on the forehead, which felt like a more distant gesture than usual.

"I'll see you later," I said. "Besides, I think I left my wallet at the winery."

"Ugh, Hannah."

He hated when I lost or broke things, which I did with regularity.

He turned and walked back toward the hotel. I stood in front of the restaurant, watching him. Wondering if he would look back. He didn't.

Chapter 3

As I watched Ethan cross the street, I weighed my options. I could follow him, tell him I loved him, and climb into a hotel bed with him. A king-size one with really nice cool-feeling sheets on it. We could cuddle, have comfortable relationship sex, and take a shower together after. I could do that and secure my future—prove to him that I wanted him, nothing else. Along with the Ethan Katz–life checklist would come a diamond ring, a house in Bedford, a personal trainer, and two well-rounded children with knowledge of Mandarin and musical theory and who played competitive youth soccer. But all of a sudden it all felt a bit forced to me. The plan. The checklist.

I'll admit that the plan was one of the reasons I had fallen for Ethan. On our second, or maybe our third, date, he'd asked me what I wanted from life. I had said something vague about how I just wanted to be happy. Besides, I had learned from dating in New York City that one had to keep one's expectations pretty low. Even though before I moved to the city, I was sure I would have a perfect life there, events conspired to disappoint me. I had once left a hair elastic in the apartment of a guy I had been sleeping with for about two months. I wasn't even at the subway yet on my way to work the next morning, when he texted to say that I had forgotten something and did I want him to mail it to me. "It was a hair elastic!" I screamed at my phone. But it was apparently too much for him. He never called me again after that, except on a lonely Christmas Eve about a year later. I was thrilled to tell him that I was in bed with his favorite bartender.

But Ethan wasn't afraid of commitment or of plans. On that same third date, when I was wishy-washy about my plan for the next hour, no less the rest of my life, he laid it all out. He had grown up in the city, but his happiest moments had been at his aunt's home in Bedford. It was a large property with horses and dogs, a large playhouse for the kids in the yard (it sounded more like a guesthouse; it had a working refrigerator and a pantry stocked with snacks) where they had sleepovers. There was a pool table in the basement and a projection television. Ethan's cousins had played on their high school soccer and baseball teams. They had learned to ride horses and played volleyball in the pool in the summer. They were always tan and seemed untroubled to Ethan. Bedford was his happy place. He wanted a big old house like his aunt's, with land and maybe a dog or two (he wasn't sure about the horse). He planned to start a business with his best friends, who currently worked at

Google, and to sell it for millions of dollars. He wanted a wife who worked but was willing to give it up for the kids. Someone would need to facilitate all of the lessons and practices, which he didn't trust a nanny to do.

At the time, I found this plan intoxicating. It was exactly (I told myself) what I had wanted as a child—fancy and stable, with wealthy parents who were devoted to the improvement of their children. The way I was raised was pretty much the exact opposite of Ethan's plan. I grew up in a tiny town in Iowa called Winthrop that had a population of 750. My father died when I was eleven, and my mother did not handle it well. My main happy memories were walking to the town library with my brother, Drew, and reading the books we picked out there in the quiet privacy of a closet. All I wanted to do was grow up and get out of there.

But the plan was also appealing after experiencing the horror show that is dating in New York. The guy who was afraid of a single hair elastic was just the tip of the iceberg. There was the guy who was dating me as well as a rich Upper East Side widow. When the widow found out about me, she had her driver take her to my building in Ditmas Park and she waited outside for me until I got home from the gym. Then, dressed in a pale pink Chanel suit while I was in my sweaty Old Navy workout gear, she came up behind me as I was unlocking the front door and threatened me, saying that if I ever talked to her boyfriend, Sloane, again, she would come back and get me. When he tried to explain the whole story to me (in secret, on a burner phone that he kept for his affairs), I told him I never wanted to talk to him or his widow again. Besides, how could someone want to date both of us? We literally had nothing in common.

There was the nonprofit publicist, with whom I spent three hours, whose only interest was going to the gym. He wasn't even interested in the very nonprofit that he was a publicist for. Needless to say, I didn't return his calls. I'm sure he's happily married by now, with 2.5 children, to a woman younger and prettier than me.

At least the publicist had a job, though. Most of the guys I dated seemed to stay home all day to "work," although it looked to me like they were mostly tweeting about sports; they called themselves a "life coach," a "freelance writer," a "drummer." They were "creative" and "consulted" and "freelanced" (I was pretty sure all they did was look at porn), while I toiled getting coffee and making fancy manicure appointments for my boss, taking the train for an hour each way to my job as an assistant to the chief marketing officer of Tiffany's. But, of course, I chased the freelancers down for a date and ended up paying for dinner, and then they would disappear in the middle of the night. It was all so depressing. I was sick of dating broke artistic guys who could easily find a prettier, richer woman at any time, just by opening their phone and swiping right. Many of them had multiple girlfriends at the same time, all ready to straighten their hair and meet for a drink without even a phone call. Sometimes even an emoji would do it.

I wanted a real boyfriend who wanted to be with me, who wanted to talk on the phone or at least text words, not an eggplant emoji. And it would be nice if he also had a work ethic and a plan for the future. So, when I met Ethan—good guy, with rich parents, a history of working, no unhinged widow exes, and a true love of monogamy—I was sold.

And up until this very day, Ethan's plan—wedding, Bedford, babies, Mandarin classes, Suzuki violin lessons—had seemed totally reasonable, albeit a little bit staid. But now I was second-guessing everything. All of a sudden, I noticed that being with Ethan was a little boring. We never talked about anything important; we just observed other people. It was something about the winery. Everett. William. All the ideas I had for them. They were starting to eat at my brain, the way the idea of going to grad school had started to take hold in the year before I applied. I could make a difference at the winery—in a way that I wouldn't make a difference at Goldman Sachs.

Of course, I couldn't discount New York. I'd be living in Manhattan with my entrepreneur boyfriend and making a handsome salary. I'd be able to pay off my grad school loans and also buy grown-up furniture and have a personal trainer. I'd be making connections that I'd use for the rest of my life. I'd be able to go for long runs along the Hudson River, go to top restaurants and plays and museums (if I ever got out of work), and I'd be there with Ethan. A real boyfriend to have brunch with and hold hands with in the park. It was crazy to give up.

I sighed and kept walking in the direction of Bellosguardo.

The walk did wonders to clear my head. The scent of juniper wafted from the trees. If I lived here, I told myself, I would have a purple house, a brightly colored hammock hung between two trees in the backyard. I'd have a porch swing in the front and a vegetable garden. I would make salad for dinner from the leafy greens and heirloom tomatoes I harvested daily from my yard, and I would take naps in the hammock with a dog. Because there would be a dog. A dog like Tannin, ideally. I would drink wine on the porch swing while classic jazz played inside the house and wafted out through the screened windows.

I wouldn't have someone who had huge expectations of me. Something about the plan that had felt so alluring when I met Ethan was starting to feel stifling. As it became more real, it got a little bit scarier. What if I wasn't ready yet to settle down? I was only thirty. I wanted life to be fun! Was that too much to ask?

I texted my brother, Drew, my lifelong confidant, who still lived in Iowa: "What do you think about Sonoma, California?"

"Love it," he texted back.

"I was hoping you'd say that," I responded. "I'm here."

"Enjoy it," he wrote.

"I will."

I turned down Old Winery Road, which wound around toward Bellosguardo. I crossed the bridge over the creek and dropped a stick in the water like they did in *Winnie-the-Pooh*, racing over to the other side to see it pass by. On the second visit, I was able to appreciate even more that the winery was a truly impressive place. The building itself looked kind of like a wine barrel, but not in a cheesy way like the commercial winery we'd been to. More like an homage. I took a mental picture, captioning it: "The first day of the rest of my life." It was a dorky habit, one that I never admitted to doing.

There were a few cars in the parking lot now, which made me happy. I approached the heavy wooden door, accented in iron, and pulled it open. I entered to find a young couple sitting at the end of the bar drinking full glasses of red wine, a plate of cheese and crackers in front of them. Tannin sat under their stools, looking up at them, awaiting crumbs. William was not behind the bar, but an older woman with salt-and-pepper hair wearing a rumpled black linen tunic was there instead. I wondered if it was William's mother.

I sat at the bar and gave her my friendliest smile, tucking my straight brown hair behind my ear.

"Would you like to do a tasting?" she asked.

I nodded.

"Reserve?"

I nodded. I already felt like an expert.

She pulled out the paper and explained it to me in a way very similar to how William had explained it that morning. They clearly had worked on the script together.

"But, for you, I'm going to start with a wine that's not on this list. It's our new Sauvignon Blanc, which we've won several local awards for. Generally, this area is known for Chardonnay, but we have a wide variety of grapes on this property, since it was originally planted so long ago by a Hungarian count. We just discovered the heirloom Sauvignon Blanc grapes a few years ago. It took us some time to perfect it, but we're really happy with it." She poured me a taste. It was perfect. Cold. Bright. Citrusy like the early notes of grapefruit juice.

"I could drink this all day," I said.

"Me too," she said, smiling. Then she started to get excited. "If you like that, there's other things I want you to taste; hold on one second." She ducked into a room behind the bar and came back with two open bottles and a bowl of oyster crackers.

"First, cleanse your palate." She held out the crackers to me and then poured another white wine. "This is a Pinot Gris," she said. "Also bright, but more like apple and pear than citrus."

I swirled, sniffed, sipped. "It's delicious," I said.

"Perfect with sushi," she said.

"Oh!" I said. "That's a great idea! Host a sushi night here. You could get a local young chef to make rolls live and serve companion white wines. Someone who would work for cheap and want exposure to fancy people. You could probably charge one hundred dollars a person for that!"

"With mochi balls for dessert?"

"Of course," I said. "Who doesn't love mochi balls?"

"Oh," she said, "you're the girl who was here this morning with all of the good event ideas. William was telling me about you. He said you had all these ideas for how to use the dog on social media and how to get more people into the winery and the wine club. I'm Linda, by the way."

I blushed. "I'm Hannah. I got a little excited this morning."

"So did I," she said. "I mean, after you left. We really need the help of someone like you. But William said you were moving to New York?"

"Yeah," I said. "I'm graduating from Haas and I have a job at Goldman Sachs working in finance, but I've always loved marketing."

"That sounds like a nice life you've got set up for yourself," she said.

"I don't know," I said. "It's a lot nicer here than in New York."

"It sounds like you have a good job, though," Linda said.

"It does sound good," I said. "But sometimes things sound better than they are. I mean, I feel lucky to have the opportunity. I'm going to make a lot of money and I'll be able to pay off my loans . . . Oh my God, am I oversharing! I don't even know you. I'm sorry . . . I shouldn't be . . ."

"But?"

"I just have a weird feeling," I said.

"I do too, actually," she said. "It just seems like you fit here . . . Okay, this might be crazy, but would you consider staying? Here at the winery? We couldn't pay you much. But you can have unlimited wine and access to our garden and stay in our guest cottage that's back behind the winery. It's a beautiful space, my favorite on the property, really. You can pour during tastings, but really, I'd love your help getting our marketing in order—events, social media, maybe some ads. Help with the wine club; that's a big deal for us. Maybe even work with distributors and trade magazines? Local stores. Our website. Oh God, we need so much help!"

I could tell that they really did need help by the frustrated tone of her voice. It was a common enough trope that we had talked about it in one of my marketing classes—small business owners often didn't know how to handle all of the aspects of running a business. "You do need help," I said. "And I'm just the person."

"Yes," she said. "You are! And really, I should be out traveling, meeting sommeliers, wine store owners. Even calling wine club members. And with William leaving . . . If you could take over some of the day-to-day for me . . . Anyway, it would be marvelous to have you."

"Can I ask you a question?"

"Of course, anything," she said.

"I saw a For Rent sign outside. What's that all about?"

"Well," Linda said. "Things haven't been great around here, so we were thinking that it might make sense to rent out the winery, and the house if someone wanted it. And let someone run it who knows more than we do. But maybe if you were here, we wouldn't have to do that . . ."

I couldn't believe she was saying exactly what I was hoping she would say. The idea had popped into my mind at lunch and I hadn't been able to shake it. But for her to be thinking the same crazy thing that I was—it meant something. Like it wasn't a silly plan that I had just cooked up in my brain, but it was a job. An opportunity.

On the other hand, I had already accepted a job that I had fought tooth and nail for all year. I had lost my friend Tyra over it. I had gotten a signing bonus, put a deposit down on an apartment in Tribeca. I had a man in a hotel about a mile away who wanted to propose to me. The comparison between working at a winery and toiling under the fluorescent lights of Goldman Sachs was pretty much the starkest contrast I could think of.

Who wouldn't choose the winery?

Well, one person wouldn't choose it, and that person happened to be the person I was dating. So, that was an issue. We had a plan and I was considering changing it, which was basically his worst nightmare. He didn't know how to go off script.

"I really want to do this," I said. "I really, really do. But I need to talk about it with my boyfriend. We were supposed to live together in New York and . . ."

"I understand," she said, looking gloomy.

"I feel like this was meant to be, though." I knew it was such an irrational thing to decide. It went against everything I had worked for at school for the past two years; it went against societal expectations that a thirty-year-old woman with a boyfriend who wants to marry her should say yes to him; it went against my own expectations of myself that I would have a wealthy, comfortable life. I knew it was literally a crazy thing to do, and possibly also a mistake. But I just couldn't stop myself. I felt a compulsion to stay. All of a sudden, I couldn't imagine myself anywhere else. "I just need to have a conversation first. And I need to finish my finals and graduate next week. So, I'd come back in mid-May. Would that work?"

"It would . . ." I could tell she was being tentative.

"The other thing is, I was going to be making a lot of money at this job. And I'll probably have to pay back this signing bonus that I got, plus deal with an apartment that I rented. And I have those student loans." Just saying it all out loud was hurting my heart.

"Would five hundred a week work? Plus room and board. And all the wine you can drink? If you stay, we can talk about equity in the winery."

"Could it be a thousand a week?" I asked.

"What about seven hundred?" she countered.

"Eight hundred?" I suggested.

"Deal," she said.

"Great," I said. "I just need to talk about it with Ethan . . . I'll come back tomorrow morning and let you know for sure."

"Okay," she said. "I hope you say yes."

"I plan to," I assured her.

"Oh," I said as I got up from the bar. "Did I leave my wallet here this morning?"

"In fact you did," she said, producing my giant pink wallet from under the bar.

"I do have a tendency to misplace things when I'm stressed," I said.

"Hopefully, you won't feel stressed here," she said.

"Hope springs eternal," I said.

Terrified, but simultaneously energized, I walked back to town with a spring in my step, already making a mental list of all the things I was going to need to do to make this happen: fight with Ethan, quit my job in New York, cancel my flight, return all the ugly business suits I had bought. I had lived in California for only two years, and part of that time I had spent in New York at a summer internship. Before California, I had lived in New York for seven years and in Iowa for twenty-one. I had only just gestated in California; I needed more time. It felt right. Rash, yes. But right. All of a sudden, my future became clear, and in Technicolor. Instead of the gray, slightly boring, generic life of suburbs and taupe couches I'd have with Ethan, I would have a colorful scene, filled with jazz and parties and wine tastings and California afternoons on the beach.

I ran back to town to tell Ethan about my offer. I knew he would disapprove, but by this point, I didn't care. As I walked, I sent a FaceTime request to my niece, Gillian. She picked up, but she held the phone so she looked upside down. "Hi, Auntie Hannah," she said. "I got a new bunk bed!"

"That's cool," I said.

"And my friend is going to sleep over for my next birthday when I turn twelve on September twentieth."

"Wow," I said. "That's a big birthday, although you should enjoy being eleven for the next few months." I couldn't believe that she was currently eleven. The same age I was when my father died. She was so much more innocent. I was jealous, but also so happy for her. Her life was going to be okay.

"I like being eleven, but I can't wait to be twelve. Where are you?" she asked.

"I'm in Sonoma, California," I said, and I turned the phone so she could see the street I was walking on.

"It's pretty," she said.

"Do you think I should live here?" I asked.

"Yes," she said.

"Why?" I asked.

"Because you're like me," she said. "You like pretty things and places."

"Good point," I said. "Say hi to your brother for me."

"Okay! I have to go have a sleepover now."

She ended the FaceTime with no ceremony, the way only a little girl on to the next adventure can do.

When I got back to the hotel, I found Ethan lying on the bed, the shades drawn, a sleep mask over his face. His bag was packed. His iPhone was playing the white noise app that he knew annoyed me. I wasn't sure if he was asleep or not, so I tried to be as quiet as possible. I crept into the room, closed the door as quietly as possible behind me, and crawled into bed. I kissed him on the temple.

"Hi," I said in my sweetest possible voice.

"Did you find your wallet?" he asked.

"Yeah," I said.

"You're staying here, aren't you?" he asked.

"They asked me to," I said.

"You're ruining your life," he said.

"I don't see it that way," I said.

"How do you see it?" he asked.

"Well, I think about how when I lived in New York, I thought everything was dirty. I hated riding the subway and how it was always smelly.

Why go back to that when I could stay here surrounded by beauty?"

"But your life in New York would be way nicer now. You could take cabs."

"Cabs are gross too," I said.

"God, you've become a snob," he said.

"I'm not a snob," I said. "I'd be giving up being an elitist for doing something real. Working here is real. Working in finance is fake. After all, it's not that cool to work at Goldman anymore."

"Ugh," he said. "Not everything is political. This is about your future."

"This isn't political," I said. "And yes, it is about my future."

"Maybe you should have thought of that before you racked up a bunch of loans in business school. When do you need to tell them?"

"Tomorrow. But I said I wanted to discuss it with you first."

"But it sounds like you've already decided," he said.

"I just . . . It feels . . ." I tried stroking his shoulder, but he turned away.

"I just feel really sad," he said. "I had a plan. And now . . ."

"I'm sorry," I said. "I know you like plans."

"I should have known when you moved in with me after two months that your impulsivity would work against me."

"I'm not always impulsive," I said. "I just don't always map everything out."

"What you're doing right now is impulsive," he said. "Moving in with me was impulsive. Even going to graduate school was impulsive."

"You have to plan to go to graduate school," I said.

"But why did you want to go? Did you need to? If you were just going to work in a winery?"

"I'm *using* the things I've learned to help them. It's entrepreneurship. You should be proud of me. It's what you do, after all."

"All of a sudden, I don't know you at all," he said. "I'm going back to Berkeley. Why don't you stay here tonight and think about it and come back tomorrow on the bus?"

"But—"

"Feel what it's like to be without me."

"Fine," I said.

"I think you'll miss me," he said.

"I know I will," I said. "That's the hardest part." I got up to go to the bathroom. When I came out, he was gone.

Chapter 4

I wasn't sure how much the hotel room was going to cost if I wasn't splitting it with Ethan, or, to be honest, letting him put it on the family credit card, which he carried around and used for things that were too expensive for graduate student salaries. I wasn't sure how I felt about his family or their money, but I did appreciate that credit card. But the problem of letting someone else make the plans for you, even if you trust their plan-making abilities, was that you lost some of the control over what the outcome was.

I was alone for the night at the very least. And my plans were my own. I decided not to wallow. After all, I was in a beautiful place. So I took a shower and put on the dress that I was going to wear to dinner with Ethan. It was a dark violet empire-waist dress with flowy sleeves, solidly in my "faux boho" style that Ethan always mocked me for. I had gained a little bit of weight in graduate school and had shifted my style from the sleeker black and gray dresses I had worn in New York to a more colorful, forgiving, billowy style that also seemed to match the California vibe. Tyra had made fun of me for this bohemian style I had adopted when everyone else in grad school was going the other way—toward business suits. But I loved pretty dresses and there were so many of them in the little shops of Berkeley and Oakland. My New York clothing had always felt like a costume to me—like I was playing the role of Serious Lady Who Goes to the Office. I put on makeup—a little bit of foundation, a pop of bronzer on each cheek, and some mascara—as well as a pair of silver gladiator sandals and went down to the lobby.

Betty was still there behind the desk, and I wondered how long her shift was. If it was legal to have her working for so long. But maybe she was the owner. I lingered around the desk for a minute until she said, "Can I help you?"

"Yeah," I said, feeling sheepish. "I'm here alone tonight, but I want to go out to dinner. Is there a good place to go? Maybe a place that a local would like rather than a tourist. And . . . I need to be able to walk there."

"Well," she said, thinking. "You've already been to the Girl and the Fig, so you'll have to go to La Salette. It's Portuguese. Sit at the bar and get the cod cakes. You'll love it."

"Thanks," I said and headed out the front door in the direction she pointed me. I walked slowly, taking in the smell and the beauty of the plaza. I walked diagonally across it, stopping to turn around and take a mental 360-degree photo of the place. Even if I never came back here, I wanted to remember the night that I took my life into my own hands. Leaving Iowa was the first time I had taken steps on my own, and here I was again at another turning point. I headed to the restaurant and sat myself at the end of the bar.

The bartender was a woman in a black tank top and black jeans with slim, sculpted arms. Her blond hair was piled on top of her head and she had a tattoo on the back of her neck that read, "In vino veritas." I smiled at her and ordered a glass of Pinot Noir.

"New in town?" she asked as she poured.

"Trying to figure out if I should move here," I said.

"Best decision I ever made," she said.

"Seems like a common consensus," I said.

"What could be bad?" she said. She put a bowl of olives in front of me. "I grew up in Alaska. I was always cold and covered in blankets and sweaters, or mosquito bites."

"There are mosquitoes in Alaska?" I asked.

"Millions. In the summer they swarm you. I once had an idea to make a clothing line made from mosquito nets, but I decided to move away instead of pursuing that goal."

I laughed. "That seems wise."

"Okay if I just bring you some things I think are delicious?" she asked.

"Perfect," I said. I wouldn't have to make decisions and I'd have a great dinner. I was already so happy. I pulled my book from my handbag (I always carry one), sipped my wine, and tried to imagine myself as a resident of this beautiful place. I was all but drawn away into the world of Tana French's Dublin when I felt a tap on my shoulder. I jumped and turned around, my heart racing. It was William. His face was red and he was wearing running shorts and a sweaty T-shirt, but he looked great nonetheless.

"Fancy meeting you here," he said. "Hi, Alexis." He gave a quick hug over the bar to the bartender. I looked away so I wouldn't know if there was anything between them that would make me feel jealous.

"Hi," I said. "Are you here for dinner?"

"I was just coming to pick up a check for the wine they bought for a private event . . ." He was a bit out of breath and he looked down at his outfit and then almost seemed to remember what he was doing. "After my run, I mean. Sorry, I'm a little smelly."

"Oh stop. You look great," I said, trying not to flirt, but maybe trying a little to flirt. "Do you run a lot?"

"When I can," he said. "I ran cross-country in high school. It helps me think."

"I like to run too," I said.

"We should go together sometime," he said.

"I think you'd be disappointed at how slow I

go," I said. I could already tell he was way faster than me.

"I don't mind being a pacer," he said.

"I'll think about it," I said. "But aren't you moving to New York?"

"Yes, but not for more than a week," he said. He looked around at the bustling restaurant. "Listen," he said. "Why don't you finish your wine and whatever awesome snacks Alexis brings you, and I'll go home and change, and then we can meet for a drink at Steiner's Tavern? We can watch some baseball and I can tell you all about working for my parents."

I nodded and sipped my wine. "Okay," I said.

"I'll meet you there. Don't be late." He turned and left the restaurant. He had forgotten the check and also hadn't told me what time "late" was. I shrugged and reopened my book, trying not to think about how he made my hands shake a little bit.

Alexis came back with a tiny dish of salted cod and the check. "Where'd he go?" she asked.

"He left," I said.

"Scaring them off?" she said, winking.

"I guess," I said. I didn't know what any of it meant, but I was excited to find out.

The food was delicious, the fish soft and garlicky but not overpowering. I spooned bits of it onto freshly baked toasted sourdough bread and savored every bite. Of all the breads

I loved, sourdough was at the top of the list. The pepperiness of the Pinot Noir was brought out by the food, and I smiled appreciatively at Alexis.

I glanced back at my book, but I was having trouble concentrating with the conversations going at the bar. I had always been a reader, despite the fact that my parents thought it was a strange habit. My brother, Drew, and I had taken weekly walks together to the Winthrop town library. It was a small library, really just a room at the back of the local post office run by a kind woman who had too many books in her house, but she kept it stocked for us—chapter books for me when I was tiny, *Little House on the Prairie* and *Anne of Green Gables* as I got older. She introduced me to Agatha Christie and even early Stephen King. I loved *Christine* and *Carrie*, but when I got to *It*, I had reached my limit. Drew, however, loved the man he called "the King" and read not only *It* and *The Tommyknockers*, but the entire Dark Tower series. While he was going in that direction, I was gravitating more toward mysteries. I discovered Margaret Truman's books about Washington, D.C., and loved the fact that she was President Truman's daughter. I can't remember anything about them now, but I remember making a little nest for myself in my closet with my nightstand lamp, the cord of which I ran in from outside of the closet, and reading those books.

The woman who ran that library was the woman who changed my life. Her name was Mary Ellen O'Neill and she had gone to the University of Iowa and studied English. She had a master's in library science and had lived in New York City. She had worked in book publishing, in library marketing, and at Barnes & Noble and the New York Public Library. She had coached me through applying to college and, in the summers after my sophomore and junior years, in what to do about getting a job in the city. She taught me about letter writing and networking. "The best thing you can ever do is to learn to write a great letter," she said. "I didn't learn until I worked in publishing, but I'm going to teach you now." She made me write sample letters to her throughout the semester expressing my interest in a variety of careers that she described to me. Then she taught me how to scour the university alumni databases for contacts. She proofread my letters. And she bought me a glass of Champagne when I got the job at Tiffany's as the assistant to the chief marketing officer.

Books had always been my escape, so I was frustrated that at this moment, when I could have used one, I couldn't get Tana French to carry me away. But maybe this wasn't a time for avoidance; maybe I needed to focus on the place I was trying to escape into, the people around me, to see if I could belong here. I gave up on the book and concentrated on my wine. I looked at all the folks sitting at the bar and tried to figure out who was a local and who was a tourist, a better game than Unhappy Couple, at least for this moment. There was a look to the locals—they moved a little slower, were dressed a little more comfortably. They glowed a little bit brighter.

I wondered how long it would take William to get home, shower, and come back to meet me. Was it better for me to be there when he arrived? Or to arrive after?

Alexis brought me a coffee and a scoop of mango sorbet. The sorbet was cool and tart and the coffee made me sit up a little bit straighter. I asked for the bill, left a thirty percent tip because she hadn't charged me for most of what I ate, and asked her how to get to Steiner's. She pointed me in the right direction and I tried to make my most grateful face.

I walked around the corner to Steiner's, where William was sitting at the bar, clean, almost sparkling actually. He had two glasses of wine sitting, untouched, in front of him. I assumed one was for me. I came up behind him and touched his shoulder, just like he had done to me. He jumped a bit but then smiled broadly when he saw it was me. "Hannah!" he said. "So glad you made it. I already took the liberty of ordering you a glass of my favorite Pinot, other than the one we make, of course. It's from a winery called Lynmar up in the Russian River Valley. We'll have to go up there. It's such a cool part of the area and they're making the best natural wines right now."

"I don't understand the words you are saying," I said. "It's like I need a Sonoma-to-English dictionary. But it all sounds good." I settled on the stool next to him and took a sip. It was slightly chilled, light, a little bit sweet, like cherries. "Delicious," I said.

He nodded. His leg touched mine just a bit and I didn't move away. "So," he said. "Tell me about yourself."

I shrugged. "I'm pretty ordinary," I said.

"I'm sure that's not true," he said.

"I'm from Iowa and then I moved to New York. Now I'm in grad school."

"And you must have a background in food and wine? Are you a cook?"

"I worked in a French restaurant in college in Iowa City," I said. "Mostly as a hostess."

One of my favorite parts about working at the restaurant was the family meal before the diners arrived, when we would test the chef's specials and tell him what we thought about dishes he was developing. He would pair the meal with wine—not full glasses, but little tastes—so the waitstaff could tell the diners with confidence that the coq au vin did pair well with the Côtes du Rhône, but it went even better with the red Burgundy. He was always tweaking the cassoulet—changing the source of the beans, putting in lamb or leaving it out, varying the number of times he cracked the crust in the cooking process. Generally, we couldn't taste the difference, but he would declare, "This is the worst I've ever made!" or "This is genius! The best I've ever made." We always had a Languedoc red to pair with it. That place, Le Milieu, was my introduction to good food and wine.

He nodded. "That must be it."

"I grew up eating food out of packages."

"It's okay," he said. "You seem to have overcome it quite nicely."

"And you're going to New York?"

"Yeah," he said. "Although now I'm regretting it."

"Why?" I asked.

"Because I didn't know you'd be coming here."

"Well, I'm not sure yet . . ."

"You wouldn't be here if you weren't going to stay," he said.

I nodded slowly. He was probably right. But I was still a little uncertain. "I don't know," I said. "It's a big decision. I mean, I'm giving up a lot for something I know nothing about. It's kind of crazy."

"I assume your boyfriend doesn't approve?"

"Absolutely not."

"How long have you been together?" he asked.

"A little less than two years," I said. "We met at orientation."

"It's your life," he said.

"I think he was planning to propose to me," I said.

He was quiet. Maybe it was too much to say on a first . . . encounter. Regardless, I could tell that he didn't like Ethan. But I didn't want him to say that to me, so I didn't press it.

"He's not so bad," I said.

"I don't need to talk about him," he said. "Tell me about your family."

"My older brother Drew's the principal of the middle/high school that we went to when we were teenagers. My dad was a truck driver and my mom is a nurse."

"A real American family," he said.

"I guess," I said. Growing up in Iowa, one did become proud of being a normal American. Maybe it was the corn. Maybe it was the election focus that seemed to be constantly surrounding us. There was always a politician or a pollster who wanted to ask you a question. My parents had both grown up in Buchanan County. Had fallen in love in high school, and my mom was pregnant with Drew before she was twenty. She had me when she was twenty-one. She was a fun, young mom, almost luminous. But when my dad died, when I was just eleven years old, all of a sudden, she seemed old. So unprepared for life. Drew and I took over. She did make money as a nurse, but we did everything else—we dealt with our own clothes for school, food, entertainment. We watched her be totally overwhelmed.

I didn't want that to happen to me. So I had run away from low expectations, to the University of Iowa (which felt far away even though it was only an hour's drive), and then to New York, to a job that I had gotten through my own networking abilities, and now to California. I had had to educate my mother about what I was doing; even hostessing in a French restaurant in Iowa City was exotic to her.

When I got the job at Tiffany's, I also had to explain to her that I wasn't going to be covered in diamonds. Everything I did was gravy as far as my mother, and even my brother, who had stayed nearby in Iowa, could tell. She didn't quite understand what I did; she appeared to be glad I was doing it. At the very least, she was glad that she didn't have to give me an allowance or babysit my kids. Even though she also thought I was an old maid at thirty without any children or a husband. So, it was a double-edged sword, but on the whole, I think she was essentially proud.

"And you, you're different. How did that happen?"

"I don't know," I said. "I always liked to read. I liked movies set in New York. I wanted to live a life like Meg Ryan in *You've Got Mail.* I also had this librarian friend, Mary Ellen, who helped me. She kind of guided me out of the town, if that makes any sense. And I just knew that after college I wanted to move far away, so I wrote letters to people in New York until I found someone who would talk to me."

"That's inspiring," he said. "I've just been here my whole life. Except for when I went to Los Angeles for college. But that's not a real place."

"Why do you keep saying that?"

"It's just not. It's all about how you look and who you know."

"New York is like that."

"No, New York is about what you do. It's about competence. LA is superficial. I was glad to leave."

"Did you want to act?"

"No, but I wanted to write screenplays and I couldn't break in anywhere, and then my parents needed help; the winery was expanding and they couldn't do it all themselves. So I came back. But now, I have to take care of myself. That's why I'm going to New York, to follow my dream. And that's why I'm so glad you'll be here to help them; they're in a bit over their heads, and recently, well, they just seem to be outpaced by other wineries. With you there, I'll worry less. Plus, you'll get to live in the winemaker's cottage."

"The winemaker's cottage?"

"My mom didn't show it to you?"

I shook my head and took the last sip of my wine.

"Oh, I'll show you later. It's the nicest part of the property."

The idea of seeing the house together made me nervous—did that mean we were going home together? I quickly motioned to the bartender for another glass of wine. "Isn't the house a castle?" I asked.

"It's not quite a castle, but it is big and drafty and we barely use any of the rooms. It was built in the 1800s by my great-great-great-something-grandfather. There are a bunch of other castles in Sonoma now—but they've all been built in the past fifteen years. So fake," he said.

"Faux," I said.

"Exactly," he said. "Anyway, we'd all prefer to live in the cottage."

"Interesting," I said. "I've always been fascinated by castles."

"Well, you'll have plenty of access to a big house," he said. "Enough to learn that you don't really want one."

At the end of the night, I had him walk me back to my hotel. I didn't feel ready to see the winemaker's cottage yet. Even though it had felt pretty electric when our legs had touched in the bar, I had to be careful. He was the son of my soon-to-be boss and I still was in a relationship. *I am a good person.* This is what I told myself as I walked up to my room, alone, having hugged William quickly on the street and given him a good-bye smile.

In the morning, I would go back to Bellosguardo and tell Linda that I was staying. I called my mom to tell her, but the call went straight to voice mail; I didn't leave a message. Same with Drew. I even tried Mary Ellen, the librarian, whom I called occasionally for book recommendations and to chat about life. Then I remembered that it was the middle of the night in Iowa. Time zones. Somehow, the thought of calling Ethan never even crossed my mind. We had never had a conversation like this before, and I didn't know how. I would tell him when I got back to Berkeley.

Chapter 5

The next morning, I walked back to Bellosguardo. I felt invigorated. I put on a dark denim A-line shirtdress that I felt looked both professional and casual. As I walked, I gave myself a pep talk: I was making a choice for myself—doing what I needed, not what was the "right" thing to do. I was good enough and smart enough and they would appreciate me working there. It reminded me of the walk I took from my childhood home to the Winthrop library to show Mary Ellen the e-mail from Cheryl Vetter, the chief marketing officer of Tiffany & Co., offering me a job as her assistant. She jumped up and down when she saw the news. She was a little past her prime jumping years, but she said the news made her feel like a kid again.

As I crossed the now-familiar bridge and approached the ivy-covered building, I noticed the castle peeking out from the hill above. I took another one of my mental pictures; this was the start of my new life. The parking lot was empty, but the tasting room door was open, so I entered the cool, whitewashed room. It was empty, as it had been on my first encounter. This time not even the dog was there. Everett emerged from the office, though, and met me across the bar. I approached and sat down. He ignored me at first until finally, turning around from organizing the bottles in the racks, he asked, "Hello, are you here for a tasting?"

"I'm Hannah," I said. "I spoke with Linda yesterday? Is she here?"

"Who?" he said. His voice was gruff and his hair was messy, making him seem angrier than I hoped he was. He had been so nice to us the day before, or nice to the dog and to Ethan. I hadn't really interacted with him.

"Hannah Greene?" I said with the up-speak tone that I knew was irritating to people, especially men, but I couldn't help it. My boss, Cheryl, in New York, had spent years drumming the habit out of me. I had finally mastered it by the time I got to graduate school, and here it was, slipping out. I gritted my teeth and told myself, *Get it together, Hannah.* "I spoke with Linda about a job here. Helping with marketing?"

"I don't know anything about this," he said. "We don't need marketing."

"Everyone needs marketing," I said. How could he not have known that I was coming? I was pretty sure that his wife had very clearly offered me a job. And I had had drinks with his son. Hadn't they talked about me? I was confused.

"What are you, some kind of college student?"

I was flattered he thought I looked so young

but wanted to establish my credentials. "I'm in business school, actually about to graduate. I fell in love with your winery yesterday when I was here? You told my boyfriend about architecture? He was the one who didn't like the dog's kisses. Anyway, I quit the job I was supposed to do in New York to come up here." Tears inadvertently came to my eyes. Not the best way to make a first impression. I sniffed them back and tried to sit up as straight as possible.

"Let me go ask Linda," he said. "You wait here." He disappeared through the same doorway from which Linda had produced our celebratory sparkling wine. The dog had apparently been behind the bar, because he appeared and went trotting behind Everett into the back room. He couldn't be too much of a bad guy if the dog loved him that much.

Before I had left the hotel room that morning, I had called my Human Resources contact at Goldman, a lovely but intense woman named Helene. I had tried to start off casually, asking her about her family, but she went right to the point: "Why are you calling? You know your start date is May fifteenth, right?"

"I know," I said. "I just—"

"Did you get another offer?"

"No," I said. "Well—"

"Who was it? J.P. Morgan? Citi? HSBC?"

"It's actually at a winery in California."

"How much are they offering you?" She was sounding combative now.

I didn't know what to say. As I was confronting this possibility, it did seem actually insane. "Eight hundred dollars a week," I said.

"What?!" she screamed.

"Plus room and board," I eked out.

"I don't even know what to say," she said. "I went to bat for you. I told them to choose you over that other girl even though they liked her better. Now . . ."

This made me mad. As if she was trying to undermine my decision. "Well, now everyone gets what they want," I snapped. I was almost crying.

"I honestly don't even understand what you're doing. You have the most coveted job and you're just giving it up?" Her voice had gone up an octave. "For *eight—*"

"Yes," I babbled. "I think it's the right thing."

"You're making a huge mistake," Helene had said and hung up without even saying good-bye. She sounded a lot like Ethan, but angrier.

When Everett was gone for more than a minute, I started to worry that Helene was right. After we had hung up, someone else from Goldman had called and left a message about me returning my signing bonus. I decided not to call that person back right away. As I waited for Everett I went down the mental path of considering whether I had made a mistake. Maybe Ethan was right. Had I completely ruined my future? What did I know about these people, whom I had just randomly stumbled upon, that I was entrusting everything to them? The Goldman job would "set the tone" for the rest of my career, Ethan said. What if the tone this job in Sonoma set was failure? William had said the winery was in bad financial shape, and I had just given up hundreds of thousands of dollars in potential income to make eight hundred dollars a week and live in a cottage with free wine.

But I had made a lot of rash decisions in my life—leaving Iowa to go to New York City for a job at Tiffany's, leaving that totally secure job that sometimes generated free diamonds to go to graduate school in California, even moving in with Ethan very shortly after I had met him. Business school was actually fun; I had liked the strategic and financial side of what Cheryl had done at Tiffany's; and the projects were creative. So, two out of the three rash decisions had been good ones. Besides, the rash decisions had taken thought, mostly. I wrote letters to successful Hawkeye graduates in New York City throughout my college years so one of them would give me a job when I graduated. After I had that job and decided I needed to get out of New York, I studied for the GMAT for an entire year on my subway ride to and from work. I learned about the top state business schools and how to establish residency in those states so my second year of tuition was lower than my first. I applied to Berkeley. I was organized. Thoughtful. I met Ethan in a bookstore and he took me to Chez Panisse for dinner, and he was better than any other guy I'd ever gone to a fancy dinner with. I gave up my apartment and moved into his almost immediately. That was perhaps *not* the best move. But if those were rash decisions, this was literally insane: In the course of basically an hour, I had changed everything in my life to work in this winery that I knew nothing about. Ethan's words echoed in my head. He was right. I was throwing everything I had worked for away on a decision I made when I was a little bit tipsy in a beautiful place.

But what a place. I took a deep breath and hopped off the barstool. I walked around the tasting room, surveying it. Above me, there was a pitched ceiling with exposed beams. A balcony ran along the outside of what would have been the second floor. There was room up there for small café tables and bistro chairs. Along the outer walls were leather couches and coffee tables. But the center of the room was empty. There was space for a dance floor in the center, a band in the corner. And up against the far wall, photos depicting the history of the winery, from its founding in the 1870s by a Hungarian count to its purchase by William Rockford, presumably William's grandfather. I wondered where William was. I couldn't remember when he'd said he would leave. If he'd said.

It felt like a place that had history; that was important. And it felt like a place that needed someone to help highlight the history, to share the greatness of the place with more people. It deserved to be seen and known, and I felt like I was the person to make that happen. It made me feel part of something. And that was what I had been missing when I thought about working for an investment bank.

I was standing in the dark corner where I envisioned the three-piece jazz band when Linda came into the bar. "Hannah?" she said loudly.

"Over here," I said, emerging from the shadows. I headed back across the room to the bar, telling myself not to have an emotional breakdown.

"I'm so sorry," she said. "I hadn't told Everett about our agreement. He's not one for change. And there's been a lot around here recently. Our other dog, Zinfandel, died. William is leaving for New York next week. Business hasn't been great. But really, I was being a coward. Because he doesn't think we need help and I didn't want to make him mad. So I didn't tell him. But now you're here and he's mad anyway."

"I thought we had a deal," I said, my voice

quiet, quaking slightly. I threw everything away because of a whim. Tears bloomed in my eyes.

"Of course we did, darling," she said, patting me on the shoulder. "I've told Everett all about it now. He'll get used to you eventually. He might even start to like you if you bring some customers into this place. There's a lot of competition around here, as you might have noticed."

"Oh," I said. "Thank you so much. I was so scared. I mean. I . . ."

"It's going to be good," she said.

"This place *is* the best," I said. "Thank you so much. You won't be sorry you hired me."

"Of course I won't," she said. "You're a good girl. Where are you from?"

"Iowa," I said.

"Perfect," she said. "Salt of the earth. Let me show you to your cottage."

"I can't stay," I said. "I mean, I can, but I have to go back to Berkeley for a few days for graduation and to move out of my apartment. I'll come back next week for good."

"Okay," she said. "But you must have a few minutes. Can I just show you the cottage? I know you'll love it. We can have one glass of wine and then I'll have Everett drive you to the bus station."

"Who could say no to that idea?" I said.

Linda put her arm around my shoulders. "I'm

glad you're here," she said. "There aren't enough women around here. Even Tannin is a boy."

"Squad goals," I said, weakly.

"Indeed," she said, looking a little confused.

It was an emotional roller coaster already.

I followed Linda through the mysterious behind-the-bar door. There was only an office back there, but it felt like I was now in the inner sanctum of the winery. A place I was excited to be. The office led to another door, which led out to a flagstone patio on the side of the building opposite the parking lot. The path transformed into a set of stone stairs. At the top of the hill was a stone cottage with two perfect front windows and geraniums exploding out of the window boxes. Beyond the cottage, what looked like a castle rose out of the hill behind the winery. Somehow it wasn't entirely visible from below, but a huge stone mansion that would have been more likely on a PBS miniseries than at a California winery was placed about a quarter of a mile behind and above the tasting room.

"The castle!" I said. "I've heard about it. But wow."

"It's pretty spectacular, isn't it?" she said. "It was built by our founder back in the 1870s. Beautiful, but it's just too much for us. We really only live in a small part of it. Your cottage was the winemaker's cottage. It's much more manageable. I sometimes wish we lived there. But it would be a bit strange to have that giant thing on our property and not use it."

"You could turn it into a museum," I said.

"You have lots of ideas," she said.

I blushed. "I mean, I would never not live in a castle if it was available," I said. "But I've never lived anywhere larger than fifteen hundred square feet, so what do I know?" I realized that I was rambling, so I gritted my teeth to get myself to stop talking. Like gnawing on my cuticles, nervous talking was a bad habit.

I sat on a little stone bench next to the front door as she dug around in the pack she wore around her waist until she produced what looked like an iron skeleton key. She put it in the keyhole. "We've never updated the locks," she said, then turned the lock and handed the iron key to me. "Sorry about that. It's a bit heavy."

I held it in my palm and turned it over. It was weighty. It had seen things. Been in generations of pockets and purses. "I feel like I'm in a Frances Hodgson Burnett novel," I said.

"Who?"

"Remember *The Secret Garden*?"

"Oh," she said. "We had a son. He only read comic books, but that sounds vaguely familiar from my own childhood."

"Right," I said. "The story is probably as old as this winery. Well, there's always a skeleton key in those kinds of novels. I've always wanted one is what I mean."

"I don't tend to read old novels. Maybe because our life is kind of like one. But the good thing about the key is you'll always know if it's in your purse," she said. "It's not light."

Inside, the cottage was the perfect combination of rustic and modern. I was glad that I hadn't come with William the other night, because now my reaction was honest. I grinned and clapped my hands. "This place is stunning," I said to Linda. But she wasn't listening. The main room was open, with lots of light—the back of the cottage, which faced east, had been renovated to have big floor-to-ceiling windows. A big overstuffed white couch faced a stone fireplace with a reclaimed wood coffee table between on rusty wheels. The coffee table sat on top of a white shag rug.

Between the living area and the kitchen was a giant farmhouse table surrounded by about a dozen mismatched wooden chairs, all painted different colors, but all fading in exactly the same way. Past the table was a large marble-topped kitchen island and a well-appointed kitchen—huge stainless refrigerator, which sat next to a fully stocked wine refrigerator. Open shelving revealed every type of wineglass imaginable. While they hadn't updated the locks, they clearly had updated the kitchen.

Our home in Berkeley was a cookie-cutter

graduate student apartment. Brown particleboard cabinets. White refrigerator. Tile table. Our furniture was all from IKEA. Ethan complained about it all the time, but he never did anything about it. Clearly he had the money; he had grown up in an apartment (and a summerhouse in the Hamptons) filled with custom pieces sourced by his mother's decorator. Needless to say, we hadn't invited his parents to our grad school apartment.

But for me, IKEA honestly was a step up from the house I grew up in. At least the IKEA furniture was new. The furniture in my tiny childhood home, which was a house not much bigger than my graduate student apartment, had all been bought secondhand or found by the side of the road. My childhood bed frame and mattress had originally been my grandfather's. My father had also slept in it as a kid and had passed it down to me. Needless to say, it was a little bit lumpy. But after he died, it felt wrong to ask for another.

All of that was to say that the "cottage" felt like true luxury.

"Thank you," Linda said, finally hearing my compliment. "I'll admit that it's one of my favorite places on the property. All of my favorite books are on that shelf, and that chair next to the fireplace is the most comfortable one I've ever sat on. I've taken many a nap on that chair."

I took a look at the bookshelf—she had *Housekeeping*, *Infinite Jest*, some Evelyn Waugh, some Michael Connelly, a Nora Roberts, an ancient-looking copy of *Little Women.* I plucked *Little Women* from the shelf and plopped down in the giant chair. "It's so comfortable!" I said. "This was my favorite book when I was a girl. I used to bring it with me everywhere and read it so I wouldn't have to talk to people. I was shy as a kid, but I think reading made me outgoing in the long run; it always gave me something to talk about."

She pulled open the wine fridge and took out an open bottle. "It's a good one. Didn't I promise you a glass of wine? I just opened this yesterday. It should be even better today. It's a Chardonnay, but a good one, not oaky, I promise. We age it in stainless steel."

I laughed a little. I wasn't a wine snob yet. Everything tasted good to me.

She grabbed two slim glasses from the stemware shelf and poured for us. "Let's relax on the back patio," she said. I pulled myself out of the giant chair and left the book on the seat. I headed to the back door to hold it open for her so she could go out with the glasses. I grabbed the bottle from the counter and followed her. We settled on wrought iron chairs with an iron bistro table between us. The chairs had grape-leaf cushions on them, the only nod to wine I'd seen so far.

Linda adhered to my rules about avoiding signs and themed décor.

The patio was surrounded by huge cedar trees, but the main house was still visible. We talked about the history of the winery and my background—I told her that my father had been a truck driver and my mother a nurse. That my older brother and I were on our own for most of our childhood and adolescence.

"You've managed to take yourself far," she said. "I grew up here. I haven't gone very far at all."

"But look at what you've done," I said, gesturing to her home, the vines, the cottage.

"This was all here for me. I just had to take it on," she said.

"What would you have done if . . ."

"If I had a choice?" She sighed. "I don't know. I never even allowed myself to think about it. I don't hate making and selling wine. And besides, I don't know how to do anything else."

The way she said it made me think she didn't not hate it either. Hating making wine was not something I could imagine, and yet William didn't want to do it, and now I wasn't even sure if Linda did either.

"This place was in Everett's family. It was founded in the 1870s by Count William, during the Wine Rush, as they call it, but it fell into disrepair in the early 1900s, during Prohibition, and Everett's grandfather resurrected it in the forties. Most people didn't have the money or the taste for wine then. He actually was using it to farm fruits and vegetables for a time and was cutting back the vines that were stubbornly trying to grow through. But when the vegetable business started to collapse, because more vegetables were being imported from South America, his son, Everett's father, had the foresight to change over to wine. Or change back, I guess is more accurate. The vines wanted to grow. My father owned the winery next door—the land is up past the castle—and he had planted his vines himself. They're much younger than the vines here but also were cultivated exclusively to be a winery, unlike here, where everything was in chaos for a long time. My father had been a food scientist and an amateur horticulturalist. He created artificial grape flavor and made a lot of money. But he started thinking the world of engineered food was disgusting and probably dangerous in the fifties, and he had the money from inventing the flavor, so he quit the flavor business and bought the land up here to farm real grapes, he said. He invested everything in the land. He had a mildly successful business, but nothing in comparison with the Rockfords' next door, who were the go-to winery around here until all of those commercial places started popping up and ruining our business, but that's another story. Anyway, in the early seventies, Everett's father wanted to buy my father's land, but my father didn't want to sell. So they worked out an arrangement that if we, Everett and I—and mind you we were children at the time—were to get married, my father would get shares in the Bellosguardo business and we would be trained to run the winery. Eventually we would inherit together."

Maybe I was a little drunk—I had had more wine during daylight hours in the past two days than in my entire life—but as I listened to Linda talk, I couldn't help but think that she had, essentially, a modern-day arranged marriage with Everett.

"Did you want to work in the winery for the rest of your life? Why did you agree to it?" I asked.

"My parents didn't want to make wine anymore, but they also wanted the land to stay in the family. I was their only child. I didn't really have a choice. I also loved the Rockford castle. It had been a second home to me growing up. The problem was, in the early eighties, right around when they were preparing to turn the business over to Everett and me, commercial wineries started popping up all around California—Kendall-Jackson and Gallo—and their wines were everywhere, and they started pushing out the smaller producers like us from shelf space and wine lists. And this was just at the same time that big-box retailers started really getting in the game of selling brands. We weren't a brand like Gallo; we just didn't produce at that level, and we didn't want to. Plus, Everett's father, who was the one who knew the most about the business, passed away shortly after William was born. Everett's mother moved to San Francisco. My parents were so happy for Everett to deal with the business that they bought a condo in Hawaii. So they left us here, in a total crisis for the business. Honestly, we haven't quite recovered from it yet. We've always made the wines here naturally and we've always grown all our own grapes, but that wasn't a selling point for a long time. Now we can call them 'estate' bottles, which means that all the grapes are grown here, on the estate. And we don't put sulfur in our bottles, which can keep them from seeming corked but also can change the taste. Recently, we've started to notice that people are more interested in independent growers and natural wine again. But if we had used the words 'natural wine' even five years ago, we would have been laughed out of the room. It's pretty wild, how the pendulum swings."

"Wow," I said. "I'm glad the pendulum is swinging your way. I'm learning about natural wine already." Or, at least, William had said words to me that sounded like he was teaching me about natural wine.

"It's the best way to make it," she said. She poured the last of the bottle into our glasses. "Anyway, that's enough about me. I know you'll enjoy graduation."

"I can't wait," I said, with only mild sarcasm in my voice. It was going to be superweird when I got back to Berkeley; I knew graduation would feel bittersweet.

She smiled and put her hand on my arm. "You're a hardworking girl, I can tell. Come back on Sunday night so you can be at our last dinner with William before he leaves for New York. I can tell that he's fond of you."

I blushed a little. I wondered what she knew. Not that there was anything to know.

"Just mother's intuition," she said. "Besides, I have a stake in it as well. If you're here and he likes you, maybe he'll be more inclined to come home."

"Whatever works," I said. "I just want you to be happy."

Linda looked down at her hands and a kind of gloom came over her face. "Everett should take you to the bus," she said and stood up from the table.

I looked around and tried to figure out what I had said or done wrong. I stood up as well, not wanting to be rude.

"I can't wait to live here," I said. "It's going to be really fun."

• • •

She walked me up to the house to find Everett, and he and I got in the truck together. Everett drove me back to the El Dorado Hotel to get my bag and then to the bus depot in silence. But he let me hold Tannin on my lap, so I just chatted with the dog and the dog gave me little kisses on my nose. I made a comment about the weather and got no response. Then I made a comment about the beauty of Sonoma. No response. Finally, I said, "Does it seem like it's going to be a good year for grapes?"

He finally answered. "It's been rough the past few years. I don't like to irrigate because then you don't get a real *vin de terroir.* We lost a lot of the younger grapes during the drought. The old guys, they're hearty; their roots are so deep, they get the water they need and they refuse to die. California rootstock is the strongest—our roots are immune to diseases that kill French grapes all the time, like phylloxera. There was an outbreak in the 1870s, right after the count founded the vineyard, but all of the vines that survived are hearty. And these vines, they lived for years here without being cared for at all. Anyway, we've finally had some rain this year, so I think we'll be okay."

"I didn't know that," I said. "About irrigation. I thought all farmers had to irrigate."

"In general, the climate here isn't ideal

for wine grapes; the temperature is, but the precipitation and the water table aren't perfect. Our land happens to be better than most. We grow the grapes on a hill to catch as much water as possible as it runs down. The count knew what he was doing. He picked the best spot in Sonoma. The drought . . . well . . . it was certainly a problem, but we're doing better than most. And now, we've got more water than we know what to do with."

I nodded. I didn't know what else to say. Everett didn't seem to be a person who was uncomfortable with silence, so I respected that. I just scratched Tannin behind the ear and his contented sighs filled the car for the rest of the trip to the bus station.

Chapter 6

On the bus ride back to Berkeley, I mostly stared out the window at the arid California landscape. As we left the fertile Sonoma Valley, we were surrounded by dry-looking, almost desertlike hills. Rocky crags plunging into deep valleys. It was in direct contrast to the flat fields of my youth, filled with corn and soybeans as far as the eye could see. Not to mention the urban jungle of New York City: One of my favorite parts of the ride into the city from Ditmas Park was when the Q train would go over the Manhattan Bridge. First you would see Brooklyn office buildings, then the glory of downtown Manhattan, and if you looked to the left, you would see the Statue of Liberty. Small in the distance, welcoming us all into her city. I said good-bye to her on my last ride into the city. Maybe I should have known then that I wouldn't go back. Now I was on my way back to Berkeley to say a different kind of good-bye.

Normally, I would have called Ethan about twenty minutes before the bus pulled into the depot to badger him into picking me up. He would resist at first, saying he was busy with something amorphous, but eventually would give in and often would arrive at the bus station with a coffee or a seltzer, depending on the time of day. In his heart of hearts, he liked taking care of me. As I was thinking about what to do after I got off the bus, my phone buzzed. A little iota of hope popped up that it was Ethan until I looked at the screen. My mom. I did not have the energy to talk to her, although I was less afraid of talking to her than I was of talking to Ethan. But since I had the option of speaking to neither, I put the phone back in my pocket and let the call go to voice mail. She always left a voice mail no matter how many times I told her that I could see that she had called. I waited until the message popped up and listened to it.

"Hannah, it's your mother. I think you're graduating soon, so I wanted to say congratulations. You're such a smart girl. I know you'll love that fancy job you got in New York City. I just wanted to say good luck and I wish you the best. I know you'll be happy. Give us a call when you can. We love you."

I sighed. My mother had never made a major choice like this; she had been in Winthrop her whole life, same job, same house. She might be able to feel sympathy, but she would not be able to empathize, no less advise. She would also be confused. She had liked Ethan when I brought him home for Christmas after our first semester together. She thought he was polite and she liked the flowers he brought for her. My high school and college boyfriend, Eric, had only ever brought over laundry to do, although my mother had liked him anyway because once he had mowed her lawn. She had been a bit suspicious of Ethan before she met him. She knew his family was rich, and that made her insecure about her house, but he made her feel at ease right away by coming in, kissing her on the cheek, and offering to fix the door on the china closet that was not closing right (only after she complained about it). She was afraid that I was quickly becoming an old maid at twenty-eight, and bringing home Ethan that first Christmas helped to alleviate her fears. I think, like all good parents, she just wanted everything to be settled for me. She had blamed me when Eric and I had broken up. Her view was that I moved to New York and left him behind. But really, he wanted to stay at the restaurant in Iowa City where we both worked, and New York scared him. He said he wouldn't even come to visit me, and I wasn't going to wait around for him. So, I left. My mother said after I was gone, he came to the house, weeping, and sat in my childhood bedroom for about six hours. She claimed I was a fool to let him go. She blamed me for that breakup and would blame me for whatever happened with Ethan. Therefore, I wasn't going to call her back just yet.

When the bus arrived at Fifth and Mission in San Francisco, I decided that I couldn't bear to ask Ethan for his help this time, so I schlepped my bag and my backpack onto the BART and took the train back to Berkeley. I walked in the door just after seven and Ethan was sitting on the couch, unshaven, wearing a Hanes T-shirt with yellow armpits and sweatpants. A beer and an empty plate with cheese residue sat in front of him on the coffee table and a basketball game was blaring on the television.

"I'm back," I said. I dropped my things near the front door and headed straight for the kitchen. "I'm starving," I said. "I didn't have lunch." Nervous talking. *Stop it, Hannah.* Ethan didn't respond. The kitchen showed signs of a frozen pizza being heated and eaten, but no remnants were visible.

I made a quick peanut butter sandwich with the Wonder Bread I had put in the freezer for just such an emergency. Bread was always getting moldy in our apartment because we would buy fancy bread at the farmers' market and then not have time to eat it. So one week, I went to Safeway and bought a loaf of Wonder Bread. I put the whole loaf in the freezer and it was a revelation. I could defrost a slice whenever I wanted. And since Ethan thought it was disgusting, he would never eat it. I spread peanut butter on one slice of bread and folded it into a half sandwich, trying to compose myself before I went back to the living room to get my bag.

Another one of my house rules was that suitcases should never be left packed. Maybe it was because when my mom brought my father's bag back after his truck crash, she left it packed in their bedroom for almost three years. We never even really unpacked it, but after three years, Drew and I moved it to the back of her closet one afternoon when she was on a long shift. I headed back to the front door to get my bag to put the Sonoma things away immediately, even though I knew I was going to pack everything up in a few days. When I went into the bedroom to sort everything, I found the bed unmade and Ethan's still-packed suitcase sitting on the floor next to the bed. I gritted my teeth. He knew that drove me crazy, and I was sure he did it just to get under my skin.

I put my clothes in the hamper, placed my shoes back in the shoe rack, and carried my toiletry bag through the living room on the way to the bathroom. As I passed by the couch, I said, "Don't you want to do the laundry from this trip so you can get ready to pack up? For New York?"

"I want to talk to you about what you're going to do about the winery," he said.

"I have to put all of this away and then I have to finish that paper for applied innovation," I said.

"I'm surprised it even matters to you," he said.

"The paper? Why?" I asked. He was staring at

me, so I brushed at my face. I had peanut butter on my lips. I licked it off.

"Because you're throwing your future away. Why would you care about grades?"

"I don't want to fail," I said.

"That sounds like not caring to me," he said.

"I care," I said.

"But you're going to stay here and work in a winery."

"Yes," I said.

He looked back at my notes for my paper, searching for an argument that would make sense. "And what about us? Do I still go to New York?"

"Of course you should go to New York," I said. "You've already started developing your app with Graham and Jesse. It wouldn't make sense for you to stay here. And who knows what is going to happen in the future."

"How can you say that so flippantly? All of a sudden, we're going from moving in together in New York to living on separate coasts," he said.

"I'm not being flippant. I'm just trying to be sensible. I want to try this thing out here. And if it doesn't work out, I can move to New York."

"But you're giving up the job you worked all through grad school to get. I feel like this is about something else. Is this about that guy who worked at the winery? The son?"

"Not at all," I said. "He's going to New York too. You can hang out with him if you want to.

I'm going to be in a winery with two middle-aged people who don't understand the Internet."

"This just feels like a breakup," Ethan said.

"Well, it isn't," I said. Being home did remind me of all the fun that we had together, and about the time he had taken care of me when I had the flu, the time he had stayed up late into the night helping me memorize a speech for Business Communication. I didn't want to break up with him, but I also didn't want to be in New York with him this summer.

"Maybe it should be," he said.

I could feel tears forming in my eyes. I blinked them away. Took a deep breath.

"Why?"

"You're not choosing us," he said.

"Aren't I allowed to explore what I want? I'm only thirty years old."

"I was three when my parents were our age." This was something I had also thought about. I was nine when my parents were thirty, Drew was eleven, and Ethan was apparently three. My father didn't go to college or graduate school; he just got a trucker's license. My mother got pregnant, and then, when she had a small baby, she got an associate's degree and took nursing courses while she worked in a doctor's office as a receptionist. And thank goodness she had done that, because she was a widow by age thirty-two. My parents lived in the town next to the one where they were born and would stay there until they died. I wanted to explore, and I knew I could fit it all in. Sometimes when I thought about it long enough, it made me angry that there's a tight timeline for women, that we have to figure things out by the time we're in our late thirties. What if it takes longer than that? I couldn't change biology, but I was only thirty and an opportunity was in front of me. I wanted to take it.

"So? It's a different world from when we were born," I said. "We have more opportunities."

"Hannah, I don't want things to change. I know I always had ideas about how things would be. About where my life would be when I was in my thirties. And when I met you . . . I thought this was going to be something. And now nothing is settled. I wanted—"

"I don't know what I want anymore," I said, cutting him off.

"Okay," he said. Now it looked like he was going to cry. "I guess for now we should just focus on getting through the next few days."

"Right," I said. "Focus. One day at a time. It's like a twelve-step program."

"Except I don't feel like I'm recovering," he said.

"It's a metaphor," I said.

I went to bed first that night, like I always did. And he snuck into the bedroom, trying to be respectful and not wake me, like he always did, but he always woke me. I always pretended that he didn't. He put his back to me, like he just wanted to go to sleep. I turned over and put my arm over him. "I do love you," I said. "I'm just really confused."

"I love you too." He sighed.

The week passed by in a blur. We respectfully slept in the same bed, not crossing the centerline. We finished up our classes and wrote papers and edited each other's work like we'd been doing all year. Tyra came by to gloat about getting my job at Goldman, but the fact that she was so happy made it hard to talk about my own conflict. I wasn't sure if our friendship would ever recover. Ethan and I packed up the apartment together and hired a storage company to come and take our things away. We would figure out what to do with them when the summer was over and I decided what to do next. We packed suitcases with what we would need for the summer. We went to graduation and had dinner with Ethan's parents at Chez Panisse. My mom and Drew couldn't make it, because Drew couldn't leave his school so close to the end of the year and my mother wouldn't travel alone. Ethan felt bad that I didn't have anyone to celebrate graduation with, and he nicely shut his parents down when they started asking when we would get engaged. He turned the conversation neatly to the renovation of their Scottsdale kitchen, and that consumed his mother for almost half the dinner. Ethan sold his car to a fellow Haas grad who was going to be working at Google.

On Sunday, May 14, at four A.M., we got out of bed and packed my car in silence. The street was deserted, all the lights off, and I imagined we were the only two people left in the world, walking up and down the steps of our building. It was like we both were making it take longer than necessary, neither one of us quite ready to go our separate ways. It was almost too quiet to talk. We passed each other sheepishly in the hallway. Ethan cleaned the bathroom mirror one last time and checked to make sure all the burners on the gas stove were turned off. We locked the front door together and walked down the stairs one final time, hand in hand, not speaking.

We settled into the car. He flipped on the radio, but I flipped it off. Then he flipped it back on again.

After a long silence, he said, “One thing.”

I took a deep breath. I didn’t really want to hear the “one thing.” I muttered a little “Hmm?”

“Where am I going to live?” he asked.

“What?” I asked.

“I can’t afford that apartment you rented on my own. Also, you should try to get your security deposit back so you can pay back your signing bonus."

"Your parents' place? Your friends Graham and Jesse?" His parents had plenty of room and were never even in their Park Avenue apartment. They spent the summer in the Hamptons and the winter in Scottsdale. He had lived there before he went to school. I didn't think it would be a problem for him to do it again.

"I was hoping to be independent," he said. "I *am* thirty years old after all."

"It'll be fun," I said.

He put his head in his hands. At that moment, I had a flash of regret at what I was doing. My decision was hurting him, and it hurt my heart. But there was also a fine line between looking out for myself and feeling like a selfish person. I had read enough articles in women's magazines about how women sacrifice their own happiness in order to keep from appearing selfish. Was what I was doing selfish? Maybe. But it was also what I needed to do. I had decided long ago that I was allowed to be selfish because so much of my childhood was stolen from me.

We pulled up to the airport and I popped the trunk. The sun still wasn't up and the lights of the departures lane created a little illuminated cocoon around the car in an expanse of darkness. He got out of the car and retrieved his suitcase. I lowered the window and he leaned back through. "I guess this is it," he said.

"I'll talk to you soon," I said. "This isn't good-bye."

"I'll be waiting," he said.

I closed the window, watched in the rearview mirror as he entered the airport, and drove away.

Chapter 7

After dropping Ethan off at the airport, I felt a bit adrift. It was too early, really, to head to Bellosguardo. It was an hour-and-a-half drive to Sonoma and it was just after five A.M. I had been invited for dinner, so I needed to find something to do for at least part of the day. All of our classmates had scattered. The roads were empty. I felt like the only person in all of San Francisco.

When I was a little girl, I made mix tapes for myself of my favorite songs from Casey Kasem's weekly Top 40 on the radio. I wanted so badly to have a copy of "Killing Me Softly" by the Fugees so that I could sing along over and over again. And even though the songs on my mix tapes had been taped off the radio, I was proud of them because they were in a specific order, an order that nobody else had. I liked to lie on the plastic lounge chair in the backyard and listen to the tapes on my father's old Walkman, the yellow one that was supposed to be for sports. I would listen and think, *I am the only person in the world listening to these songs in this order right now.* What were the odds that someone else wanted to listen to "Killing Me Softly" and then "Me and Bobby McGee" and then "Who Will Save Your Soul" and then "Tainted Love," a song my sometime babysitter, Julie, from down the street had always liked? I adored the idea of being the only one doing something. Of being unique. At age eleven, all I should have wanted to do was fit in; something about the fact that I loved to read books and to make radio mix tapes, and the uncool clothes that my mother bought me because they were affordable, just didn't allow that to happen. In retrospect, I was cool. At the time, I felt just strange.

Now, at five A.M., with no old home to go back to and no new home to get to yet, I felt like the only person on earth. So I headed to Golden Gate Park to watch the sun rise. The park was on the way to Sonoma, but if the weather was nice, it wasn't a bad place to spend time. I was a pretty good sleeper—insomnia hit me in only the most stressful of times—so it was rare for me to see the sun rise. I pulled into the parking lot and got my running shoes out of the trunk. I was already wearing my gray-and-black running pants and flowy gray running tank top underneath a cowl-neck tunic, more out of comfort than out of any plan to exercise, but now I was glad I was. The running clothes looked just like the Lululemon ones that I coveted but were from the remarkably more affordable Old Navy. I took off the tunic and put it and my clogs in the trunk. I laced up my pink-and-gray Brooks running shoes from Nordstrom Rack. I left my music in the car and decided just to be alone with my thoughts. Running had always been the way I processed what was going on in my life. I had started on the track team in high school. I was never very good, always near the back of the pack, but I liked the other people on the team and nobody seemed to begrudge my slow pace. I never complained about the workouts and I slowly got in better shape. I never was fast, but I learned to love the feeling of running, the calm it brought to me. I'd fallen out of the habit a bit in graduate school, partially because of stress and partially because I spent most of my free time with Ethan, but I was going to get back into it this summer.

As I ran, I thought about my classes in graduate school, Strategic Leadership and Problem Solving, and about the winery, what could make it tick. Sure, they needed some fun social media, and a party to engage the locals and some tourists would be good. But what could really make them increase their sales? Restaurants and wine stores buying by the case was good, but it was better to have a chain store that needed a bigger order. Maybe having sales reps out there selling wine would help, a kind of distribution deal. I wondered if they even had the wine-making capacity to handle bigger orders. I would need to ask. William had said they sold three thousand cases a year but wanted to sell more. I didn't know what capacity was needed to make and sell five thousand or seven thousand cases, how much space for fermentation, but Everett seemed like the kind of person who would know such things. I would ask him when I got to Sonoma. The sun peeked out from behind the hills as I ran and tried to do math in my head. Math wasn't my strongest suit; it was the part I struggled with the most on the GMAT and in my finance class. But sometimes when I was running, a little bit of arithmetic was just the thing to make the run go by faster. Concentrating on a math problem, and on the way the sky was filling up with pink and orange light, made the miles go by less painfully. I still hadn't figured out what was going to save Bellosguardo, but I was going to try.

I wished there was somewhere to take a shower, but doubling back to the Berkeley gym felt completely out of the way, nor did I know if I could even get in there anymore. Besides, that would be like going back into my past when I needed to take steps toward my future. So I stood behind my car after my run and looked into the little compact mirror in my makeup kit. I brushed my hair into a ponytail and tapped some concealer under my blue eyes and some mascara on my lashes. My cheeks had some color from the run, but I figured that would be gone by the time I got to Sonoma, so I put some cheek stain on my cheekbones. I pulled the cowl-neck tunic back on over my running top and ran a little rollerball of perfume over my wrists. I nodded at the mirror. It wasn't great, but it would do. I got back in the car, put on my Lady Power mix, which included songs like "Miss Independent," "Brass in Pocket," and "Hollaback Girl," and I drove over the Golden Gate Bridge toward my summer adventure. I was pretty sure I wasn't the only person to have made such a mix, but at that moment, I felt like the strongest woman in the whole world.

The Lady Power mix, and a little NPR thrown in for good measure, propelled me through the ninety-minute drive. It was a little early to go to Bellosguardo still, though, so I parked in front of the wide window of Sunflower Caffé.

As I sat in the car, I sent a FaceTime request to my niece. Talking to her always made me feel better; her view of the world was always positive and unfiltered. She said exactly what she thought, and all of it was on instinct; it was refreshing. "Aunt Hannah!" she yelled as she picked up. She was in the backyard wearing a bathing suit. "It's hot out today and we got out the sprinkler!"

"That's fun," I said.

"What are you doing today?" she asked.

"I'm moving to a new place and starting a new job," I said.

"That sounds fun," she said. "Maybe we'll get to come visit you."

"You're welcome anytime," I said.

"And Patches too?"

"If he can walk that far," I said.

"We wouldn't walk to California, silly. We would drive and he loves the car. He misses you, Aunt Hannah," Gillian said.

"I miss him, and you, and Duncan too," I said. Duncan was not as chatty as Gillian, so I spoke to him less, but I adored them equally.

Gillian pointed the phone at the dog, who was soaking wet. I felt sorry for Drew and Elise, who would have to clean it all up.

"I love you," she said.

"Love you too," I said.

I headed inside, gave an "it's too early for this" smile to the barista, and ordered a latte, bravely resisting the pastries. I picked up a relatively current copy of *Sonoma Magazine* from the table next to where the sugar and milk were kept, and I settled myself, my latte, and my magazine on a high stool near the window so I could watch as people walked by. It was a relatively older crowd, people not afraid to wear shorts and white socks. I assumed those people were tourists. There was also a fashionable element, women in slim-fitting dresses and stiletto sandals carrying colorful Marc Jacobs handbags. I assumed those were locals.

I was reading about how the proceeds of a wine auction were benefiting the children of local migrant workers when a tall, slim woman with a blond pixie cut wearing a white leather jacket and a pair of cuffed jeans approached me. “You’re the new girl helping out at Bellosguardo.”

I turned and raised my eyebrows. I had been in town for less than an hour and I hadn’t met very many people—William, Linda, Everett, Reed, Betty at the hotel, and the bartender at La Salette whose name I had forgotten, and that was more than a week ago. But maybe in a small town, that was enough.

“I’m Celeste,” she said. “I make it my business to know everything that’s happening around here. And besides, I’m friends with William. He told me. And then I found your photo on Facebook. I know, I know, I’m a stalker.”

I had so many questions: How did she know William? How close were they? She was pretty and thin, so that made me feel jealous too. But I was new in town, and *you have a boyfriend,* I reminded myself as she sat herself down right next to me. “I’m Hannah,” I said.

“Welcome,” she said. “How are you finding Sonoma so far?”

“I just got here,” I said. “But it’s pretty.”

“Pretty,” she said. “Not beautiful.”

“I think it’s beautiful here,” I said.

“I was talking about you,” she said. “You’re pretty, but not beautiful.”

“Thanks, I appreciate it,” I said as a way of

ending the conversation. I turned back to my magazine. Who was this person? And had she heard of girl code? Even if I wasn't beautiful, no woman wanted to be told that to her face.

"Don't be offended. You don't want to be beautiful," she said, as if she knew what it was like to bear that burden.

"I think all women want to be beautiful," I said. If I was honest with myself, I had never thought of myself as beautiful. I had thought of myself as strong. As athletic. Pretty. I was tall enough to pull off a jumpsuit and a maxidress, and thin enough to wear a pencil skirt. Not a model, but I was in shape. There were days in New York when I worked at Tiffany's and I wore heels and the black Chanel suit edged in white that my boss had given to me as a Christmas gift and the vintage coat that I had bought for one hundred dollars on MacDougal Street with fur lollipop arms and a fur collar and a wool body, my brown hair highlighted and cut in a reverse bob and big sunglasses over my face, and I felt fabulous. Walking into Tiffany's in that outfit and taking the elevator up to the ninth floor, using my staff ID, I felt like I belonged. Like I was somebody. And maybe that wasn't exactly beautiful, but it was something. I needed to figure out a way to feel that way about working at Bellosguardo. Like I belonged there, and belonged to myself.

"You want to *feel* beautiful, but you don't want

to *be* beautiful. *Being* beautiful means nobody ever leaves you alone."

I mumbled something under my breath about how I was learning what that was like.

"I'm sorry," she said. "I feel like we've gotten off on the wrong foot. Sometimes I don't have a filter. I'm a Sagittarius. I mean well. I just . . ." She put her hands up to her face.

"It's okay," I said.

"Listen," she said. "I grew up here. William and I were raised on the same blanket together. My parents make wine on the other side of the hill from the Rockfords. I know everyone here. And I sell real estate, so I know everything. Where the sinkholes are."

I nodded and tried to smile. I wasn't entirely sure what was happening. "It must be a nice place to grow up," I said.

"I love it here. I could never live anywhere else. It takes a certain . . . kind of person to live here, and I'm that kind. I don't have any other skills other than being a person who lives in Sonoma," she said. "Of course, William always had bigger dreams. But he'll be back. He'll realize."

She opened her purple Mulberry handbag and pulled out a bedazzled business card case. She snapped it open and took out a letter-pressed card. She put it on the counter next to my coffee and hopped off the stool. "Celeste Davis. Call me."

I took the card and put it in my pocket. I was not going to. As if she could read my mind, she came back. “You know what?” she said. “You better give me your number, too. Just in case I need to reach you first.” She handed me her phone so I could put my number into it. And for some reason, I did. Everyone needs a friend. Even a kind of stalkerish crazy one.

Chapter 8

When it was a reasonable hour for me to head to the winery, I threw away my coffee cup, got back in my red Hyundai Accent, and drove up to Bellosguardo. The parking lot was full, which I took as a good omen. I parked my car and left the suitcases in it. I headed into the tasting room, where Everett was in the far corner behind a card table leading a wine tasting for five middle-aged women wearing matching purple fedoras, Eileen Fisher–style tunics, leggings, and clogs. Linda was behind the bar, so I headed to her instead. She was pouring a tasting for a young couple, both of whom had a baby strapped to their backs. Twins. I sidled up beside the woman. They were on the reds, and I looked down at her notes. She had checked off the Pinot Noir and had written a star next to the Cabernet Franc. "Good choices," I said. The woman was a little startled but looked at me and smiled. Linda noticed me next.

"Hannah!" she exclaimed. "You're here!"

"I start tomorrow, don't I?"

"You do!" she said. "And I invited you for dinner tonight, didn't I? It's William's last night before he goes to New York."

"You did," I said. "Do you want me to get anything ready?"

"Don't be silly," she said. "Just go get yourself settled in the cottage. Do you know how to get there? Just pull your car around behind the tasting room and go up the stone steps."

I nodded and turned back toward the door. The women in the back were giggling. Everett must have had some wine-tasting shtick that he did. So far I hadn't found him to be warm, or even conversational. Plus, I knew that he didn't want me here in the first place. But the group seemed to be enjoying themselves, so who was I to judge?

I went back out to the lot and did as Linda said, pulled the car around back, got my suitcases and my backpack out of the trunk, and pulled them up the stone steps. I hadn't showered after my run and I was feeling pretty salty.

The front door of the cottage was unlocked and there were flowers, a bottle of Pinot Noir, a block of Comté, and a jar of quince paste out on the kitchen island. A note from Linda in flowy penmanship read, *Welcome, Hannah.*

I smiled, unwrapped half of the cheese, and broke off the front of the wedge. I ate it, rind and all. The only thing that could have made it taste better was a slice of focaccia. But I'll eat cheese with or without carbs, and this was a cheese that could stand alone. As I chewed, I went straight into the bathroom to shower.

The bathroom was all marble and the shower

was the kind that sprayed water not just from the top but into my back as well. There was also a steam setting that I was excited to learn more about. It was just the right temperature and pressure. I felt myself relax. After all that had happened, I was finally in the place where I was meant to be.

Wrapped in a soft towel, I went back to the bedroom, which was also gorgeous—a king-size bed with a gray fabric headboard. There were books neatly stacked on each nightstand. One stack contained books about wine. The other, contemporary novels—Elin Hilderbrand, Meg Wolitzer, Ann Patchett. I loved them all. There was also an overstuffed chair with a perfect reading light over it and a walk-in closet.

I launched myself onto the huge bed and looked at the clock before giving in to a nap. I had, after all, been up at four A.M. I slept a dreamless, drooling sleep and woke at six. I felt groggy, but I forced myself to wake up. I riffled through my suitcase and put on my nicest dress, a gray sleeveless shift from Theory that I had planned to wear my first day at Goldman Sachs. I grabbed a light blue cashmere wrap that I had planned to use in the office to fend off aggressive air-conditioning. Evenings did tend to get chilly here, so it could fend off the natural chill instead. I applied a light lip stain from Fresh on my lips. It woke up my face but didn't make it seem like

I had tried too hard. When I was ready, I put the rest of my clothes and toiletries away, trying to make the room feel like my own, even though it clearly wasn't.

I walked out into my living room, intending to have a little bit of water, maybe make a coffee to further perk myself up. There was an incredible built-in espresso machine in the kitchen that Linda had left instructions for. I took my espresso and settled myself on the couch that felt like a hug when you sat on it. Linda had left a stack of books on the coffee table as well, including *The Secret Garden* (which looked new) and the copy of *Little Women* that I had taken off the shelf on my last visit. I tried to read, but my brain just couldn't concentrate on the words, even though they were so familiar to me, I should have had them memorized. I remembered how much I idolized Jo March, the second sister, the writer, the one, I had learned as a child, whom Louisa May Alcott modeled on herself. She had wild brown hair that she couldn't control and was always obsessively writing plays and making her siblings perform them. She had a desk in the "garret" of the house (which I had assumed was a fancy word for attic; I later confirmed that it was), where she would write wearing a hat with a feather in it. She was a true artiste, in my opinion. Even though the youngest sister, Amy, wanted to be a painter and had gotten lessons from the man next door and had gone to Italy, it was Jo, who eventually chose to be a teacher, whom I admired. Maybe it was the brown hair or the childhood love of reading, both of which I shared. But Jo had settled; she had given up her desire to be a writer to be a wife to Professor Bhaer and to run the school with him. I never felt disappointed in Jo when I was younger, but I also wasn't an analyzer of literature. As I thought about her now, I thought maybe she had compromised too much. But, of course, Jo was based on Louisa May Alcott, and she herself did not compromise, or if she did, I didn't know about it. She did become a writer after all. She followed her dream. She wrote the books in 1860s Massachusetts that I as a little girl in late 1990s Iowa devoured. If that wasn't success, what was?

I leafed through that book and also through some of the design magazines that Linda had scattered on the coffee table. I found an old copy of *Sonoma Magazine* with a profile of Everett, Linda, and William in it. William looked about fourteen and the interviewer had asked them about the competition from what she called "mega-wineries" in the area. Linda had been demure and stated, "Of course, it's a thing that worries us, mass producers taking shelf space away. But we've always been independent and we'll stay that way. We grow our own grapes and we stand behind the quality of our wine. It's a family business and it won't ever be anything but." I thought about them all together—Everett, Linda, and William—and I wished my family was that close. Although, being the one who lived far away and didn't return my own mother's phone calls, I was probably the reason my family wasn't that way.

At around seven thirty, I headed up more stone steps to the castle. I was approaching from the back, but it was still majestic, made entirely of gray stone, with carvings of grapes above the center of each window. And there were dozens of windows. The stone path that continued from the steps wound around to the side of the house, where I found Everett and William sitting at a wooden picnic table adjacent to a side door. They were drinking wine and had an extensive spread of cheese in front of them.

"Welcome," William said, winking at me. "My mom's in the kitchen; go grab a glass." He pointed toward the door.

I nodded and headed into the house. In comparison with the kitchen in the cottage, this kitchen was shabbier—linoleum tile, old appliances, a movable butcher-block center island that reminded me of the one I had in Berkeley. The breakfast nook looked like a booth from a pizza place—two orange benches with a faux wood-grain table between them. Linda was next to the sink slicing vegetables into a huge bowl—she was surrounded by zucchini and asparagus and cherry tomatoes. "These were all growing in the garden until a few minutes ago," she said.

"That's amazing," I said.

"You must have had garden dinners when you were growing up in Iowa."

"We weren't farmers," I said, trying not to sound too snarky. I'd always been slightly irritated by the stereotype that everyone from Iowa was a farmer. I grabbed a wineglass from the drying rack next to the sink.

"Neither are we," she said. It was kind that she chose to identify with me rather than pick up on my rankled feelings. "But it's so fun to grow these things yourself. The garden is out back. Feel free to help yourself to anything, especially the lettuce. It grows faster than we can eat it, even if we have it at every meal."

"Thanks," I said. "This takes farm to table to a different level."

"Let's call it garden to table," she said. "I'm just going to roast all these vegetables a little and put them over this cavatelli that I made this morning." She showed me a bowl of pastas that looked like tiny hot dog buns.

"You made this by hand?" I asked, incredulous.

"It's so easy if you have a pasta maker. I find it therapeutic. It requires just enough attention that you don't have to think about anything else. But not so much that you're tired."

I nodded. "It sounds like meditating."

"Kind of," she said. "But you're not here to talk about that, and the wine is outside. Go join them; I'll be out in a minute."

I looked down at the glass in my hand and headed back outside, realizing that I should have brought flowers or some sort of contribution to dinner. I eased myself onto the picnic table bench across from William. He poured me a glass of red and they continued their conversation about Tannin's limp. I didn't have anything to contribute to that conversation other than the fact that I thought he was pretty cute whether he limped or not.

When the conversation lulled into comments about the quality of the wine and the temperature of the evening, both of which were generally approved of, I decided to venture into possibly dicey territory, so I looked at William and asked, "Where are you going to be living in New York?"

Immediately, Everett made a snorting noise and got up from the table. "I'll go check on Linda."

William smiled. He clearly liked making his parents uncomfortable. "I'm staying with my friend Simon in the East Village for a few days and then I'll find a sublet or a roommate situation in Brooklyn."

"I used to live in Ditmas Park," I said.

"Oh," he said. "I don't know where that is."

"It's a supercute neighborhood in Brooklyn. And it's affordable, or it was when I lived there. My apartment was tiny, but I loved living there. I had this big couch that was blue and kind of shaggy that I found at a thrift store. My best friend, Nicole, called it Grover. She lived next door and would come over almost every night. Even though the apartment was small, I set up a full bar right outside the tiny kitchen, so people loved coming over. Nicole and I were always experimenting with new cocktails. One year, I threw an epic New Year's party where everyone brought sleeping bags and we set them all up like a patchwork so everyone could crash after they were done drinking. You could fit about eight people in there with the bags all side to side. Even though most of my friends lived within a five-block radius, the sleepover part was the best part."

Life in New York may have been stressful at times, but it was never boring. I liked the pace of it, that it was never quiet, that it was never predictable. I loved the fact that I could just walk to the bar on my corner and know half the people in there. But even with all the people around me, I will admit that sometimes I was lonely. I wanted someone to love me. That was probably why I fell for Ethan. But life with Ethan wasn't what I wanted either, it turned out. I wanted more. I wanted all the fun and variety that my life had in Brooklyn, plus a great job and someone who adored me. Was that too much to ask?

"That does sound fun," he said. "And you worked at Tiffany's? That must have been weird."

"Yeah, it was, like, behind-the-scenes stuff, though, not like I stood at a counter and sold diamonds to rich people. I made sure that my boss, Cheryl, went to all of her meetings and that the advertising proofs got circ'ed to the right people and that the invoices got paid on time. It was a long commute and long hours, but I learned a lot and got these earrings out of it." I pulled my hair back to show the 1.5-carat studs Cheryl had just pulled out of her desk one afternoon a few weeks before I left and given to me. She had said that I couldn't be in business without a proper pair of diamond earrings. I did wear them to my Goldman interview and on my first date with Ethan. And today. I liked to think they brought me luck.

"Nice," he said, clearly uninterested.

"I'm more excited about the wine here, though," I said.

"More than diamonds?" William asked.

"Absolutely," I said. "Although I'm sure that one of those Disneyland gift shops up the road has a T-shirt that says, 'Wine Is a Woman's Best Friend,' with a picture of a dog and a wineglass on it."

William laughed. “Those places are pretty ridiculous, aren’t they?”

“Terrible,” I said. “Terrifying, actually.”

“Do you think Bellosguardo needs a gift shop?” William asked. “I think we should have one even though they’re tacky. People ask about it and it’s another way to make money.”

“I don’t think so,” I said. “I mean, if people want to buy the branded glasses, you should sell them at a markup. But I think those gift shops are pretty lowbrow, and that’s not your brand.”

“Good answer,” Everett yelled from the door. He was opening another bottle of wine but clearly had been listening the entire time.

Linda came out of the kitchen carrying a huge bowl of pasta covered in vegetables. “Pasta primavera!” she said, setting it in the middle of the table.

“It looks amazing,” I said.

We each heaped piles of pasta onto our plates and murmured our approval.

“This is delicious,” I said, genuinely impressed.

“What grows together, goes together,” Everett said.

“I love that saying,” I said.

“It’s especially true here,” he said, “because of the history of fruits and vegetables growing on this property along with the grapes. The grapes take on the flavor of the other food growing here. So you might notice a little hint of rosemary in the Zinfandel that we're drinking. That's because we have rosemary planted all along the side of the vineyard. Mostly because I like how it smells."

They were so devoted to the beauty of their land, to the perfect taste of their food and wine. I wondered why their kitchen was so shabby in comparison to the one in the cottage and what the rest of their giant house looked like. I hadn't had the wherewithal to look around when I'd gone in for a glass. Dinner chitchat was casual, about the time that William should leave for the San Francisco airport in the morning, about how Everett disapproved of a fellow winemaker irrigating his fields so early in the season, about how a new restaurant was opening in Petaluma that Linda wanted to target for getting Bellosguardo wines on the first menu. As they chatted and I only half listened, I couldn't help but stare at William. He had great posture sitting at this picnic table, which made me think he had great abs, not that I had any proof. A long face with pronounced cheekbones. His style outside of the tasting room was casual hipster—an artfully fraying plaid shirt and a tattoo of a wine bottle peeking out from his left short sleeve. It was a good look on him.

"Did you know that William didn't like grapes when he was little? Even delicious, sweet ones. What kid, especially one who grew up in a vineyard, doesn't like grapes?" Everett asked.

"I still think you gave me the bitter ones," William said.

"You never wanted to really be in the business," Everett said.

I started to feel uncomfortable.

"I just want to try something else out. I've given lots to this business. I came back here after college, didn't I? I could have stayed in LA," William said.

"That was because of—"

"Let's not talk about that now," William said. He shifted his attention to me. "Do you want to go see the vines before it gets too dark?" he asked. Linda was nervously stacking dishes to bring them back into the kitchen. "Great time of day; the bees are mostly asleep so you can get close enough to taste the grapes."

"Mostly asleep?" I asked.

"You're not allergic, are you?"

"Not that I know of," I said. "But I don't want to get stung to find out."

"Don't worry," he said. "I'll protect you."

I teased, "Kind of hard to do with bees. Unless you have a spare beekeeper's outfit that I can borrow."

"I'll see if I can find one before our walk," he joked back. He punched me in the arm really lightly, and it felt electric. The spot where he touched lingered warm long after.

I loved how we were already familiar, how

it felt like I was part of the family. I was ignoring the fact that Everett and Linda had been scowling as William and I talked about Brooklyn neighborhoods. Instead of interpreting their scowls as discomfort with me, a relative stranger, being part of this family discussion, I chalked it up to their disapproval of William's summer plans. I so wanted to be a part of this family. Besides, I was beginning to disapprove of William's plans too. I wanted him in the same place as me, not in the same place as Ethan.

We brought the rest of the plates into the house, refilled our glasses, and headed out to the vines, as he called them.

The vines were old in this part of the vineyard. Many were ones that the count had planted when he originally settled the land, but the growth was young, William told me. It was the beginning of the season, so the grapes were still tiny, like little rocks, and tasted sour. He picked one and fed it to me, but I puckered at the taste and spit it out.

"I'm sure the rabbits will appreciate that," he said.

"There are rabbits?" I asked.

"And mice and even marmots. But we hate the marmots. They make too many holes."

We walked together through the rows and he told me which wine would be made from each grape. How they would taste. How long they would need to be aged. Where each vine had originally come from. How long it had been growing. At the end of each row was a rosebush. William plucked a rose for me.

"We keep roses at the end of each row because roses get the same mildew diseases that grapes get, but they get them first. They're like our canaries in a coal mine, but for wine."

I sniffed the lush pink rose. It was so fragrant that it made me sneeze. "But you're allowed to pick one for me?"

"Just doing research. Looks healthy," he said. "And bless you."

"Thank you!" I said, almost singing. "You know so much about this place." I skipped ahead down the row of grapes, which seemed to go on for miles, sloping downhill. The vines wrapped tightly around the trellises set up for them and the tendrils snaked toward me, as if they were reaching for me. The ground was soft and gave way under my flip-flopped feet. It felt slightly like a Disney movie, but in the best way possible. "It must be hard to leave it."

"It's where I grew up. But I need to see new things, you know?" He walked leisurely behind, occasionally stopping to look at a grape.

"I know," I said. "I was dying to get out of Iowa."

"Do you ever think about going back?"

"Never," I said. "But I do want to have a home

one day. Eventually I want to know somewhere like you know this place."

"I'll come back here one day," he said. "My parents think I won't. But I will. I just want to try something else. I don't know if I'll be any good at it, at making movies. But you only live once."

I stopped and touched the stony grapes with my hand, the tiny grapelings hard against my fingers. I plucked one from the vine. "What's your favorite?" I asked, holding one of the tiny grape rocks up to the sky.

"Grape? Probably Pinot Noir."

I laughed and dropped the grape. "No, silly! Movie."

He sighed. "Hard question to answer. I always say *The Conversation.* Because that's what a film person would say. But the truth is that I love John Hughes movies the most. First is probably *The Breakfast Club*; who doesn't love that one? Then *Weird Science* and *Planes, Trains and Automobiles*. I love how they create a world."

"Will you set your movies in Sonoma?"

"How could I not? It's the only place I know. But I also have to leave it to write about it."

"That makes sense." I had always wished I was a creative person—an artist—but the closest I ever got was knitting a scarf for my mom one Christmas. An ill-formed scarf no less. "So you haven't started yet?"

"I've started a million times, but I haven't made

much progress. They let me in on the back of a documentary short that I made about this place. I interviewed my parents and spliced in some old photos and took some B-roll in the vineyard."

"I'd love to see it," I said.

"It's terrible," he said. "It has fifty-one views on YouTube and approximately thirty-eight of them are definitely by my mom. But she loved it so much that she put it up on the vineyard website."

"Oh, the website," I said. "It's actually not a bad site. But I didn't see the video when I looked at it. She must have put it in kind of a weird spot."

"She's doing the best she can," he said.

"I'm impressed she can do it at all," I said. "But I can't wait to help her."

"You're sweet," he said.

"Anyway, the film must not be so bad if it got you into NYU."

He smirked, but I could tell he was proud of it. "Okay, I'll go grab my computer and meet you at the cottage."

We separated and I meandered back to the cottage, ducking under and around the vines, feeling elated. I tried to remember what it had been like when I'd met Ethan during business school orientation. We were both in the giant UC Berkeley bookstore. He was trying to decipher the codes on the course books to figure out what the reading lists would be for the classes he was interested in taking before attending them the first week. I was looking at the shelves devoted to undergraduate English classes with names like History of the English Novel and The Legacy of *The Odyssey*: Quest Novels. I'd picked a few things off the shelves; I'd left almost all of my books behind in New York and needed something to read before classes started in earnest. He'd come over to tell me not to poach books from the course selections because they were ordered with specific quantities in mind. "There has to be an overage," I'd said.

"You'll mess everything up," he said. "I used to work in my college bookstore. I know how the ordering works."

"How do you know I'm not just getting ready to take one of these classes?" I asked.

"You're wearing a Haas T-shirt," he said. "There's no way you have time to take these undergrad literature classes."

I looked down and it was indeed true. I'd been given the T-shirt when I registered and I hadn't unpacked my suitcases yet. "Good point," I said. "But I really want to read this." I held up a copy of *Ulysses*. "And they must account for some people who buy the books but don't take the classes. Or someone who will buy the books from somewhere else."

"I can't imagine you will be able to read that this semester. Just give up now and buy a romance novel." He was wearing a monogrammed shirt from Brooks Brothers tucked into perfectly pressed khaki pants; his hair was short, his neck perfectly shaved. He had aviator sunglasses on his head and was carrying a beat-up, but clearly fancy, leather briefcase. I wondered if it had been his father's before him, like the kind of family heirloom that is passed down on the first day of work. He looked straight out of prep school, like he had never figured out another way to dress. He wasn't unattractive; he had a strong jaw and a Roman nose. He was a regular guy. There was no way he had ever dated a dominatrix, and he wasn't fit enough to be gym obsessed.

I tried not to feel insulted by his romance novel comment. I wasn't against them, although I hadn't read one since my Mary Ellen library days. But he had said it with such a sneer that it made me defensive. Did he think I wasn't smart enough to read *Ulysses*? "I don't read romance novels," I said. "This is much more up my alley. And if that scares you, you can walk away right now."

He seemed a bit taken aback by my forwardness.

"Okay, okay," he said. "You read what you want."

I still thought he was condescending, so I

decided to give it right back to him. "What are *you* doing here?"

"Shopping classes before they start. You can know a lot about a class by the reading list, and the reading list is always right here in the bookstore before you have to sit through seventy-five minutes of class."

"I might be in denial about classes starting," I said. "I forgot that I was wearing this T-shirt. You are a very prepared person."

"Thank you," he said. "I'm Ethan Katz." He shifted the macroeconomics textbook in his right hand to under his left arm and held out his hand to shake mine.

"Hannah Greene," I said. I offered *Ulysses* as a means of a handshake. He shook the book, which made me smile.

"You're going to buy it, aren't you?"

"Just to annoy you," I said.

He followed me up to the register, bought *Ulysses* for me, and then asked me out for dinner at Chez Panisse. I had been in Berkeley for about a week, existing solely on ramen noodles and peanut butter sandwiches. How could I pass up an opportunity to eat at one of the best restaurants in the country? So, I had said yes. I hadn't felt a physical spark with him, but we clearly had plenty to fight with each other about from the very start. Ethan didn't want someone to flirt with him; he wanted someone to converse with, so my instinct toward low-grade conflict worked for us. It was a peculiar aspect of our relationship, mine and Ethan's, that often led to a kind of verbal combat and one-upmanship (combined with put-downs).

It wasn't the kind of relationship my parents had, and I'm not sure how I got that way. I remember when I was little, before the accident, my parents would never fight. They were brooders. If they were sad or angry, they would just go be by themselves until they figured it out. I swear there was an entire year where my parents barely spoke to each other, other than saying necessary things like "please pass the salt" and "the phone's for you." My dad was on the road a lot that year—sulking in his truck, most likely. I never knew quite what brought them back together, but then after that year, he was around more. And they were happier; they went out on dates, bought each other little gifts. He started bringing back pig figurines from each long haul that he went on, and pretty soon she had an entire windowsill of tiny pigs above the kitchen sink. "My mini farm," she used to call it. I'm so glad they had that year, because it was their last good one. That mini farm is still on the windowsill in my mother's kitchen. Lovingly dusted, but unchanged. That was how they showed affection in my family—with small gifts, a pat on the back, a smile. And anger and disappointment were never displayed with fighting.

Even as a small girl, I had been kind of the black sheep of the family emotionally. If I was sad about something and was asked about it at the breakfast table, I would start to cry. If I was mad, I would throw a toy. I became an expert at slamming my bedroom door. I once even broke the lock on the front door of the house by slamming it on my way out. It upset my mother, father, and brother so much when I was angry that I got angry more often. They called me "our little teenager." After my dad died, things did change; even I became a brooder. There wasn't energy or time to be passionate anymore.

Ethan's family had been intense: Dinnertime was a kind of interrogation, where you had to detail what you had done that day, prove your worth. His father, who was a high-powered hedge fund executive, always took time when Ethan was little to have dinner with the family, even if he went back to work late into the night after, so that mealtime was sacred, valuable. The idea of quality over quantity was important in the Katz household. If the answers weren't robust enough, Ethan's father challenged, asked more questions. The conflicts were always out in the open. Ethan didn't say he liked that approach to family bonding, but he also couldn't help but sometimes fall into the twenty-questions version of an interaction.

So, my attraction to Ethan was one of otherness,

strangeness. He was from a world I wished I could be a part of, the family I never had. The only problem was, I didn't always know what the line was between playing and fighting. For me, everything kind of felt like fighting, although I knew that for him mostly it felt like playing. Until it wasn't playing at all.

With William, the attraction was physical, a rumbly stomach, sweaty palms, a loss for words. Wanting just to touch each other. With Ethan, our relationship felt mature, grown-up, like we had been together forever. Dare I say boring? Or was physical attraction just a fleeting thing? I didn't know. Everything felt confusing, up in the air, adrift, and I felt like a teenager with a major crush.

William showed up at the cottage about forty-five minutes later carrying a laptop, a cable that would connect it to the TV, and a bottle of Port. I'd already taken a bottle of Pinot Noir out of the wine fridge, but he insisted that it was past that time of day. It was the time when you had to drink Port. "It's the ultimate nightcap," he said.

"Baileys on ice is the ultimate nightcap," I said. "Puts you right to sleep."

"That's what the movie is for," he said, his eyes twinkling. It was clear that despite his earlier protestations, he was proud of the film. "Also,

Baileys is gross. It's just chemicals. You should stop drinking that."

"I'm not sophisticated like you," I said.

"You used to work at Tiffany's," he said. "That sounds sophisticated to me." His hand lingered next to mine, his leg just adjacent, but with only a hint of closeness.

"But I'm from rural Iowa," I said. "I grew up on Wonder Bread and Chef Boyardee. Highbrow and lowbrow."

"You'll be one hundred percent highbrow by the time you leave here at the end of the summer," he said. "You might not even like California wine by then. You might only drink Italian. Some French."

"That doesn't seem possible," I said.

"Just wait," he said. "My dad can make a wine snob of anyone."

After he set up all the technology, we settled on the overstuffed couch with our glasses of Port and the film. It was indeed short, about fifteen minutes. It covered the history of the winery, some of which I had heard on my first visit. But it was romantic and elegiac. The violin music he had scored it with as he showed the rolling hills and the portraits of his ancestors really got to me. And he did this amazing time lapse of grapes growing on the vine. I wondered how he did that.

"I loved your film," I said when the credits rolled.

"Thanks," he said. "You don't have to say that."

"I am so impressed that you did it all yourself. And it brought tears to my eyes. The violin music was so beautiful."

"I really appreciate you saying that," he said. "It took a long time to get that fifteen minutes down."

He took my hand and I felt fluttery.

"Do you really have to leave tomorrow?" I asked.

"Yeah," he said. "The program officially starts in September, but I was eager to get started, so I'm taking some summer classes and working as an assistant to one of the professors, who is cutting a short film."

"Oh," I said, disappointed.

"If I'd known that you would be here, I'd probably have waited. But how could I have known? I am glad we met, though, and that you'll be here with my parents."

"I like your parents a lot," I said. "They like to explain things."

"Be careful," he said. "They're more complicated than they seem."

I nodded, not knowing what to make of that statement. My family was what you saw on the surface. My mother was lonely, living in the past. My brother was the good, strong one who took care of her, as well as his own family. And I was the one who ran away. When I took Ethan out to Iowa to visit on the Christmas trip we named "Meet the Greene," my mother behaved as well as I could have possibly expected. She wore clothes that weren't her hospital scrubs. She made my favorite food from childhood, macaroni and cheese with hot dogs in it, even though I had repeatedly told her that I didn't like that anymore. She told her favorite childhood story about me: about how she couldn't find me one morning for school; she checked everywhere in the house and called the neighbors and then called the school to tell them that I would be absent, and they told her that I had gotten to school at six thirty A.M. and was found waiting outside when the principal got to work at around seven. I had asked if I could go into the library because I had finished reading my book and needed a new one. Ethan asked what book I had finished, but I was pretty sure the story was apocryphal. After all, Mary Ellen kept me pretty well stocked. After dinner, we sat in the living room and silently watched a hockey game together. My father was a long-suffering Blackhawks fan and my mother, even though she never liked hockey, had taken it up after his death. She watched every Blackhawks game and, by now, even knew the players and the strategy. Even though she still claimed to hate the sport.

I knew that Ethan thought hockey fans were philistines, a fact he had admitted to me before I told him that my mother loved the Blackhawks. "It's different in the Midwest," he had said. "It's colder there." I liked seeing him backpedal. But my mother seemed to like Ethan, although she managed to bring up my high school and college boyfriend, Eric. She reported to the table that she had seen Eric himself with his daughter at the A&P and Drew had seen Eric's mother at the gas station.

"She lives in the past," I told him that night as we tried to get comfortable on the foldout couch in the basement; it felt like we were sleeping directly on the bars that held it up. The next day, we'd had brunch with Drew, his wife, Elise, and their kids, Gillian and Duncan. Elise and I had mimosas and we all watched the Vikings on a giant projection television.

"Welcome to the Midwest," Drew had said.

"It's not so bad," Ethan had said as he drank an Iowa microbrew. I could tell that at that moment, he meant it.

It took longer for me to meet Ethan's parents than it had taken for him to meet mine. After that first Christmas in Iowa, we had gone back to California together. He hadn't seen his family that holiday, claiming, "We don't celebrate Christmas. Why would I go visit my parents?"

It took until the spring when I was interviewing for my summer job at Goldman Sachs for us to fly together to New York. We stayed in the hotel Goldman had booked for me, so there was no weirdness about staying in the Katzes' apartment. But we also barely spent time with them. We met Franklin and Bunny (as she was called) Katz for dinner at the Four Seasons. Ethan's father didn't even let us see the menus, just ordered a round of martinis and steaks and lamented that the place would be closing soon. "It's an institution," he declared. "It's a travesty to mismanage a landmark." Then he delivered an extensive lecture on derivatives and their impact on the economy. Ethan's mother had told a remarkably boring story about a fund-raiser she was organizing to support artists in the public schools, not that she had ever set foot in a public school. Ethan had warned me about her boring stories and I had thought he was exaggerating, but she could make even a gossipy story about an artist having a nervous breakdown before her art was to be delivered to the auction sound truly tedious. Ethan kept squeezing my hand under the table as if to assure me that it would be over soon. After their monologues, they had asked me about my family and I had skirted the question a bit, which they hadn't really noticed, saying just that my mom lived in Iowa and was a nurse. "What a noble profession," Bunny said. She never asked a follow-up about my father, and it seemed too much to tell them. I didn't know if Ethan had briefed them on my father's death before the dinner or if they just didn't care enough to ask anything else.

They asked me about my plans after business school. They appreciated my answer about the summer job at Goldman and after that pretended that I wasn't there, discussing their plans for Passover in the Hamptons and Memorial Day in Scottsdale, although wouldn't it be oppressively hot there by then? Bunny gave me a kiss on each cheek at the end of dinner.

She patted Ethan on the head and said, "Don't mess this one up." I assumed that meant that she liked me. That night, he said, "I think they liked you because they just acted like they always act, like self-involved narcissists." I decided not to comment on that. It seemed like the type of thing you were allowed to say about your own parents but probably didn't want feedback from other people on. While I was at my day of interviews, Ethan went to see his friends and start-up cofounders, Graham and Jesse, in Brooklyn. Somehow I didn't get to meet them on that trip, which was disappointing. I had heard way more about them in our eight months of dating than about his parents. To me, it seemed like they were more like family, and he'd known them for almost as long. I tried not to be offended that I never got to meet them. He chalked it up to them working on their business plan, but it made me wonder if he was embarrassed by me. I never had the guts to ask.

I had never thought my family was strange—the prolonged silences, the lack of conflict, the disappearing act that my father did when he was unhappy, or the days he spent in dark rooms. Nor did I really have the space to evaluate all of the extra work I had to do taking care of my mom after my dad died. Even though I knew in theory it was unusual for an eleven-year-old to be responsible for making a grocery list, making sure dinner was available for anyone who wanted it, and cleaning the bathroom, it was my normal. It was a bit of an awakening when I started spending time with my high school boyfriend Eric's family. Eric had three sisters and about twenty first cousins, and their house was always filled with home-cooked food, lots of clutter, and laughter. There was always music playing on the radio or music being played on a piano or songs being sung. There was dancing. They played whiffle ball in the yard. I always wanted to be part of a family that was fun like Eric's, and I wondered sometimes if it had been a mistake to leave him behind. At the very least, he understood where I was from. What my roots were. And he would always be proud of me. He just wanted me to be happy. That was why he let me go; he knew I would be happier.

Ethan's family was intense. They had high

standards for themselves and their son. Ethan did brag about me once during the meal to his father, saying I was one of only a few members of our class to get this far in the interview process, that everyone was jealous of me. That was the one time his father perked up and looked at me kindly. Like I was more in his image than his own son. They didn't seem supportive of the tech start-up that Ethan was starting, which they found confusing and risky. "Why not just come join the old family business?" Franklin had asked. But Ethan had said, "Let me just try this, Dad." At least with my family, the expectations were so low that I never had to worry about disappointing anyone.

"You're different," I said to William.

"From who?" he asked.

"From other people I've met," I said.

"I'll take that as a compliment," he said.

"You take things in stride. And you're proud of what you've accomplished. But you want more. I find that inspiring."

"That's very sweet," he said.

"What do you mean about your parents being complicated?" I asked.

"Still waters run deep, I guess," he said.

"I still don't really know what that means," I said. "Are they sad that you're going to New York?"

"They get it," he said. "But really they want me to stay here and marry a girl named Stacey Rowley. Her family owns a winery in Oregon."

"The ultimate girl next state," I said.

"The girl next state who has a strain of Pinot Noir grapes that they want access to. And family money to prop up the business here."

"The most classic arranged-marriage story ever," I said. "I wonder why they would do the same thing to you that happened to them. But you loved someone else? Someone from the wrong side of the tracks? Who didn't have any wine strains at all?"

"I had a girlfriend in college named Antoinette. She was from a family kind of like mine—a family business, but shoes, not wine. From Orange County. My mother hated her. Wouldn't stop talking about Stacey around her. I'm actually surprised she didn't mention Stacey tonight; that's actually a good sign. Anyway, Antoinette was beautiful and fun, but she also had no empathy. She could walk right by a quivering dog or a crying child and not even notice. And she also didn't have empathy for me. The worst was when I told her this story about when I was a kid and someone at a party that my parents were throwing gave me a little glass of sweet ice wine. It tasted amazing—supersweet, like liquid Popsicle, really. So I drank it and then I felt dizzy and went out to the garden with my dog, Sevvie, short for Reserve—we always named the dogs after wine things—and I felt horrible. I lay on the ground and rolled around and the sky was spinning and then I threw up. And Sevvie ate it. I was so embarrassed. I never told anyone that. Not my parents, not anyone. And her only response was, 'It's amazing you're not an alcoholic.' "

"I'm so sorry," I said, our hands still lingering. Fingers lightly intertwining. "It must have made the things that your parents made be scary. Like they could poison you. And your dog."

"Yeah," he said. "Something like that."

And then he very smoothly moved himself toward me, put his arm around me. I leaned against him and looked up at his face. I wanted him to kiss me, but I couldn't yet. But I won't say that I didn't nuzzle my face into his neck and inhale a delicious earthy smell, a combination of wine and vegetables and, yes, maybe just a hint of dirt. But it was a smell, not a taste. I knew what good dirt smelled like.

Chapter 9

The next morning, as the haze of the previous evening wore off, I realized that I had cheated on Ethan. Emotionally. I had talked about my family and my hopes and dreams with another man. A man who put his arm around me and tucked me into my couch to sleep. A man whose family I was spending the entire summer with.

I would need to call him later—Ethan, not William; I could never talk to William again. The idea of a new crush was terrifying. I had been with Ethan for almost two years and I had kind of decided that this was it. That he would be the last person I would sleep with, the last person I would kiss. I had mentally closed up the dating shop. Maybe I was lazy, or just exhausted after going on first date after first date with men who either couldn't stop talking about themselves or had nothing to say at all; going for months without hearing from someone, only to have them pop up with a witty text message at the most inopportune time.

The other thing that was amazing about singledom was that everyone in relationships would say things like, "You're so great, Hannah. I don't understand why you don't have a boy-friend. A guy would be lucky to have you." And then when I would ask if they knew anyone single, they would think about it for a second and say, "Sorry, I don't, actually! Let me think about it."

I'd thought regularly about going back to Eric, who was working his way to becoming the chef at the French restaurant I'd hostessed at in college. But no matter how bleak the life of a single woman in her twenties in New York could be, something kept me from giving in, from returning to Iowa, a sense that there was more for me if I just kept at it. I would get that perfect Nora Ephron life that I saw in *When Harry Met Sally* and *You've Got Mail*: a beautiful apartment (or at least a separate bedroom), a great career, and a wagon-wheel coffee table to fight over. Besides, I had mentally decided that Eric (and Iowa) would always be there for me if I needed them, but that I needed to charge forward, even if it made me sad and exhausted. Of course, if you wait long enough, your backup plan can betray you. It seemed that now Eric had a daughter and, presumably, a wife.

But I told myself that I had to swear off William. He was on his way to New York. I was settling here. It was my first day of work in a job that I felt I was made to do, working for his parents. I was still technically with Ethan; maybe there was a way for me to have this life and for his plan to work out also. This is what I told myself as I showered and made coffee and toasted an English muffin that I found in the refrigerator. I covered it in the quince paste that Linda had left on the island the night before. I wondered if she made it herself. The label read Old Winery Road, and it was entirely possible that there were quince trees on the property. I sat on the patio for a few minutes drinking coffee, eating my breakfast, and smelling the air—moss and dirt and a hint of the roses planted all around the cottage. This was better than what would be happening in New York, right? I took out my phone and looked at Instagram. The first icon that came up was a new follow from Celeste and a tag from Tyra of a Venti Starbucks with her name on it. Caption: "Fueling for first day at Goldman in NYC. Thanks to @realhannahgreene for passing up the best job on earth." I commented back, "You're welcome," and then went back inside to get the quince paste and a Champagne flute. I filled the flute with orange juice, took a croissant out of the freezer, and set up the flute, croissant, and Old Winery Road quince paste on the wrought iron patio table. My caption: "Heaven on earth. #Ichooseme." I tagged Tyra just for fun. She didn't heart my post.

At around ten, I headed down to the office in the back of the tasting room, but it was locked. I went around to the front door and it was also locked. I remembered that Everett was driving

William to the airport today, but I wondered where Linda was. She hadn't said anything specific about when we would start working today, but she also hadn't said we wouldn't start.

I wasn't sure what to do. I had gotten dressed for work in a knee-length skirt with a bird embroidered on it and a supersoft T-shirt, so it didn't make sense to go for a run. Instead, I decided to go for a walk. I headed back toward town, and as I walked, I called my brother, Drew. He was whom I turned to when I didn't know what to do. I was lucky to catch him during a quiet moment in his office. School was still in session, and usually in the mornings he walked the hallways, talking to students.

"Hannah," he said. "What's wrong?"

"Nothing," I said. "I'm walking through paradise. I have a babbling brook below my feet and can reach out to touch a redwood tree."

"You only call me if something's wrong."

"Nothing's wrong," I said. "How are you?"

"You're stalling."

"So, remember when I texted you about Sonoma?"

"Sure," he said.

"Well, I decided not to go to New York for that job at Goldman that I got and instead work in this winery in Sonoma, but it's already weird. I'm falling for the son of the winery owners and the parents weren't even at work this morning."

"What time did you go in?"

I loved that my brother didn't ask me any other questions about why I had made the decision or what was going on with Ethan. He knew me well enough to know that I didn't want to talk about that.

"Ten," I said.

"And it's a winery? In California?"

"My first day."

"You've got to chill out, my sister. All will be fine. And the son, well, I wouldn't worry too much about it. You've got to figure things out."

"He's going to New York."

"Perfect. Listen. You're living the life. You made a decision and now you have to embrace it. Go enjoy your morning. Drink some coffee. Eat a pastry. Talk to a local. All will be fine."

"So wise. Thanks," I said. "How's the family?"

"Elise is finishing up the year. Gillian is going to sleepaway camp for three weeks and Duncan is on a traveling soccer team. We're all ready for school to be over, but we have a few weeks left."

"Tell them I say hi," I said. I loved my niece and nephew, had made it my business to be home when they were born and for most Christmases. They also once came to visit me in New York (with their parents, of course) and I got to have the perfect kid New York vacation with them. We went on the Staten Island Ferry, to the Prospect

Park Zoo, and on the Dumbo carousel, and they got unlimited artisanal ice cream, which Duncan declared "much better than boring Iowa ice cream." I hoped that one day they would run away from Iowa to stay with me. Not that Drew and Elise were bad parents; they were amazing. I just wanted the kids to feel like they had somewhere else to go, a feeling that I never quite had. That was one of the reasons I kept in touch with them via FaceTime, so they would know I was out there for them. A friendly face who could provide fun times and good snacks.

"Sure," he said. I could tell he was getting distracted.

"How's Mom?" I asked.

"Fine," he said. "She'd love to hear from you. She said she called?"

"Yeah," I said. I called my mother only rarely. We didn't seem to have much to talk about other than Drew, and I talked to him twice a week. I was just . . . different from her. Mostly she didn't understand what I was doing or why. Our conversations didn't feel supportive, or even really congenial. "It's hard for me," I said.

"She does love you," he said.

"She doesn't understand me," I said.

"You need to give her a chance to try," he replied.

"Fine." My walk had taken me back into downtown Sonoma. "Tell her I'm okay. I guess

I should go," I said. I clicked my phone off and walked right into Celeste.

"Fancy meeting you here," she said. Her hair was in a high ponytail and she was wearing workout gear and carrying a yoga mat in a yoga mat–shaped bag.

"Good morning," I said.

"I've been up for hours," she said. "I like to go to sunrise yoga and then do the Pilates class right after. Really gets me ready for the day."

"Sounds exhausting," I said.

"You should come with me," she said. She rooted around in her purse and handed me a coupon. "Here's a free class."

I shook my head. "I don't know what my schedule will be."

"Just take it," she said. "I mean, you are allowed to take care of yourself. You have to, really, if you work in hospitality. You need to look and feel good to deal with the general public."

Celeste reminded me of my parents' next-door neighbor, Mrs. Anderson. She knew everything about everyone in Winthrop. She called my mother once a day to tell her what she had learned via her phone calls with Mrs. Holliday (Justine's mom), Mrs. O'Callahan (David's mom), and Mrs. Carpenter (Alexandra's mom). Each of those women got similar reports, I was sure. Mrs. Anderson's calls kept my mother entertained, but they were the way that I found out when Justine started wearing a bra, when David had been rushed to the hospital with dehydration after a particularly nasty bout of diarrhea, and that Alexandra wanted a dog but hadn't remembered to water her "pet" cactus, which had withered and died. I'm sure my mother told their mothers things about me that I didn't want known. And now that we were all out of the house, I'm sure the conversations were even more invasive, although my mother rarely reported on them. Mrs. Anderson was a bit of a busybody, but she was also the person who brought my mother soup when she was knocked out with the flu. Celeste seemed to have similar qualities.

"Do you want me to drive you back to the winery? Did you walk here?" she asked.

I nodded. She shrugged and put her arm around my shoulders. She walked me two blocks farther into town and opened the door of her white Mercedes SUV. "Get in," she said.

The thing was that she didn't drive me right back to the winery, which made me a little nervous; it was my first day on the job after all. She gave me a tour. We drove out of town and onto winding roads. I didn't quite know where we were, but it reminded me of the movie *Under the Tuscan Sun*. "It's really beautiful here," I said.

"Just wait until I bring you farther north," she

said. "But this place is pretty nice. Has a nice view at least." We drove up a winding road to a new building at the top that had a fountain in the courtyard. "A little cheesy," she said. "But just wait until you eat their salami on their patio."

"Do you think I should call Linda and tell her where I am?"

"Don't worry about Linda," Celeste said.

We walked through the courtyard and into the tasting room, which reminded me a bit of the one Ethan and I had been to on our first day—the Disney one.

"We'll skip the tasting," she said. "Their reds aren't great. But we can get a glass of sparkling wine and sit outside." She whispered to the woman at the hostess desk for the patio and we went out and sat at the table in the corner with the best view. The wind was blowing a bit, but it was warm and sunny. All of a sudden, overflowing flutes and a plate of meat and cheese appeared in front of us.

"Welcome to Sonoma," Celeste said.

"Thank you," I said. We clinked glasses. "I love this Champagne," I said.

Celeste looked appalled. "Just so you know, you can't call it Champagne here. Even though it's made in exactly the same way as French Champagne, with the same grapes and the same process, we have to call it sparkling wine. Except for Korbel, André, and Cook's; they were calling their wine Champagne before that ruling came down, so they can."

"Crazy," I said. "I have so much to learn."

"You're smart," she said. "It'll be fine. So let's get to the good stuff. You fell in love with William at first sight, broke up with your boyfriend, and moved here for the summer?"

"I wouldn't say exactly that," I said. "But you seem to know so much about me; why don't you tell me about you?"

"Not much to tell," she said. "I'm from here. I went to UC Davis. I moved back here. I sell real estate. I just got divorced. It was a mistake all along; you know, high school boyfriend. We'd been together forever and it was like: either break up or get married. And I felt like I should, you know? I was twenty-five. Everyone else from my sorority was doing it. But it didn't last. We pretty much knew by the wedding that it was a mistake, that we had nothing in common anymore, but by then, it had all been planned."

"The world does sometimes make us feel like we should do what it thinks," I said. "I'm sorry."

"Water under the bridge," she said, waving her hand. She picked up a piece of sliced meat with the other.

"I've never been married," I said.

"Better that way," she said. "I won't do it again. I mean, maybe I would. But he'd have to be rich."

I smiled. She was a ridiculous person, but she was entertaining.

"Tell me about Everett," I said. "I can't get a read on him."

"A serious man," she said. "He loves that winery. It's his life. It was his father's. He has a pretty incredible palate. Hard to talk to, though. You should read some books about wine. It's easier to talk to him about wine than anything else. He can't really do small talk."

"I noticed that," I said.

"And he's trying hard; so is Linda, but the world is changing and how wineries succeed is changing. They've been falling behind despite having a good product."

"Are they in trouble?" I asked.

"They can use a lot of help," she said.

I nodded and wondered again if I had stepped onto a sinking ship that I was unqualified to fix. I ate a piece of cheese.

"The cheese is delicious," Celeste said, although I was pretty sure I'd eaten most of the cheese and she'd just sipped her sparkling wine. "I'd say we should have more, but I should get you back to work. They usually open up around noon. And it's already one."

"It is?" I asked.

"Time flies here," she said. "Get used to it."

I reached for my wallet, but she shook me off. "It's all taken care of. I have an account. Let's go."

We walked back out to the car and she brought me back to the winery.

"Do you want to go to yoga together tomorrow?" she asked when we stopped in front of the winery. Then before I could answer: "I'll pick you up at seven thirty. It'll be great."

I didn't want to, but I didn't know what else to do and I could already tell that Celeste would be the kind of friend who more or less maintained the friendship for me. I wasn't great about reaching out or making plans or keeping in touch, which was why my friendship with Nicole in New York had faded away. Neither one of us ever really reached out. I assumed the same would have happened with Tyra if we didn't part ways over the job. "Okay?" I asked.

She peeled off without a word.

Chapter 10

Celeste had dropped me off at the front door of the tasting room, which was finally open. I went inside to find Linda in the office, telephone headset on her head, concentrating deeply on her computer screen. The room was disorganized—paper piled on every surface. There were two desks and a bookshelf, about six laptops stacked on one chair, and file folders on another. There wasn't really anywhere for me to sit. They clearly hadn't thought about the logistics of me actually working there.

"I can work up in the cottage," I said, looking helplessly at the mess.

"Oh," she said. "I'm sorry. I'm used to working alone. We can clear off a table for you." She also looked a bit helpless. "I don't even know what's in here."

She stood up, but I waved her off. I rearranged a few things, filed a few of the papers in the filing cabinets that were actually clearly marked. I then wedged myself into a little niche of emptiness that I created at a table near the back of the room. There was one dusty laptop among the papers. I took it and held it up to Linda. "Okay if I use this? Or should I use mine?"

"That one should work," she said.

"Thanks again for dinner last night," I said as I opened the computer, which was unsecured and already connected to Wi-Fi. I logged in to my Gmail. It was filled with sales and offers for stores like Pottery Barn and Zappos, but nothing personal, no messages from Ethan, no letter from Goldman saying anything positive or negative, nothing from school. I was like a blank slate. My new job was just beginning, but my old life was gone. I couldn't help but check William's Instagram; it showed a photo of an airplane tray table covered in tiny liquor bottles. He was having fun already.

"Of course," she said. Her tone was curt, as if she wasn't used to having an office mate and wasn't interested in a casual chat. Maybe small talk also wasn't her thing. I had always been impressed with the type of people who embraced silence over mindless chatter. I wasn't one of those people; I was great at mindless chatter.

"I met Celeste in town," I said, unable to settle into the silence that Linda obviously wanted.

"She's a piece of work," she said. "Don't listen to anything she says. She just likes to get a rise out of people." It was as if she had been listening to our very conversation.

"I didn't mind her," I said. "She took me on a drive. Showed me the neighborhood."

"She's lonely in her heart. That's why she is the way she is. Sometimes the things she says . . .

Well, I guess she was always that way even when she was little," Linda said. "We tried to take care of her when she was young. She was here a lot. Her parents traveled all the time." She squinted at her computer screen. She typed for a few minutes and I stared at my screen, not sure where to begin.

"I did think it was weird that she had already researched me before I got here," I said.

"She'll do that," she said. "She's always trying to sell something."

"Maybe she just wants friends?" I asked.

"Oh, she definitely does," Linda said. "And you two would be good for each other."

"She's already making me work out with her," I said. "So that's a good thing, I guess."

Linda laughed. "She does love those exercise classes."

"Who's pouring in the tasting room today?" I asked.

"Oh, I will be if anyone comes. It's a Wednesday, so maybe one or two people later in the day. I'm not too worried about it. A bell rings in here when the door opens and I just scoot out and do my show."

"What would you do if more people started coming for tastings?"

"Well, now that you're here . . ."

I smiled and decided that I should start on the things I had promised. I opened the winery website, Facebook page, Twitter, and Instagram, which William had given me the passwords to. I read the entire website from top to bottom, including the history section and the description of the wines and the wine club. Those parts seemed to be in good order. On Facebook and Instagram, I posted a photo from the previous night's dinner: We had posed Tannin with the bowl of pasta and a bottle of Pinot Noir. Then I shared it on my personal Facebook and Instagram: "Summer job. For real." Comments were already popping up on my accounts and likes were transferring over to the winery pages. Not that my social media acquaintances were going to change the fate of this place, but they were a start.

"I'm game for anything," I said as I typed. "I'm updating your social media, in case you notice things happening. And I was thinking the first thing I would do would be to plan an evening tasting and jazz night."

"Great," she said.

"Do you have a marketing budget at all?" I asked.

"It's around here somewhere," she said, gesturing toward the piles of paper. "I mean, to be honest, there's not a lot of extra cash around. You can spend a few hundred dollars; I'll give you cash out of my pocket if I have to, but things are tight. And you charge for admission?"

"Yes, but I don't know if that'll cover everything. I want the tickets to feel binding enough for people to show up, but cheap enough that they're not a purchase you worry too much about. We can maybe charge for extra wine, too, like beyond the first glass. And we can sell bottles. I bet people will take a bottle home. But I think we need to provide entertainment and food."

"For music, ask Jackson Hill," she said. "He's my old friend from high school and he lives in town and is a great saxophone player. He'll bring some guys and probably will work for food and wine if you're nice to him."

"That's perfect," I said.

"Oh, and he doesn't like the phone, so you'll need to go up to his place to ask him. I'm sure he'll be happy to see you."

"Okay," I said, warily.

"To be honest, he's not the most social guy. But he won't slam the door in your face. I'll draw you a map," she said. "Good thing you're pretty. That'll help." My looks had never been discussed so much. She handed me the map and pushed me toward the door as if she was glad to get rid of me. It was going to be hard to convince her that having me around was going to be fun and would make her life better. In practice, she was used to working alone.

I headed out to my car and propped Linda's map on my dashboard. I sat there studying it and thinking about what I would say when I arrived at Jackson's. "Hi, I'm this random new person in town who Linda hired, and today's my first day and I'm coming to ask you a favor out of the blue." It seemed crazy, especially since Linda was the one who knew Jackson. I took a deep breath, turned off the car, and headed back inside. Linda was standing at an overflowing filing cabinet and making a squinty face.

"I'm back," I said. She jumped a little, clearly she wasn't expecting me to come back.

"You startled me," she said.

"I'm sorry," I said. "I realized that it would just be so weird for me to show up by myself to Jackson's house. I mean, maybe it wouldn't be for someone like Celeste, but for me . . . Anyway, I wonder if you would mind coming with me."

She paused for a moment, as if she was really considering it. A kind of panic passed over her face and then a smile. "I just haven't seen him in such a long time," she said in a dreamier way than she had spoken in the past.

"So, you'll do it?" I asked.

She sighed. "Okay. I must have secretly wanted to see him when I suggested it. Can I have a few minutes? I need to call Felipe and ask him to cover the room."

"Of course," I said. I settled in my desk chair and she disappeared. When she returned, more than a few minutes later, she was wearing a tasteful chambray shirtdress with three-quarter-length sleeves. She'd put some bronzer on her cheeks and a light gloss on her lips. She'd pulled her salt-and-pepper hair back from her face with a comb. She hadn't been wearing makeup at dinner the night before or any of the times I'd seen her in the office or tasting room. I wondered if she was trying to impress Jackson, or me.

"You look nice," I said.

"I can clean myself up every once in a while," she said. "Mostly it's just easier not to, though."

"I get it," I said.

"Oh, to be young," she said. "You don't have to worry about cleaning yourself up."

"I wear makeup every day," I protested.

"Well, you should stop," she said. "You don't need it."

I blushed. "That's nice," I said.

I wasn't sure what to say next, but then Felipe entered the room. "Here I am," he said. He was around my height, with bright blue eyes and dark brown hair, closely cropped. He looked to be around my age. But he was an expert winemaker. How was that possible?

"Hi," I said. "I'm Hannah, the summer . . . something. Marketing person?" I wasn't sure what I was.

"It is very nice to meet you," he said. He had an accent, which manifested itself in his pronouncing every word distinctly.

"Likewise," I said.

"You got this?" Linda asked.

"I am getting this," he said.

"It's good for you to be in the room every once in a while."

"Last time nobody came," he said. "I am hoping for the same this time."

"I'm not!" I said. "I'm going to tweet that our expert winemaker is pouring tastes for the rest of the afternoon."

He blushed and laughed a little. "I do not appreciate that."

"You'll love it," I said.

"Let's go," Linda said. "You drive, I'll direct. Thanks, Felipe."

"Safe traveling," he called after us.

We walked out to my car and I drove away from the winery in the opposite direction from town. After about five minutes we found ourselves in pure countryside, surrounded by grapevines in long, straight lines. Linda put on NPR and listened silently, lost in her own thoughts. As I wound up into the hills, the roads narrow and bumpy, signs peppering the shoulder: SICK OF POTHOLES? GO TO POTHOLEGUYS.NET. The route could use a good resurfacing. Tiny corkscrew roads with few residents. They must be hard to maintain. Then again, it would be horrible to get a flat out on one of them where you might or might not have cell service and there wasn't another person for miles. I did my best to avoid the holes, as my car, a ten-year-old Hyundai that I had bought for a thousand dollars when I moved to Berkeley, wasn't the most robust car in the world. It shook when I drove it above sixty miles per hour and didn't have any shocks at all. Ethan called it "the go-kart." But it got me from place to place and barely used any gas. And rarely broke down if I kept the oil changed and rotated the tires. "There's nothing *to* break," he would mock me. "It's like man's first car." The car had crank windows and a tape player, and you had to physically unlock the doors; no remote keyless entry for me. But I liked it that way. After seven years on the subway, my one-thousand-dollar Hyundai Accent was the height of luxury.

"Sorry about the car," I said.

"What about it?"

"It's not the smoothest ride," I said. "Ethan called it the go-kart."

"Oh, I don't mind," she said. "We aren't used to fancy cars. And I know these roads . . . They haven't been attended to in a long time."

"I wonder why," I said.

"No need," she explained. "It's not like a lot of people drive on them, and we don't get the snow and ice like out east."

"It is paradise," I said.

"Sometimes," she said.

As I drove, I saw cows and goats in pastures and farmhouses set back from the road, all of which seemed to be positioned for the best views of the valley. I wondered how long these farms had been in the families of their current residents, how one came to be a California farmer or a small-production winemaker. There had been many children of farmers in Iowa where I grew up who didn't come to school during planting and harvesttime. I would ask my parents if I could skip school too, but my mother told me I was lucky not to have to do manual labor and I could get a job if I wanted one, but there was no way I could miss school. The kids who had to work on the farms never seemed too happy about it, and once one told me that he much preferred math class to feeding a thresher. But I was still jealous.

"So, you and Jackson went to high school together?" I asked.

"We did," she said. I could tell she was being evasive. Her makeup sparkled.

"Do a lot of people that you know from that time still live around here? It seems like you grew up with Celeste's parents also."

"Some," she said.

"Why did Jackson stay?"

"He didn't, but then he always had the house here. When his parents died . . ."

"Oh," I said, sympathetically.

"He has a lot of land," she said. "He can make as much noise as he wants."

"That's good for a musician," I said.

"Just up here," she said as we went around what felt like a hundred curves.

Jackson Hill's house was at the end of a long, winding mountain road. He had a wooden gate that I had to get out of my car to open, and then I drove up a dirt road that continued past a small pond surrounded by ducks and a garden surrounded by a high anti-deer fence, a few grapevines, less tidy than the ones I had seen from the road, and a woodpile, complete with ax. It looked as if he had just stopped chopping to run into the house.

The house at the end of the road was a log cabin that looked like it had been built in the 1800s. Solid but small. A large Doberman lounged in the shade under a giant tree that grew beside the house. He looked up and yawned when I drove up, gravel crunching under my wheels. He gave a small bark when I stopped the car, but then went back to sleep.

The front door opened as I turned off the car, and an extremely tall and thin man with curly gray hair that seemed to grow vertically up out of his head appeared in the doorway. He looked like Lyle Lovett. His limbs were long and gangly and he held a cup of coffee in bony fingers.

"Who's there?" he asked as I got out of my car.

“I’m Hannah Greene. I work at the Bellosguardo Winery. Linda sent me to talk to you about a gig.”

“I’m not playing anymore,” he said, and turned around and went back into the house. But he didn’t close the door behind him, so I took that to mean that the conversation wasn’t entirely closed. I followed him and stood in the doorway. Linda was still sitting in the car, with the window rolled down, and he didn’t seem to see her.

“It would be a huge favor to Linda. And to me, not that you know me.” His brusqueness made me feel sheepish. I looked back at Linda and gestured that I needed her help.

“I don’t,” he said, loudly.

Linda got out of the car and approached the door. “But you know me,” she said.

“Linda,” he said. He made the same face that she had made when I had suggested that she come. A shy smile.

“I knew you would give her a hard time,” she said, approaching the house.

“I give everyone a hard time,” he said. She approached and he hugged her tight. He even lifted her off the ground a little.

“Well,” she said. “Now you have to at least invite us in and offer us some iced tea.”

“How do you know I have iced tea?” he asked.

“Because your mother taught you well,” she said.

He nodded. “I do have some that I made yesterday. Sun tea, in fact.”

“I knew it,” she said.

He held the door open for us. “Welcome to Chez Hill.”

“Thanks,” I said.

“Don’t have much of a choice, do I?” he muttered to nobody in particular.

We walked directly into the kitchen, which was open to the rest of the house. A classic log cabin, clearly decorated by a single man. There were leather couches and a large television. A California flag hung on the wall, as did a gold record and a flattened saxophone.

“Have a seat,” he said, gesturing toward a wood table that looked like it was made from unfinished branches. He busied himself with the tea while I tried not to smile too broadly at Linda.

He brought the tea in mason jars to the table and sat next to Linda. He looked at me. “I played at their wedding, you know.”

“Were Everett and Linda high school sweet-hearts?”

He laughed. “Not exactly. More like high school enemies. Linda was actually my high school girlfriend.”

Linda shot a look at Jackson that said, “Stop it, now.”

“The plot thickens,” I teased.

"We haven't seen each other in a long time," he said. "What's it been . . ."

"Five years?" Linda asked.

"Maybe longer," he said. "Did I play at William's graduation party?"

"You did," she said. "But he's thirty now, so that's nine years."

"Time flies," he said. "How's he doing?"

"He's in New York for the summer," she said.

"But that's not why you're here," he said.

"We," I said, interrupting their banter. "Well, I, if you want me to be specific. I'm trying to help them grow the vineyard. So we're going to have an event. A party. For locals and tourists. And we'd love for you to play at it."

"I'm busy," he said.

"I didn't tell you when it was yet," I said.

"Good point," he grumbled.

"I can work around your schedule," I said. "You're the first person I'm talking to about it. I want it to be on a Friday. In the summer. But again, flexible."

"Okay," he said. "I'll look at my calendar and call you."

"Can you look now?"

"You don't trust me, do you?"

I made a noise that indicated wavering trust. He nodded and pushed himself up from the table. His body was gangly and oddly flexible, as if he had also been doing yoga for forty years. That was entirely possible; he did grow up in Northern California after all. He ambled over to an old rolltop desk. When he rolled the top up, it looked like it was stuffed to the brim with paper. The only thing keeping it from exploding was the roll top itself. He reached behind the crumpled paper and pulled out a well-worn pocket paper calendar. He flipped through some pages. "Looks like I'm free in June."

"All of June?"

"Looks like it." He didn't seem insecure about this, which I loved. I wondered why he needed a calendar. Maybe it made him feel better. The idea of future plans. I, too, was free for all of June, but I was new in town. He seemed wise to me. I wondered if he regretted letting Linda go.

I smiled. "So what's the first Friday in June? We can call it First Fridays at Bellosguardo."

"June second."

"You're booked! I'll pay you in wine and tips."

"I don't love the wine, though . . . You might have to cough up some beer," he joked.

"Done," I said.

"Wait. I have one more question."

I raised an eyebrow at him. "Yes?"

"Just wondering what today is."

I consulted my iPhone even though I knew exactly what day it was: the day I wasn't starting at Goldman Sachs. "May fifteenth. We have about three weeks to get ready."

"Okay," he said. "We can do it."

I thanked Jackson and got up from the table. I walked out in front of Linda but heard tense murmuring behind me. I tried my hardest to listen.

"You always do this . . . ," he said.

". . . miss you . . . ," she said.

". . . when things . . . okay," he said. "I was always a sucker for you, Lindy."

"I'm sorry," she said.

When she met me at the door, there were tears in her eyes. I knew better than to say anything. I held the door open for her and followed her to the car.

We got in and drove in silence, not even the radio playing, until we got to the bottom of the long, windy road that led to Jackson's door. Once we were back on the main roads, she started to talk.

"So, that's my Jackson," she said.

"You were together in high school?"

"We were really in love," she said. "But it couldn't be. And now, he's right, every few years, I get an itch. Like regular life isn't enough and . . ."

"You go back to him?"

"Well, usually, I just call him and then we have a drink and get in a fight and I realize things with

Everett are fine. There was one time when we really did get together for a summer; things were so bad at the winery, financially, and Everett and I just could not get along at all. But it was so hard on William. I eventually came back."

"How was it between you two, you and Jackson?"

"Oh, that time?" She stared out the window. "It was good. Until it wasn't."

"And he's never been married?"

"No," she said. "He's had girlfriends. There was even one who moved in for a while. But you must have seen, he's not the easiest . . . I know how to pick them, don't I?"

I had so many questions, but I let her keep talking.

"It was never practical," she said, as if she was trying to tell herself the story to confirm she had done the right thing. "I had to stay here. My parents needed me for the winery. He wanted to be a rock star."

"And?" I asked.

"I did. And he was. For a bit. Went down to LA, to Nashville. Played on a lot of records. Had a band. What were they called? The Fugitives? The Rascals? The Jailbirds? I can't quite remember. It was a kind of fusion jazz. They had a trumpet and a saxophone. Anyway, they came up here and Everett and I went to see them in San Francisco. At the Fillmore, opening for B.B. King. I remember they played a mean version of 'The House That Jack Built' in their encore. He did a solo. Changed the way I thought of that song. I think I was pregnant with William."

"Not the most fun time to go to a concert," I said.

"Well, it meant I couldn't really go to any more concerts. And Everett wasn't that happy about it."

"It's sad," I said.

"Why?" she asked.

"That you loved each other but couldn't be together."

"Everyone's living the life they wanted to live," she said.

"And you and Everett?" I asked. My only impression of him so far was that he was a bit of a blowhard, and also not the most generous of people.

"We work well together," she said. "We combined two wineries. Built all of this. Well, some of it was here. But it needed rehabilitation, you know? We did that. And William; he's a good kid. We did that too."

"It's amazing," I agreed.

"It was important to our families. His father was dying. Mine wanted to retire. We were so young."

"I get it," I said. "Priorities. History took precedence."

"Right," she said.

"Do you ever regret it?" I asked.

"You ask a lot of questions," she said.

"I've been told that before," I said.

She looked out the window for a moment. "And how are you doing? Settling in okay?"

"Change is hard," I said, accepting the shift in topic. "But I'm excited. I just have to figure everything out . . ."

"You followed your heart," she said. "That's important."

"It's weird," I said. "I mean, I've made decisions before, but I've never had to give up one thing for another, something big."

"I'm sure it feels scary," she said.

I nodded, trying to keep the tears out of my eyes. It was scary. And I couldn't imagine what was going to happen next. Up until now, I had been deciding. Now things were happening outside of my control.

When we got back, we found Felipe in the tasting room, surrounded by beautiful women. I laughed at him, gave the thumbs-up, and headed into the office with Linda. He followed us in and said, "Please, let me to go back to the wine cellar. These women!"

"You love it," Linda said. "I promise not to tell Maria José when she gets here."

He smiled. "Okay. They are buying lots of wine."

"Of course they are," Linda said.

"Good work," I said.

"The tweeting," he said, shaking his finger at me.

"The tweeting," I said.

I grabbed an open bottle of wine from the office refrigerator and headed back up to my cottage. I took the wine, a plate of cheese that Linda had left in the cottage fridge for me, and a glass out onto the back patio. After the day talking about Jackson, I couldn't help but think about Ethan and what he was doing in New York. He didn't have an office, and because of me, he also didn't have a home. I had no idea where he was or what he was doing, and I was too scared to call him to find out. If he was in fact crashing in a gross apartment in Brooklyn with Jesse and Graham, he could have been cursing me daily. Or he could be enjoying it. As fancy as he acted with his rich parents and his private school education, he loved drinking a Miller High Life in his boxers at nine A.M. and yelling at a DVR'd edition of *Pardon the Interruption* on ESPN. It was the life he never had, that of a male sloth. He'd spent his entire life in a suit and tie: in his private school uniforms, in bespoke suits as an undergrad at the London School of Economics, at his dad's hedge fund after graduation. At Haas. Sometimes he didn't wear a tie, but he always wore a blazer. Again, the life he wanted; he chose it for himself, or at the very least his parents chose it for him, but he wasn't opposed to slumming it occasionally.

I was definitely the one in the relationship who tended toward getting off message—I could get sucked into a Netflix series that would prevent me from leaving the apartment for two days. I could eat a block of cheese for dinner and be perfectly happy. I often ran out of basic supplies like milk and eggs and regularly forgot to restock the toilet paper. These were qualities about me that drove him crazy. He liked schedules and well-planned meals and having a pantry full of backup paper products. But his family also had a full-time housekeeper when he was growing up and my family was catch-as-catch-can. He was also used to regular vacations planned by a travel agent and, often, led by a tour guide. Drew and I had to plan our own fun in the summers, which included sneaking into the town pool to swim with our friends, playing soccer at the school field with other unsupervised children, and visiting our friend Mary Ellen the librarian.

I hoped Ethan would just move back in with his parents. That would be comfortable. His mother, Bunny, still had the cook and the housekeeper in the city even though they were rarely home. Maybe he would even have the entire Park Avenue apartment to himself. He could move the start-up in there. Fanciest start-up setup ever.

Instead of making up stories about what Ethan was doing, it probably would have made sense for me to call him. To see how he was doing. But my fear led to many scenarios. I was afraid that he wouldn't pick up. Afraid that he would. Afraid that he would yell at me. Afraid that he never wanted to speak to me again.

And then I thought about William and I got more confused. I knew I wanted to hear from William, but I hadn't heard from him, either, since he had departed for the same city that my ex-almost-fiancé was in. William was most certainly living in a dirty hovel with black soot on the windowsills, clangy radiators, and some overweight cats. But in my mind that seemed like the right place to write a screenplay about a winery in Northern California. I knew that he would be successful. Something about the film that he had made already, which showed that he had talent, and the way that he talked about the film that he wanted to make. It just sounded good.

As I was wallowing, I got a FaceTime request from my niece. She always cheered me up.

"Hi, darling," I said.

Gillian went on to tell me about how she wasn't allowed to get a haircut and was sulking. Being a child was simple. I was jealous. She recovered from her hurts and slights so quickly. Her emotions were more flexible.

Feeling remarkably inflexible, I kept meaning to call Ethan over the next few days, but life kept getting in the way. It also is worth noting that he didn't call me, either.

Chapter 11

After our first-day adventure, we settled into a routine. I would go to yoga or Pilates or a very torturous Bar Method class that I protested vehemently but attended because it was easier to just go than to resist in the morning with Celeste. One morning, I made her go running with me, and she hated it so much that I was able to get a pass from her on going to classes by telling her that I was going running. The weird thing was that I actually did the runs and I even enjoyed them. After exercising, I would come back and shower and drink homemade espresso, make an egg-white omelet, and then head down to the office. Linda gave me a key so I could come and go as I pleased. I found that she wasn't a morning person and really didn't get going until around noon. She preferred to work late into the night, while I was winding down around six.

In the office, first, I organized all of the paper and detritus that was cluttering up the office. I found a few really nice bottles of wine, some unpaid invoices, and a newer Mac laptop computer, which I requisitioned for myself. After the place was clean, I focused on updating the social media—I liked posting photos of Tannin in places around the vineyard, but I also would include quotes from people whom I talked to in the tasting room: "Jane from San Diego says the sparkling rosé is 'to die for.' " I took Tannin out to the fields with Felipe and posted them together testing grapes, with the caveats "#dogsdonotdrink" and "#donotrythisathome," because I knew Tannin's ever-growing fan base would also ask questions if it seemed like he was doing anything dangerous. In the tasting room, I also started coming up with specials—a discount on a third bottle of wine if you bought two, free delivery on cases within ten miles of the vineyard. To keep the burden of my new ideas off of Linda, I decided to handle the ensuing deliveries. It was a nice way to learn the area and check out where people lived. And it gave me something to do on the long, lonely evenings.

And, of course, I worked on the plans for First Friday. It may have been ambitious to set the first one for just three weeks after I started at the vineyard, but plans seemed to be coming together, especially with Celeste's help.

I had also taken over all of the billing and wine club business. When Linda showed me the spreadsheet she was using to track orders, I tried to contain my horror. It was disorganized and confusing. Definitely making her job much harder. All I said was, "I think there are new softwares that could make all of this a lot easier."

"But I'm used to this," she said. "I made it myself."

She didn't seem like the type of person who would want me to say, "I'll just handle that for you." But she did respond well to me saying, "What if I take a look at your existing orders and numbers and get it all set up and then I can show you? And if you hate it, you can go back to the old system."

She agreed, so I downloaded QuickBooks and moved over all of the restaurant and liquor store accounts, as well as the wine club orders. The system automatically sent invoices and tracked payments; it even sent reminders. It handled the entire wine club business, which was a little bit complicated because it involved preferences, and sometimes people ordered extra things or wanted to change the basic package, which Linda allowed because she was too nice. I wasn't going to mess with the rules of the place (although believe me, I wanted to). When I was finished setting up the system, I sent a test invoice to Linda. I was sitting across the room from her, so I watched her face as she opened it on her computer.

"Wow," she said. "This is a beautiful invoice."

"And it's automatically generated," I said.

"You are a genius," she said. "But I'll never figure all of this out."

"It's so easy," I said. "I promise you'll like it when I teach you how to use it."

"Okay," she said. "But can you just use it for a little while?"

"Of course," I said. And that is how I became in charge of billing. As I went back through the accounts, I realized that they just weren't getting paid on a regular basis from the restaurants and stores they served. Getting completely paid wouldn't fix everything, but it couldn't hurt. If I helped them with one thing this summer, getting some cash flow into the winery would be a great thing I could do. It wasn't all about social media after all. Just boring old cash flow.

Planning the party helped break up the monotony of billing. I researched companies that provided temporary party help. I also signed up for Eventbrite to sell tickets, created fun little Facebook and Twitter posts about the party, and drove around town posting physical posters on actual corkboards. When I was out doing my deliveries, I also left postcards, which I made myself, with different inns and wine shops around town. Everyone seemed willing to help Everett and Linda. "That place is a Sonoma institution," the manager of the El Dorado told me.

"I hope you come to the event," I said.

"I'll do my best," she said.

As I was doing all of this, though, I couldn't help but look at Tyra's Instagram. She posted a photo of a new Chloé bag, which I knew cost more than two thousand dollars, almost an entire month's salary for me here at the winery. She also posted photos of a steak dinner at the Palm, a pedicure at the Great Jones Spa, and a red Egg chair (with ottoman) that I was sure was real. All with the hashtag #thanksgoldman. I tried not to cave.

I rarely saw Everett; he was always off somewhere mysterious with Felipe or up in the house doing research or on what he called restaurant research trips. I kind of didn't blame Linda for wondering what life would be like with Jackson. Life without William and with a barely present Everett in a giant castle couldn't be that fun.

On the Saturday after I arrived, my first more casual day—I was due in the tasting room but not in the office—I was sitting on my patio, reading *Housekeeping*, and drinking Sancerre. I had made a big salad with the vegetables from the garden and had covered it in goat cheese that I had bought at the farmers' market. I planned to have a piece of defrosted Wonder Bread with Nutella on it for dessert and I was going to pair it with the Syrah Port that William had introduced me to. Highbrow and lowbrow. It was going to be perfect.

As I finished my salad and poured a dash more Sancerre into my glass before switching to dessert and Port, I felt sophisticated, like I knew what I was doing. I was living the Sonoma life. Just so I could get some witnesses, I posted a photo of the salad on my personal Instagram with the caption "Look at me, being healthy. #Ichooseme." The first like was from Ethan. I felt guilty that he was seeing that sentiment. I wished I could hide my happy Instagrams from him.

Just as I was weighing the options of calling Ethan or not, my phone rang. It was my mother. I figured Drew had told her by now that I was staying in California for the summer. I hadn't been in touch in a while. But I just wasn't ready to talk to her. I let the call go to voice mail and then listened when she had hung up.

"Hi, darling. It's your mother. I saw Drew and Elise and the kids today. They said they miss you and love you and they liked the singing California Raisins that you sent them. They're about to get out of school for the year and are so happy. It was such a nice day. We went next door to the Andersons and swam in their pool. They're such nice people. Trudy was there with her daughter. Can you believe our little Trudy has a twelve-year-old daughter? Amazing to think that you two are the same age. I wonder what your daughter would be like if you had one. Anyway, he, Drew, told me about your big California adventure. I wish you would have told me yourself. You know I'm proud of you no matter what. I just like to hear from you, you know? Anyway, I don't want to criticize. I just want to hear from you. Please call me."

The stuff about kids really got to me. But she didn't know any better. She was from a world where everyone grew up and just had kids; they didn't think about it.

She was a good mom. She meant well. Even though the message hurt my feelings.

But I still didn't call her back. Sometimes, I wasn't the best daughter, and I did feel guilty about it. I wanted to be better. Maybe it was because I had this idea of having raised myself and taken charge of my family after my dad died, even though it was my brother and me together. But I was the one who felt resentful about it. I felt like I had done my time. On the other hand, the longer I acted like a jerk, the worse I felt. I had been playing the role of an adult for the past few years, but I was still acting like a resentful teenager. Maybe it was time to grow up a little bit and take responsibility for myself. And yet, I still didn't call my mom—or Ethan.

Part II

MAIN COURSE

Spicy almond flour–encrusted chicken on a bed of freshly picked avocado and arugula

PAIRING

Lynmar, Pinot Noir 2014
(Russian River Valley, California)
Tart plum, raspberry, and touches of cola

Chapter 12

At the start of my second week at Bellosguardo, after my morning run and my gluten-free breakfast, I went down to work to find Linda in the office, wearing a suit, putting wine into a rolling suitcase.

"Are you going on a trip?" I asked. Usually she wasn't even there when I got to work, and today she was all dressed up and about to walk out the door.

"Sales call," she said. "Want to come? Felipe is in the tasting room."

"Am I dressed okay?" I asked. I was wearing a green-and-white-print floor-length maxidress that I had bought in downtown Sonoma at an adorable store called Perlé. I hadn't been able to afford it, but it was exactly the thing I needed for my Sonoma life. I had put it on the interest-free credit card that I had gotten for the summer and hoped it would never come due.

"Perfect," she said.

"Do you want me to drive?" I asked.

"That would be great," she said. "Then we don't have to drag this thing up to the house, where my car is." She looked honestly grateful. It made me feel like I was starting to figure her out. She just wanted someone to offer to help. We walked through the tasting room, where I gave Felipe a high five.

"Are you ready for the crowds?" I asked.

"Please don't tweet again," he said.

"I can't help it!" I said. "You're our most popular pourer. And I'm supposed to improve the winery social media." I snapped a photo of him with a bar towel and posted it to Twitter, Instagram, and Facebook before he could protest.

I dragged the suitcase out into the parking lot and Linda followed, carrying her laptop in a Copperfield's tote bag and staring at her phone as she walked. "We're going to Healdsburg," she said. "We'll take CA 12 to the 101."

"Okay," I said. I didn't want to remind her that I didn't really know the area, but . . .

"I'll show you," she said. "Don't worry."

Highway 12 was a beautiful side road; we passed small houses, a few farms, some wineries. "That's where Celeste grew up," she said, pointing to a sign that had only a dirt road next to it that led up to a huge house on the hill (although it wasn't close to a castle). "Her parents make beautiful Chardonnay. They pick their grapes a little earlier than most places, so they minimize the sweetness and use steel instead of oak to keep it crisp. We made ours a little more traditionally, until last year, when Felipe came. Now we're using steel too, but I keep some of the older style around. Some people still like it. Especially older people. It's like classic rock."

I smiled, but I kept my eyes on the road.

"Am I boring you?"

"Absolutely not," I said.

"Have you heard from your boyfriend?" she asked, taking a different tack.

"No," I said. "Although I feel like I should probably call him. I don't even know where he's living."

"He'll reach out to you when he's ready," she advised.

"We left on pretty bad terms," I said.

"They always come back," she said.

"Did Jackson come back to you?"

"Once." She sighed. "Right around when William went to college. We hadn't opened the tasting room yet, so I was really just a glorified bookkeeper and shipping agent. Everett was out in the fields and in the cellar with the barrels, but I was lonely. I was pretty sure a monkey could do my job. So, I started spending a lot of time at the Girl and the Fig, at the bar."

"Was Reed there?"

"Reed? Oh, that self-righteous former teacher? No, he wasn't there yet."

"Oh," I said, a bit dejected.

"You liked him?" she said, laughing. "I guess I can see that. He makes a good first impression, but he's really only got one story. A little annoying if you ask me. Anyway, I went there almost every day at around two. I was lonely and I always would run into someone to talk to, and then I could come home at seven with some takeout for Everett and go straight to sleep."

"So even though you were depressed and not around, he still depended on you to eat? He couldn't cook his own food?"

"He can," she said. "Sometimes he would make dinner. But mostly, you know, men would rather not eat or just eat a spoonful of peanut butter and a frozen waffle than do a little work."

"Yeah," I said, thinking about my Wonder Bread dinners. "I guess I do know."

"Anyway, one of those nights I ran into Jackson. And we'd seen each other around town, but we hadn't really talked since shortly after my wedding. He played at it; did you know that?"

"I believe you already told me that," I said.

"Maybe I'm just trying to remind myself," she said.

"That must have been painful. It wasn't long after you two broke up, right?"

"At the time, I was angry. I felt betrayed by him, even though I was the one who made the choice. I realize that now. But I felt like he should have changed everything for me. So, to answer your question, when it was happening, it was okay. But when we started talking again, it all came back."

"That's lovely," I said.

"Maybe," she said. "Anyway, instead of going to the Girl and the Fig for a glass of wine, I started just going to his cabin, and at first it was innocent. We'd just sit on the back porch drinking wine, talking. But then it wasn't so innocent. And I kept going."

"Did Everett ever find out? Why did you stop?" We were passing little houses with goats and cows in the pastures. Bigger properties with rows and rows of wine grapes. Everything was green. Lush. How could you not be in love in such a beautiful place?

"He never did, but I got diagnosed with breast cancer at around the same time. And Everett was there for me. He drove me to the hospital, helped me when I was just so sick I couldn't move. And Jackson was a little scared of the whole thing. He kind of disappeared. He sent flowers, I think. I can't remember. But it did make me realize that I loved Everett, that he was good in a crisis. We'd been through so much together . . ."

"Wow, I'm so sorry. About everything."

"Well, it brought us back together. I guess that's why 'in sickness and in health' is in those vows. It also did make me admit to him that I was bored. So that's when we decided to reopen the tasting room. He said he wanted me more involved in the business and he knew that I was good with people, so we redid that room—it was in pretty bad shape—and we've had it ever since. About ten years. It's been good for business. Helps with the wine club and locals. It could be bigger, I guess."

"That's amazing," I said. "Was Jackson sad?"

"He understood that Everett knew how to take care of me when I was sick. He tried, but he's just not that kind of person. Then he went away for a while. He rode his motorcycle to Mexico. Probably did some stupid things."

"So you've broken his heart twice?"

"I guess I have," she said. She reached for her handbag and pulled out a tissue.

"I'm sorry," I said. "I shouldn't have said that."

"It's true," she said. "My heart is broken too, though. There's all those myths in our society about the happy ending. Shakespeare—how the wedding is a comedy. But there's no such thing as a happy ending. Just one day after another. Some days you're happy and some you aren't. You do the best you can. But none of it is what you think. I haven't been single a day in my adult life, and I'm lonely every day. So much for having someone to complete you."

"Do you think Jackson completes you?"

She paused, like she was really thinking about it. She took a deep breath. "I don't think anybody can complete anyone. You've got to do that for yourself. I've been doing better these past few years, but I'm not the champion."

"That's excellent advice," I said. "I'm trying to figure that stuff out this summer."

"You are several years ahead of me," Linda said. She looked away from me out of the window. We were just merging onto the 101 to Healdsburg. "I love this drive," she said. She leaned her head against the window and stared away into space. I concentrated on the road and wondered what it was like to feel complete.

We drove in silence for a while, until the signs started to indicate that we were near downtown Healdsburg. "Where are we going?" I asked.

"Oh," she said, shaking herself out of her reverie. "I should have told you that. We're going to see Chris Crane at the Shed, which is a seafood restaurant. He's had this restaurant for a few years. Before this he had a little wine bar in Calistoga. Maybe he still has it? We'll ask. I've known him for a long time—he also makes wine out on Dry Creek Road and he sells some of it at the Shed, but he loves our whites. So I've brought him some today. If there's time, we can also go visit my friends at Copperfield's. I hear they might want to serve wine in their café."

"Sounds fun," I said. "What should I be doing?"

"Just listen," she said.

The Shed, she explained, was not on the main square of Healdsburg but on a side street. But she wanted to park in the square so that I could see how lovely it was. It was not unlike Sonoma, which also had a center square, but Sonoma's was larger and airier. Healdsburg felt cozier. We parked on Plaza Street and walked through the beautiful square to the other side. We passed Copperfield's, a beautiful bookstore, and then finally turned onto a sunny side street. We walked by a few tasting rooms and a taco shack and finally got to the Shed. It was a large open space that looked to be made of tin. Kind of like an old gas station, but classier. There was outdoor seating, where a family was sitting with a baby in a high chair and a golden retriever lounging under their chairs. A carafe of rosé sat waiting in an ice bath. Their plates were heaped with greens and fruit. Through the huge open barn-style doors, there was an enormous square white bar adorned with large urns of pussy willow. The bartenders stood inside, all wearing black headbands and wristbands. Linda walked in front of me, nodding at the hostess, and headed back to the kitchen, which was open, with two line cooks and a man in a big chef's hat who was slicing beef.

"Chris!" she said, tapping on the counter lightly. Her voice took on an airier tone now that we were out of our regular environment. This was saleswoman Linda.

He looked up and smiled broadly. "Linda! It's so good to see you!" He tapped one of the other workers in the room to continue slicing the beef, washed his hands, and came around the counter to give Linda a big hug. He looked at me quizzically.

"Oh," she said. "This is Hannah, our summer . . . associate?"

I held out my hand, "I'm just here to learn," I said. "Pretend I'm not here."

"A summer associate? What's that all about?"

"She's been helping me with a bunch of things," Linda said.

"Wow," he said. His eyes twinkled. "What could you possibly need help with?"

"Oh, stop. I know you've been telling me to hire someone for years."

"You're just too easy to tease, Lindy! Are you two hungry?"

"No, no," Linda said. Although as he said it, my stomach grumbled. I coughed to cover it up.

"Let's go sit over here." He gestured toward a booth at the back. It was around noon, but the place hadn't filled up yet for lunch. I assumed it would.

Linda zipped open the bag and pulled out two whites and a rosé.

"So," Chris said. "How's things? How's life? How's the family?" He spoke fast, like a New Yorker, which I hadn't heard in a while.

"Good, good, good," she said. "William just left for New York. He's pursuing his movie dreams."

"In New York?"

"He wants to write," she said. "He's taking classes at NYU."

"He always was a dreamer," he said.

"Indeed," Linda said. She opened the bottles and he gestured toward one of the waitresses who came by. She was wearing a green bandanna like a headband and matching bandannas around her wrists. I noticed that all the waitstaff wore similar adornments, but each in his or her own color.

"Eve, can you bring us three glasses? Actually, make that six, just in case." She nodded and came back quickly with glasses. "Things are good here," he said, unprompted. "It's a big space, so in the winter, we tried having a little art gallery in the back, hung art by people in the area, to kind of make them feel like coming. Brought folks in during the evening for a glass."

"That's a good idea," I said. Then I remembered that I wasn't supposed to talk. But I filed the idea away for Bellosguardo. We could absolutely show local artists and host an opening. We could even sell their paintings and take a small commission.

"It was fun," he said. "So many of our regulars are artists. It made sense to give them a little group show. A few even sold some pieces."

"I might copy you," I said.

"You're welcome to," he said. "You're far enough away." He winked.

Linda opened the first wine and poured little

tastes for all three of us. "This is our early-harvest Chardonnay. Our new winemaker, Felipe, started doing this one two years ago, and I think it's one of our best."

"You make it in stainless?" he asked.

"Exactly," she said. "It's almost effervescent because we bottle it so early."

"It has citrusy notes," he said.

"Exactly," she said. "It'd pair well with a crudo or one of those fruity salads you do."

"Good," he said. "I'll take a half case. What else you got?"

Half a case? That didn't seem like enough. But Linda didn't blink. She opened the second white. "This is our 2014 Pinot Gris. A little heartier, more apple and pear than citrus. But not sweet. This is one of our old-vine wines. These grapes are descendants of the ones the count planted when he got here in the 1870s."

She poured. He swirled. Tasted. "Wow," he said. "It's an intense white."

"We leave this one on the vine a little longer. Let some of the sugars build up. But I wouldn't call it sweet."

"No," he said. "But I don't know what I'd pair it with. What else do you have?"

She uncorked the rosé. "I just opened this last night because, weirdly, it tastes better the second day. This is another Felipe wine, a rosé of Pinot Noir that he did in the *saignée* style."

Chris savored this one longer than he had the Pinot Gris. "Nice," he said. "We have our own rosé from the farm on tap here, so it's hard to sell bottles, but I'd take a half case and see how it sells. It's richer than the one I make."

I tried to read him. He wasn't taking second sips of the wine and he didn't seem to be ordering very much. We'd come a long way and it seemed like not a very big order.

"Great," Linda said, making a note in her iPhone. "I'll bring the bottles up next week."

"How do you handle bottles here?" I asked. "How big is your list, I mean?"

Linda shot me a look, but I put my hands under my chin, batted my eyes, and tried to look innocent.

"We have about six reds, six whites, and two rosés at any given time," he said.

"And you print the menu once a week?" I asked.

"About that," he said. "Sometimes twice a week."

"So, if you're going to have a bottle on the menu, doesn't it make sense to have more than six of them?"

"Well," he said, looking uncomfortable, like I had maybe called him on something. "We do more by the glass since we have our own wines on tap . . ."

"But a big table would order a bottle, wouldn't they? Do they order your bottles?"

“Kind of depends,” he said.

“Okay,” I said, not wanting to push too hard.

“Did you bring any reds?” he asked.

“I have two,” she said. “I didn’t think you’d want them, though, with yours being so good.”

“Sometimes it’s nice to show that we don’t *only* sell our own stuff here.”

Linda smiled. “I didn’t dare bring you a Pinot. But I did bring you a Grenache. Which we make in the Châteauneuf-du-Pape style. Although we only aged this one for eight months, not six years.”

“It’s delicious,” he said. “Earthy. Maybe even leather? We could pair this with our portobello burger.”

My stomach growled.

“You’re hungry!” he said.

“Oh no,” I said. Eating seemed wrong somehow.

“Let me just get you some olives,” he said. He gestured to the waitress. This time a brown-haired one in a pink headband and wristband came by. “This young woman is hungry. Can you bring her some olives and bread?”

“Of course,” she said. She disappeared and returned almost immediately with a small dish of olives of various sizes and a basket of bread. I ate an olive, which melted in my mouth. And the bread. How did he know?

“Wow,” I said. “So good.”

Linda looked irritated, but Chris also took an olive. "We grow these ourselves," he said. "You've got to have one, Linda."

"Fine," she said. She picked the smallest one in the bowl and smiled after she ate it. "They are good."

"I'll take a case of the Grenache," he said, winking at me. Was he flirting? "And why don't you up my order to two cases each on the whites."

"Really?" she asked.

"I'm feeling adventurous," he said. "Do you want lunch? We have a great mango salad today."

"No, no," she said. "We should be going. They want to buy some wine at Copperfield's."

"Ah yes, I like that idea," he said. "I gave them some rosé for a pilot program."

"Well," Linda said, standing up and zipping up her bag, "it's been so great seeing you."

"Tell Everett I miss him," he said.

They hugged and we walked out of the restaurant.

"I try not to eat when I'm on these calls," she said.

"I'm sorry," I said.

"You can't help your stomach growling," she said. "But we should remember to eat a snack before we go in next time."

"So I can come again?" I asked.

"Of course," she said. "It's the only way to learn."

She didn't mention the fact that I had upped her order from two cases total to five cases. Ever since I had started doing the billing, I thought more about return on investment. Five cases seemed worth the drive back to Healdsburg. I wondered how many of her other accounts could be worked into ordering more. I would have to look at the billing when I got back to the office. I made a note to myself about that and about the art show. And tried not to notice if Linda was mad on the car ride back.

Chapter 13

I followed Linda up to the house when we got back. She went into the kitchen to "throw together a little dinner," as she said, the first words she'd said after an entire ride home in silence. Everett was sitting at the outdoor table doing a crossword puzzle. Felipe was next to him, texting with his family in Chile. I sat across from them and poured a glass of Sancerre. Neither one acknowledged me right away. Everett looked up when he filled in the last answer. "You have a good day?" he asked.

"Yes," I said. "I went on a sales call. We sold seven cases. Five to the Shed and two to Copperfield's. Linda told them all about your innovations, Felipe."

He looked up, smiled with pride, and went back to typing into his phone.

"That's good," Everett said. "But I wish Linda would give it up. There are people who make these deals for you. A sales rep, a distributor. But Linda's a control freak. We could sell more wine if there were more people out there selling it. Anyway, I don't want to fight with her about it, but if you wanted to say something to her, maybe she'd listen to you."

I nodded. "I don't know if she would listen to

me. Although I will say that I've started to notice places where we—I mean, the winery—could become more efficient." I restrained myself from telling him that I had gotten the orders higher in both places. Maybe it was just beginner's luck. Instead, I tried to be positive. "What I loved about her pitch was the stories she told about how you pick the grapes and when you bottle it. She knows so much about the origins of the bottles."

"That's the joy of a family winery," he said. "But we can tell those stories to the reps. We can put them in the sales catalog."

"Do you ever wish it was bigger?" I asked. "The winery? William told me that you sell three thousand cases a year. Could you get up to five thousand or ten thousand?"

He shrugged and idly unfolded the newspaper that he had been doing the crossword in. "We own the land and the house outright, and we grow more grapes than we need. So it's really just covering the costs of making the wine. Right now, in a good year, we break even. But a bad year . . . that would kill us. Last year wasn't great. So that's why we put up the For Rent sign. This year was slow to start out. We lost a few restaurant accounts and a few wine club members."

I nodded, trying to figure out the math of it all in my head, which, after half a glass of wine, felt impossible. I was never great at math, and drinking really didn't help. I wondered if I would improve my tolerance this summer. I certainly wasn't used to drinking wine with every meal like we did here. I also wasn't sure if I should tell Everett what I had discovered about the billing and that many people were so late with their payments. Maybe it didn't quite matter at the end of the day. Regardless, it made sense to bring in more money. "So, you have the capacity to make more bottles?"

"Sure," he said. "Last year I even sold some grapes. That's actually a great business. These dot-com millionaires want to make wine, and they have a lot of money and they hire some experts. But they don't have land and they don't know how to grow grapes."

"Did any of them make anything good?"

"Who knows," he said. "One guy sent me a bottle of Merlot, but I didn't drink it. I thought the label was ugly."

"Life can't be too bad when you turn down free wine," I said, trying to make a joke.

"Wine is the only thing we have in abundance," he said.

"Wine is life," Felipe contributed.

"Felipe, tell me about your family," I said.

He smiled and showed me the lock screen of his phone—a photo of a beautiful brunette with blue eyes and two small children, a boy and a girl who looked around the same age. "This is Maria José, Alejandro, and Lucia. They are in Santiago now, but we, Maria José and me, are from Viña del Mar. Her family also has a winery. My family worked in one, not hers, though."

"Viña del Mar sounds like a perfect place," I said.

"It is," he said.

"Do you miss it?" I asked.

"Sometimes," he said. "I wish they were here. But one day we will be together again. This is such a good opportunity for me. It will help me to prove myself in Chile that I succeeded in California. They understand. And they will come here after the harvest."

"How did you meet your wife?" I asked.

"At a wine tasting," he said. "We were . . . fifteen? I've been tasting wine since I was four. And she too."

"How did you know? You were so young." I was truly curious.

"It just felt right." He blushed a little.

"That's a nice story," I said. Felipe was always communicating with Maria José and the kids, texting, video chatting. They were definitely the happiest couple around this place. "You inspire me that true love is out there."

"Just keep going to wine tastings," he said.

"Good advice," I said. Now I was the one blushing.

• • •

Just then, Linda came out carrying a plate of chicken. "Hannah," she said, "can you be a dear and run in to get the salad? I've already dressed it and the wooden tongs are on the counter next to it."

I nodded and pushed myself up from the table. My head was aching. Maybe it was from being on my best behavior or trying to learn or just being polite for so many hours in a row. I found the salad just where Linda said it would be, on the counter, next to the tongs. It looked amazing—fresh-picked lettuce with little slices of clementines, raisins (which I assumed came from their own vineyard), goat cheese, and orange peppers. I was about to pick up the bowl when the house phone rang. By instinct, I answered it.

"Rockford residence. This is Hannah speaking."

"Hannah!" It was William, and my stomach jumped a little.

"Hi," I said, a bit sheepish.

"How's it going? I wasn't expecting to talk to you."

"I know. Me either. Things are good," I said. "I went on a sales call with your mom today and I even made a friend."

"Celeste?"

"How'd you know?"

"She's everyone's first friend. A little needy," he said, "but harmless."

"Okay," I said, "good to know. I haven't had a friend in a while."

"I'm glad to hear it," he said. "How are my parents?"

"Fine," I said. "I think. I'm planning a party for the tasting room. To drum up new business. It'll be the first Friday in June."

"Fun," he said.

"Jackson Hill is going to play the music." I wondered if he knew about Jackson's relationship with his mother.

"He's got a good sound," he said. "Has a thing for my mom, though."

I smiled. So he didn't really know. "Who wouldn't?" I asked.

"That's gross," he said.

"Sorry," I said. "How's New York?"

"Okay," he said. "I randomly saw your boyfriend the other day. I passed him on the street in Soho, and I recognized him. I don't know if he saw me or not. But I noticed him because at first I thought he was homeless. And then I wondered if maybe he was someone I knew from college, but then I realized who it was. He looked like shit. He hadn't shaved. He was wearing the same outfit he'd been wearing at the winery, and it kind of looked like he hadn't changed in weeks."

"Ugh," I said.

"I wasn't going to tell you," he said. "But . . . since you picked up the phone . . ."

"It's okay." I said. "I appreciate it. That makes me worried about him. But what can I do? Do you want to talk to your parents?"

"No, it's okay. Actually, don't tell them I called. I'll call later. I'm glad you're there with them. It keeps them occupied. Creates a buffer."

"Do they fight a lot?" I asked.

"It's just not always easy," he said. "Be kind to them."

"Of course," I said. "I like them. I think we're getting along. It's nice to be part of a family. Okay, I guess I should go back out. I was just in here to get the salad."

"Right," he said. "Talk to you soon."

The conversation made me feel sad. Poor Ethan. I needed to call him. But I wasn't ready to have him tell me what an awful person I was. How I had ruined his life. I sent him a quick text that read, "Hope all is well in NYC," to assuage my conscience. When he shot back, "I feel like garbage," my conscience was not comforted, but I also decided not to respond. He was trying to make me feel guilty. And I did. Calling him would acknowledge what was going on between us (or not going on, as the case may be). I knew it was cowardly to ghost on your own boyfriend, but I just wasn't ready to acknowledge anything quite yet.

I went back out with the salad, explaining that I had gone to the bathroom to wash my hands before eating. Felipe, Everett, and Linda were already eating their chicken, legs and thighs covered in a mushroom lemon sauce, in silence. I felt like making conversation was my job. "I learned a lot on the call today. What do you do next?"

"Oh, I'll drive them up next week, like I told him."

"Is delivering yourself a good use of your time?" I asked.

"Who else is going to do it, especially now that William is gone? Usually when I get there a nice young barback or kitchen hand will help carry the boxes out of the car."

"Seems like a lot of work," I said. "Is there a delivery service?"

"That would cost money," she said. "This way, we make all the profit."

"But your time," I said. "And gas . . ."

"It reinforces things, for them to see me again. And I'll make another sales call when I'm up there. We have a few restaurants we work with. It's like a rotation."

"It's not efficient, Linda," Everett said. "I've been telling you this for years."

"If we had a distributor, we'd lose twenty percent."

"But the costs of travel and maybe you'd sell more?" Most of what I had learned in business school didn't apply here—they didn't teach us about the ins and outs of wine making (how could they have missed that important topic?), but I did know about the basics of running a small business—about sunk costs and efficiencies. About the importance of timely invoicing and good bookkeeping. Linda was doing her best, but efficiency was not necessarily her forte.

"I don't know," Linda said. "How would I know that they would pitch my wine correctly and to the right people?"

"I'm sure you could give them all the background. Maybe there's, like, a small local distributor who could help you? Or maybe just a part-times sales rep? Or I could do some of it? At least the delivery?" I said.

Linda nodded and served herself salad. I sipped the Sancerre, which had started warming up in the evening air. It tasted less crisp, but no less peachy. "I'll think about it," she said to me. "You put her up to this," she said, turning to Everett. There was anger simmering under the surface; it made me nervous. Especially after having seen how Linda was with Jackson.

Chapter 14

"I'm afraid that you aren't ready for First Friday," Celeste said. It was a week and a half away. She had barged into the cottage while I was still sleeping and jumped onto my bed, startling me.

"I think we have plenty of time," I said.

"You need to be prepared," Celeste said. "You're taking this all too casually."

"I feel like we have everything under control," I said.

She arranged the pillows behind her head and started leafing through the design magazine that Linda had left on the bedside table. "Isn't this marvelous?" she asked, showing me a photo of a waterfall in a rock garden. "Linda should do this here. She has great rocks."

Celeste was fun and she was helping me a lot, but I didn't love how familiar she felt in my home. We had really just met, after all. And what did it say about me that I had someone storming into my home all the time trying to take care of me? I guessed it was mildly my fault for not locking the front door, but I could never find the key in my bag. Besides, in New York, my friend Nicole and I had gone back and forth into each other's apartments like we lived together. But we always knocked before we entered. In retrospect, though, it was a friendship of convenience, because neither one of us kept up with the other now that we lived three thousand miles apart.

"You've already talked to Jackson about the music?"

"I did," I said.

"Great," she said. She continued flipping. "Wouldn't it be nice to have an ocean view?" she muttered.

"He's in for Friday. I'm calling it First Fridays at Bellosguardo. And I found some servers. A bartender. I set up a ticket website. No caterer, though."

"Brilliant," she said. "I have the perfect person. Annie Sanders will cater it at cost. We'll have to do the shopping, though. And what else do we need? A few decorations. I'm sure we can dig something up in Linda's house. She doesn't even know what she has."

"Thanks . . . ," I said, feeling a tiny bit defensive. The party was my idea, and I weirdly wanted the credit for it, but I also knew that without Celeste's help and knowledge of Sonoma, I wouldn't be able to make it perfect.

"So, how's it going otherwise?" she asked. "Your boyfriend break up with you yet?"

"What?" I asked.

"Well, the other morning, you weren't sure."

"I don't know," I said. "I talked to William last

night and he said he saw Ethan on the street in the city and that he looked really pitiful. But I just didn't have the emotional energy to call."

"Well, he can call you too. He's a grown man with a phone." She stood up and dropped the magazine on the bed. "Annie will be in touch about her menu. Make sure you have her make the mini sliders. They're always the most popular! See you soon."

I wanted to call Tyra to tell her that William had seen Ethan. To see if she would check on him. They were friends too, after all, and they were in the same city. She couldn't be mad at me anymore; she had gotten what she wanted. I checked her Instagram before texting her, though, and found a selfie of her in a new Armani business suit with the caption "First major client meeting today and I feel fabulous." She didn't have time to chase Ethan around the city. I put my phone back on the bedside table.

Celeste left as quickly as she had come. I wasn't even quite sure what had happened to me. She was a whirlwind. Loud voice, long nails, ultrablond hair, Lilly Pulitzer prints. But with her help, the party was planned in one day. Now we just needed people to attend. Her relationship advice was less sound than her party advice, but what could I do? I pulled on leggings and a tunic, ran a brush through my hair, and headed down to the office to talk to Linda about the idea of hiring Annie Sanders for the catering. I was sure that Linda would know her if she was, as Celeste claimed, a local.

The office was unlocked, but Linda wasn't in it, although her usual mess was. I ventured into the main tasting room and found her curled up on the leather sofa using what looked like a pashmina scarf as a blanket. I didn't want to wake her, but I was also worried about her. I went back into the office and got the Penny Vincenzi novel that had been sitting on Linda's desk since I started, unopened. I settled myself in the overstuffed leather chair across the coffee table from the couch that she was sleeping on and started reading. I was immediately swept away by the story of the rich London publishing family and the intrigues that could happen between parents, siblings, colleagues. Family business was family business, I guessed, no matter what the type of work. I had read about thirty pages when Linda started stirring. She turned over to face me and looked shocked. She also looked puffy, like she had been crying.

"What are you doing here?" she asked.

"I'm sorry," I said. "I had something to tell you. An idea that Celeste had. I figured you'd be in the office, but then I found you sleeping here and I wanted to stay to check on you."

"Oh," she said. "I had a hard night. Everett and

I got in a huge fight after you left. One of the biggest. Now that William isn't here, it's just . . ."

"I'm sorry," I said. "About the distributor?"

"About everything. My role. His role. The business. How best to grow it. Why maybe we shouldn't grow it. How we don't respect the work the other does. That kind of thing."

"I'm so sorry," I said. I felt that somehow the fight was also about me, but neither of us brought that up. "How did you leave things?"

"Well, then the argument devolved into more what I don't do for him, what he doesn't do for me. How we are just business partners at this point."

"Oh," I said. This was a kitchen sink fight—the kind where you just said everything that you had ever thought about the other person. It was hard to recover from such fights. I decided not to say that, though, because what did I know about marriage in general and their marriage in particular? Nothing. "But you guys have such a long marriage. You can survive a night like this."

"We have before," she said. "But I'm done. After seeing Jackson the other day, and this fight, it makes me realize I'm just wasting away here. I'm sorry that you're here while this is happening. You can stay or go. I know you don't have the best relationship with Everett, but he'll probably need you more than ever with me gone. You already have all the billing under control.

I'll tell you about the deliveries. But that's easy. He'll see how much I do when I'm not here to do it. I know he thinks it's unnecessary, that I create work for myself, but nobody else does."

"Of course," I said. "You do so much." My mind was racing. What was I going to do? I was supposed to learn from her. How would I keep the place afloat? What was going to happen? I just wanted to plan a party and post cute photos of a dog on the Internet. Not take over for the woman who ran the business side of the winery.

She sat up on the couch and shivered into the thin cashmere shawl. "What's going to happen to me?" she asked.

"Maybe you'll be happier," I said, trying to push my own anxieties aside.

"Maybe," she said. She looked like a little girl at that moment, red eyes, messy hair, a too-big shawl, an oversize couch. I hadn't realized how tiny she was until this very moment. She had such a loud voice and a big personality and was always moving so fast that you didn't notice that she was small—petite, fine boned.

"Whatever you need to do to make yourself happy," I said. Although I wanted to scream: "Don't abandon me! I am totally clueless!"

"You're sweet," she said. "I admire you."

I didn't know what to say to that, so I just moved next to her and gave her a hug. She snuffled a bit more, then stood up. "I guess I need to get some things in order."

"I guess," I said. "I had originally come down here to tell you that Celeste is going to help me with the party—organize the catering and decorations."

"That's great," she said. "I'm sorry I'll miss it."

"You can still come," I said.

"Oh, Hannah," she said. Fresh tears came to her eyes and she walked ahead of me into the office.

Chapter 15

Linda spent the next few hours narrating her day. She showed me how she tracked the inventory, how she filled orders like Chris's from the day before, the list of wines that would be ready for the next season. She had highlighted a few restaurants and wine stores that I could just call on the phone to see if they wanted to restock. Some needed more handholding. I nodded. I was planning to call a local wine distributor as soon as she was gone to have them take on the existing accounts and try to grow the business. I could deal with the wine club and the tasting room and the social media and planning the party on my own—with a little help from Celeste, of course. But I also needed to show Linda that I respected what she did.

At the end of the day, she pushed back from her desk, took off her headset, and closed her laptop. She wrote down a list of her passwords and her cell phone number. Then she gestured for me to follow her into the tasting room, where she opened a bottle of Taittinger 2011 Domaine Carneros Brut Cuvée. It was frothy, but she poured it into our glasses so that the froth grew just to the very top.

"This is one of the best out there," she s
"Cheers. To new beginnings."

"To new beginnings," I said, feeling a bi
terrified for both of us.

We clicked our glasses together. She smiled. "I smell honeysuckle," she said. "Maybe also violets."

"That's still hard for me to notice," I said. "I still just taste fruit. Maybe like bitter strawberry?"

"Yes," she said. "Bitter strawberry; that's exactly it. And maybe a hint of wasabi? I've been saving this for a long time. This is the perfect time to have it."

"Also, you won't be able to take it with you," I said.

"Good point," she said. "I should go throw some things in a bag."

She walked out of the office and I sat down at her desk with my flute of sparkling wine mostly full. I put her headset on my head. But it bothered my ear so I took it off. I looked around at everything Linda had built and I had organized. We had worked together for the past week, and now she was gone. I would have to fill her shoes. I knew I could do it. I had learned a lot, but there was something to be said for having that institutional knowledge there. The person who knew everything. I was starting from scratch.

I texted Drew a photo of the office and made

ude the open bottle of Cuvée. "This is
k now," I said.

an a school," he wrote back.

true," I wrote.

"I'm sure you're killing it," he wrote. "Now I have to go check in on the kids in detention."

I liked how he could always remind me that his life was way weirder than mine.

After I finished texting Drew, I went out into the tasting room and sipped my Cuvée behind the bar. It was a Tuesday, so it was not entirely guaranteed that someone would come into the tasting room, but it wasn't out of the question either. I sipped my sparkling wine slowly and mentally tried to envision the room filled with a jazz band and partygoers and passed hors d'oeuvres. The party. It was coming up. I felt like things were organized, but I wasn't sure. I was sure about so little all of a sudden. So I decided to call Celeste. I told her about the open bottle of Cuvée and she arrived in ten minutes flat.

She walked through the door wearing a backless Lululemon top and white lace short-shorts. "Bubbly!" she said, smiling.

"It's like your bat signal," I said. "Who knew?"

"I mean, it's not just any bubbly," she said. "I wouldn't rush over here for Prosecco."

"Duly noted," I said as she settled herself at the bar.

“This is one of the top ten wines of the region,” Celeste said. “I have a case in my basement, but I never drink it; I just give it as housewarming gifts to my clients. I do so much for them. I give them tours; I take them to parties; I introduce them to new friends, who are, of course, other clients.”

“Real estate isn’t easy,” I said.

“Finding the property is the least of it,” she said. “The negotiation. Dealing with lawyers. Renovations. Architects. Contractors. I’m just involved in everything.”

“That’s why you’re good at what you do,” I said. “Are you bringing any clients to the party?”

“Oh,” she said. “I hadn’t thought about that.”

“Not fancy enough?” I joked.

“Not that,” she said. “But maybe. Maybe if it was at the house and not at the tasting room. So it would feel more exclusive. But that house is like a mausoleum, isn’t it?”

“It is kind of like a mausoleum,” I said. “I wonder why they keep all those nice rooms so dark and all the furniture covered. Why not enjoy it? Instead they just sit in that ugly kitchen.”

“So weird,” Celeste said. “But that’s what rich people are. Weird. If I know anything from my job, it’s that.”

“They’re not rich, though,” I said. “Everything is kind of falling apart behind the facade. They were thinking of renting the place when I started.”

“They live in a castle,” Celeste said. “They’re rich even if they are cash poor. And we’ll help them. You’re growing the business already; just look at all the RSVPs for the party. And the social media. I can’t believe that dog already has over a thousand followers.”

“Good point,” I said. “I just want to do the right thing for Linda, you know?”

“I do,” Celeste said.

We polished off the last of the Cuvée and headed into town to eat lavender crème brûlée.

The next morning, feeling only a tiny bit foggy because of the sparkling wine and the sugar, I found a couple standing outside of the front door of the tasting room just as I was opening. “Good morning,” the woman said, and walked right past me as if she had been expecting me to open the door for her and had timed our arrivals simultaneously. The man walked in behind her but immediately took her hand after they passed the threshold. They were laughing and pointing at the details in the tasting room. I walked around to the other side of the bar as they got themselves situated, but I overheard her say, “The outside looks like a wine barrel, how clever.” I liked them immediately. Their faces were young, but their hair was gray. I was impressed that in the world of eternal youth we all lived in, they had embraced their own gray hair. I resolved right then to let my hair go gray naturally rather than fighting it with dyes and pigments. They settled down at the bar and I introduced myself and asked them if they wanted the reserve tasting.

"Oh, we so do, sweetheart," she said, in the least condescending way someone can say "sweetheart." "But this is our first stop of the day. Can you just pour us your best white, your best Pinot, and your best Cab?"

"Of course," I said. I pulled out the early-harvest Chardonnay that Linda had poured for Chris on Monday. "I love this wine," I said. "It's a Chardonnay, but we age it in steel, not in oak, so it doesn't have that buttery taste."

"So glad that's gone out of fashion," he said, swirling his glass.

"This is delightful," she said. "I taste snap peas. And I smell . . . rosemary."

"We grow rosemary next to the grapes," I said, remembering what Everett had told me that first night at dinner. "Grapes tend to take on the elements of what grows around them."

"How interesting," she said. "I didn't know that."

I smiled. It was nice to finally feel like I knew something about what I was doing. I pulled out the Private Reserve Pinot Noir and poured them each a taste. We rarely opened the Private Reserve for regular tastings, but I had a sense that they might buy a case of it. They seemed fancy.

And then I could finish the bottle in my cottage that night.

"Wow," he said.

"This is a limited-edition wine," I said, "that we grow in our coastal vineyard, because it needs a slightly cooler temperature than here. It's cooler on the other side of the mountains near the ocean."

"Coastal vineyard?" she said. "That sounds like a great place to have a vacation."

"I smell cherry pits," he said. "And a berry flavor."

I nodded. I hadn't been to the coastal vineyard and I wasn't even sure it was part of Everett and Linda's actual property. But I knew they didn't buy grapes from other people, so there must have been an explanation that I didn't understand. I made a mental note to ask Everett about it.

"Where are you from?" I asked.

"Colorado," he said. "A blond woman in a pink print assaulted us at the coffee shop this morning and told us this was the best wine in Sonoma."

"Celeste?" I asked.

"That sounds right," she said.

"She's quite friendly, and really, she's your best advertiser," he said. "She insisted that we come here. You should pay her!"

"She means well," I said. "She's helped me a lot with a party I'm planning here."

"Party?" the woman asked.

“We’re going to have music and a food and wine tasting here the first Friday of June.” I said.

“Oh,” she said. “We’ll be back home by then.”

“You can fly back out for it!” I said, only sort of joking. “I swear it’ll be great.”

“Our son is out here,” the woman said, shaking her head like he had been a massive disappointment. “We don’t know what he does. But he seems to manage. Though his apartment is disgusting. So much dust. It’s amazing they can breathe.”

“That’s all we can ask,” the husband said. “Food. Shelter. Some modicum of happiness.”

I wondered if my mom talked about me in such hushed tones. The daughter who left. The one in “business.” The world I lived in wasn’t one she understood. She understood that Drew was a principal. That made sense. Lawyers, doctors even. But business. Marketing. She had no idea what that was. I’d tried to explain once after my first few months in New York. Trying to explain what I did at Tiffany’s was a bit of an uphill battle. “Sounds like you’re an over-paid secretary is what you are,” my mother had said.

“It’s like an apprenticeship,” I had said.

“Do you think you’ll ever have your boss’s job? Do you even want it? Are you being trained for it?" my mother had asked. Training was important to her. She was always taking classes to improve her nursing skills.

"I mean, I guess one day. It's not really what I want, but it's good experience."

"So why are you doing it?"

"To learn."

"I don't understand," my mother had said. "It sounds to me like they're just taking advantage of a smart girl and making her get coffee and print out reports."

"You learn from those things," I'd said.

"You don't have to go to college to get coffee," my mother had said. "You went to college, Hannah. Why don't you use some of those skills? Become a teacher like Drew."

I wanted her to think what I was doing was worthwhile. Explaining this would be even harder. So probably I wouldn't even bother. Maybe that was why I wasn't taking her calls. I just didn't want to explain. Maybe Drew would tell her if he was feeling generous. But he probably wouldn't. I just felt stuck.

I poured the final wine for the Colorado couple, and we had moved from talking about disappointing children to discussing good restaurants in the area, which was a topic I much preferred, when Felipe came running into the tasting room breathlessly, his short brown hair mussed. “It is Mr. Everett,” he yelled. “He has had an *accidente.*”

“An accident?” I asked.

“He needs . . . He fell from ladder. Now he is not moving.”

I could tell that Felipe’s English was starting to falter under the stress. I tried to be calm, but I didn’t know what to do. My own English disappeared. I was struck dumb with silence, staring at Felipe, who was fumbling for his phone. I looked to the couple at the bar.

“Don’t move him,” the older man said. “He could have a concussion or worse. Have a local ambulance come. Bring him to the hospital here and they’ll decide if he needs to go somewhere else.”

“You’re a doctor?” I asked.

“I’m a nurse practitioner,” he said. “I work in a hospital every day. There’s nothing worse than moving someone who has a neck injury.”

“I’ll do it,” I said to Felipe, and I ran into the office to call 911. I screamed that somebody needed to come out to Bellosguardo right away. We then all sat in silence for a moment and waited for the sounds of a siren. Then I ran to the office and looked at the list of numbers Linda had given me. I tried to type hers into my cell phone, but I kept messing up. Finally, I got it to work. “Linda,” I said. “There’s been an accident.”

“What?!” she said. “I’m in San Francisco. I told Everett.”

“You have to come back,” I said.

“Okay,” she said. “I was so close to getting away . . .”

“The ambulance is coming. You have no choice.”

I went back into the tasting room. “His wife is coming. But it might be a little bit of time. Should we go to where he is?” I asked Felipe.

He led us out into the parking lot and down a dirt path toward the vineyard. The nurse practitioner and his wife trailed behind us.

As we jogged through the vines, I asked, “How will the ambulance get up here?”

“There is a service road,” he said. “Where we bring the picking trucks.”

I nodded. “Should we tell William?” I said to nobody in particular. “He’s the son in New York.”

“Probably best to get Everett to a hospital,” the older man said. “You’ll know more then, before people start getting on planes. He might be fine. Just in shock.”

“Thanks,” I said. “I don’t even know your name.”

“Walter,” he said.

“I’m glad you were here, Walter,” I said.

“Me too,” he said. “This is Nancy.”

I shook Nancy’s hand and strained to hear an

ambulance. "We should go out in front. In case they come."

Four hours later, Linda and I were huddled together in the waiting room of Santa Rosa Hospital, anticipating the results of an EKG, an MRI, and a CT scan. They didn't know if it was a stroke, a heart attack, or both. I didn't know what to say, so I concentrated on basic needs—did Linda need coffee? A sweater? A snack? The answer to all was no, although I did wrap the shawl I had been wearing as a scarf around her just in case, and she didn't complain.

When she arrived at the hospital a few hours after I had, I just hugged her and said, "Sorry your trip to the store got interrupted."

She nodded at me, like she knew what I was saying. She didn't bring up William, so I didn't either, although I was itching to call him. It was true that he wouldn't really need to know what was happening if his father was going to be okay, but likely he would be angry not to have been informed. When my father died they kept it from me for as long as possible. My mother had gotten a phone call in the middle of the night and had woken me up to tell me that she needed to go on an emergency call at the hospital and would we be okay by ourselves? I could get breakfast for myself and Drew and get us both to school, right? She didn't even wake Drew. She just disappeared. She didn't come back for two days. She called and made sure we were okay. She sent over her friend Mrs. Anderson, who wouldn't answer any of our questions, but who let us have French toast for dinner. And even let us use the real maple syrup, which my mother kept in the top of the cupboard for really special occasions. I can't eat maple syrup to this day.

We found out after two days that my father had been in a truck accident. His truck had slid off the road on a night that was plagued by black ice in the middle of Nebraska. The front cab had gone into an irrigation ditch, jackknifing the tractor-trailer, and my father had been knocked unconscious. Luckily, another trucker had seen it happen and had called for help. My father ended up in an Omaha hospital and my mother drove out there to be with him. But she hadn't told us that he was in a coma; she didn't keep us updated on his progress; she tried to make us think it was going to be okay. Maybe because she thought it was going to be okay. Who knows. But all we knew was that after two days, Mrs. Anderson told us that he was dead and that we needed to go to the store to buy black clothing for a funeral. When our mother got home, she looked like a ghost and just sank into my dad's chair in the living room, turned on a hockey game, his favorite sport, and rarely got up again. I never really forgave her for not telling us what was going on as it happened. We deserved to know. I know the way she dealt with it was the only way she knew how, but I wished it was different. And for that reason, I felt like William deserved to know. Although it also wasn't my decision to make. So, I bit my tongue, as much as it killed me.

Linda had fallen lightly asleep on my shoulder, but I had to wake her when the doctor came out. He pulled her aside and whispered to her and then brought her with him behind the doors that read: IMMEDIATE FAMILY ONLY.

I waited for what felt like an interminable amount of time, leafing through old issues of *Us Weekly* and *Psychology Today.* I wondered if they merged the two magazines whether they could figure out what was wrong with the Kardashian family. Or maybe they were all the sanest people on earth, and they had just figured out a way to make money off of their family drama. I knew that I was tired when I started rationalizing the behavior of the Kardashians.

I bought a mocha from the coffee-dispensing machine hoping it would taste less like flavored water than the drip coffee I had ordered earlier, but it didn't. They had improved on this technology elsewhere. I wondered why it hadn't hit hospitals yet, a place where people ostensibly needed caffeine.

Finally, Linda came back out, crumpled, a nurse holding her up.

"How is he?" I asked, rushing to her.

"He had a heart attack," she said. "They aren't sure if it was what caused the fall or if the fall caused it. But regardless. They have to do a double bypass. They think he'll be okay, but . . ."

"Oh, Linda," I said. "I'm so sorry." I hugged her and she allowed herself to be hugged, although all energy seemed drained from her body.

"I'll stay here tonight with him," she said. "Can you call Celeste and ask her to bring me some things and some things for Everett too? She has a key. And of course she knows where everything is. And can you go back and run things while I'm here? Just basic things—answer the phone and deal with any of the restaurants or shops that buy from us if they call. Try to keep the tasting room open the rest of the week and this weekend?"

"Of course," I said. "Whatever you need."

"I should call William," she said. "But I think I'll wait until tomorrow. Please don't tell him until I do."

"I won't," I said, although it made my head ache. I really, really hoped Everett would be okay.

The days after Everett's heart attack were a blur. It was a good thing that Linda had given me that impromptu lesson in how the business worked, because while she was at the hospital with Everett, I dealt with shipping and invoices and even had to drive two cases of wine to Corte Madera for a Pinot Noir emergency at a pizza restaurant. I checked on my old apartment when I was down in Berkeley. When I drove by at eleven P.M., no cars were in the driveway and no lights were on, so I assumed the Harvard MBAs were working hard and barely in the apartment.

Most of the time that they were in the hospital, though, honestly, I poured wine in the tasting room, took photographs of wine, and wrote Facebook posts about First Friday. I posted a picture of Tannin with one of the centerpieces I was developing that featured bottles of wine that told the history of the winery on their labels. I posed him with the 1965 Cabernet, the first wine from Bellosguardo ever to get a medal. He licked the bottle (because I put peanut butter on it).

> @TannintheWineDog: "Just One Week Away! All the wine you can taste, food by @AnnieSanders, and music by Jackson Hill. Plus, a petting booth of me!"

It got over 150 likes.

I kept the office neat, the tasting room swept, and the QuickBooks up to date with phone orders that came in. In my downtime, I went through the old order spreadsheets and made phone calls to older, slightly dormant accounts that looked like they might need a reorder. I sold a few cases to each. Even so, I was a little bit lonely. This wasn't exactly the summer I had in mind when I decided to work at a winery. I had envisioned fun afternoons behind the bar, serving wine. I hadn't pictured spreadsheets. But I felt like I really had a job. I got up early. I went to bed early. Some nights I didn't even have a glass of wine before bed I was so tired. Celeste came by regularly with updates. Everett was awake. Everett was sitting up. Everett was talking. Sort of.

Keeping things going reminded me a little of how things were after my dad died. My brother and I didn't really have time to mourn because our mother was so debilitated. We heated up casseroles that people brought to us and put portions in front of our mother. When the casseroles ran out, we went to the store and made ourselves food. We got ourselves to school and home and made sure the electric bill was paid. Now, even though I still wasn't quite sure what I was doing, I knew that I was bringing in money for the winery and that I was keeping things on track. I liked being important. I know I felt resentful about keeping things on track when I was a kid, but now it just felt good.

On Memorial Day, the Monday before the party, the beginning of my third week at Bellosguardo and my fifth day of running things without Linda and Everett, I was pouring sparkling wines for a couple from France in the tasting room when William walked through the door. But instead of being happy to see me, he barked, "Do you have cash? The cab driver will only take cash and I owe him a hundred and fifty dollars."

I hadn't been expecting him, and seeing him made my stomach immediately do ten somersaults. "I'll check in the petty cash," I said. I ducked into the office and pulled out Linda's cashbox, which held 300 dollars. I marked down that 150 dollars was for William and brought it out to him.

"You're a lifesaver," he said. He went back out to pay the driver and then didn't come back inside. I guessed he went up to the house or off to the hospital. I tried not to be offended by the fact that he didn't even seem to register who I was.

I went about the rest of my day, trying not to think about him being there, or not being there. I stayed late in the office updating the inventory and then brought an open bottle of rosé back to the cottage. I was pretty sure there was a veggie burger in the freezer that I could heat up. I would need to restock the fridge at some point. I was trying to remember if there was any cheese to go with the burger as I unlocked the front door. I flipped on the light but noticed that the light on the back patio seemed to be on. I grabbed a candlestick from the front table and walked toward the back. I was entirely alone on the huge property right now, aside from Felipe, who was in another cottage completely on the other side of the vineyard. He lived in a converted bunkhouse that was originally built for grape pickers, but which Linda had converted into a loft-style house that would be able to accommodate Felipe's wife and children when they arrived after the harvest. But even though I knew Felipe was fifty acres and a quick text message away, it was a little bit spooky. To think about acres and acres of land and a giant castle all devoid of life. Just little me in a cottage, with a candlestick. Ridiculous. I couldn't see anyone on the patio through the kitchen windows, so I threw open the door.

I was both relieved and a little angry to find William, asleep on one of the padded reclining chairs. "Hey," I said, putting the candlestick down on the iron café table and settling myself on the end of his chair.

"Did you think you were going to defend yourself with that?" He laughed, waking up.

"It's heavy," I said.

He shook his head. "Do I need to get you a baseball bat?"

"The only intruders I have here are people I already know," I said.

"Sorry," he said. "I've always liked to nap here. And it's been a long day."

"It's your house," I said.

"You live here too," he said. "More than I do now."

"Are you okay?" I asked.

"It's scary," he said. "To hear that your dad is in the hospital. And that they don't know if he's going to get better."

"I know," I said. "I've been there. But I am glad your mom called you. When my dad was in critical condition, they didn't even tell me."

"What?" he said.

"I mean, I was little. Eleven. They thought they were protecting me."

"That seems counterproductive. But I also feel guilty because I so wanted to be away from here. And now I'm back."

"You don't have to stay forever," I said.

"I know," he said. "But . . ."

"I know," I said.

We sat in silence for a few minutes. I decided not to tell him what had happened with his mom right before his dad's accident. Maybe it didn't even matter anymore. Maybe everything she had said would just evaporate in the face of Everett's accident and she would stay at Bellosguardo forever.

"I'm glad you're here," he said. "It makes me feel a little bit better about them. I feel like they need someone to watch over them. To care."

"You barely know me," I said.

"That's not true. Besides, I see what you're doing," he said. "You're helping them."

"I selfishly don't want you to go back," I said.

"I know," he said.

"But I know that you selfishly don't want to be here," I said, trying to walk back my oversharing.

He shrugged and tucked my hair back behind my ears. "You must be starving."

"You're avoiding so many things," I said.

"There's piles of food up at the house and it's all about to rot. We must go and eat it."

My stomach growled audibly and he laughed. "I'll take that as a yes."

"You're still not off the hook," I said.

"Neither are you," he said.

William was digging through the refrigerator pulling out pâté and double-cream Brie. "Look at all of these snacks!"

I smiled and exclaimed, "Snacks for dinner!"

"Snacks for snacks; we'll eat them as we cook. There's also steaks. We have to eat them today or else they'll go bad. And we'll make mashed potatoes. And salad. We can pick it in the garden." He was joyously pulling marked Ziplocs out of the refrigerator.

"Did you not eat in New York?"

"I did. But I didn't cook. I miss cooking. I tried to buy a chicken breast there and I swear it cost twenty dollars. For *one*. This is food! People are even bringing over food, not that my mother would ever eat it. She's a better cook than any of them."

"She is a good cook," I said, laying out all of his finds on the butcher block. "It's funny that people always bring casseroles when someone is sick. I wonder what it is about casseroles. Anyway, how's New York?"

"It's a crazy place," he said. "But it's amazing. Everyone I've met is creative, is working on a project. They know people. But not like how people in LA know people. They know interesting people."

I nodded. He handed me a bag of potatoes and a peeler.

"You peel. I'll go get the grill started."

He went outside and I peeled a few potatoes, but I really wanted to see the house, and so far nobody had offered that, so I left the fruits of my labor on the counter and went into the rest of the house, ostensibly to look for a bathroom, if anyone asked. The remainder of the house was quite grand, decorated in a Victorian style. There were rich drapes, dark-wood sideboards, and handwoven rugs with floral designs. A giant portrait of a man and a horse hung over the grand central staircase, dominated by a multitiered crystal chandelier. I snuck into the living room, where the floor-to-ceiling windows were covered with shiny yellow brocade curtains. But the sofas and grand piano were all covered in white sheets. Yellowed formerly white sheets that had clearly been there for ages. I walked through dark-wood pocket doors to a grand dining room. A giant table had sixteen chairs around it, but the furniture in that room was also covered and the blinds were drawn. I wondered why they would live in this grand home with classic furnishings but not use any room except the shabby kitchen.

I was heading through the pocket doors back toward the kitchen when I heard my name being called. “Hannah! Hannah!” It was faint and far away.

“I’m in here!” I yelled.

William found me in the dark living room. “What are you doing?” he asked. He didn’t seem angry, but I wasn’t one hundred percent sure.

“I was looking for the bathroom and I got distracted. Why don’t you use these beautiful rooms?”

“Expensive to heat. Fancy family heirlooms that we didn’t want to ruin. My mom always claimed that it was uncomfortable, although that was just to keep us out of the rooms, I think.”

“I just can’t believe you sit at a pizza booth when you can sit in there.” I gestured toward the dining room.

“When I was little, we would use it sometimes on Easter or Christmas, but even that became a pain because everything needed to be uncovered and then cleaned and re-covered."

"It's just so pretty," I said. "And it's the story of your family. My family just has a few kind of faded photos in frames from Walmart on the mantelpiece."

"One day, we'll open it all up," he said.

I smiled. I wasn't sure if I was included in the "we" or not, but I wanted to be.

"More important, you've abandoned your potato post," he said. "And we need to get the mashed potatoes going, so now we both need to peel."

We headed back to the kitchen and he told me all the stories he had made up about the people in the portraits when he was a kid. There was one of a man with a beard holding a shovel that he called "The Gravedigger," although it was actually a portrait of a relative who had come to California to find gold. Another painting depicted a man in a very fluffy fur collar. William had always thought he had a pet fox around his neck and called the man General Fox, "but I recently realized he was just wearing a really ugly fur coat."

"There's no accounting for historically bad taste," I said. "But it must have been a fun place to be a kid."

"It was," he said as he peeled potatoes. But I could sense a hesitation in his voice.

"And it wasn't?"

"And it wasn't."

I continued peeling as well, deciding to be quiet for once in my life.

"Lonely," he eventually said. "There weren't other kids around. The dog was always my best friend. Sevvie, the one I told you about, short for Reserve. I told him everything. But you need other kids to play with. Celeste would come by, but she wasn't any fun; she just wanted to talk about the kids at school and dress Sevvie up in costumes. And my parents were both busy. Even busier than they are now, because they were setting the business up. And they fought a lot. I always was worried they were going to get divorced. There was one summer when my mother just disappeared. She said she was going to visit her mother, but she'd never done that before. I never found out where she went. My dad and I ate a lot of frozen burgers that summer."

"I'm so sorry," I said, realizing that all families have times that aren't perfect. Even this one.

"It actually wasn't that bad, that summer," he said. "Since my dad was kind of lonely and needed a friend, we did things. But I could tell he was happier when she came back. I hope she remembers that now."

I didn't know what to tell him. I felt like Linda and I had a private bond that I wasn't quite ready to break with her yet. And there were things that a son shouldn't know about his mother. I wouldn't want to know what my mother's true feelings about my father were. "They seem like a good team," was all I could bring myself to say.

"They are, in business," he said. "But I think as life partners they aren't great. But there's lots to do and this house is big, so they often just kept to themselves. My dad would watch baseball games in the evenings upstairs. And my mom would sit down here and knit or read or do puzzles in puzzle books. It always just felt sad. Like they both wished they were doing something else, but they were stuck here with one another. But alone. They loved me and paid attention to me, but I could feel that they didn't want to be with each other. If that makes any sense."

I sighed and reached over to put my hand on his. "That sounds hard."

"So I'm determined not to have that happen to me. I don't want to be miserable across the table from someone I don't like. Or, I've compromised so much to be with, I start to resent. I'd rather be alone," he said. "And that goes for the business too. I've helped them for a long time, but I don't want to do it forever."

I nodded. I wondered if I'd be miserable for my entire life with Ethan. With his incessant planning. His life checklist constantly being checked off. "I get it," I said. "That's why I'm here. But isn't it also possible that you could find happiness? I feel like I will one day. I'm not giving up on that."

"I don't know," he said. "But I'm pretty sure with my parents that they knew it was wrong from the beginning but they did it anyway. To merge businesses. Property. Because they had complementary skills. Reasonable things like that. I don't think you should get married for reasonable reasons. It should be because you're madly in love or nothing."

"You're a romantic!" I said, pinching his cheek. He blushed a little and smiled. But then he steeled his face.

"It's not a joke," he said. "I mean it."

"I believe you," I said.

We were done peeling the potatoes and I swept the peelings into a bowl to put in the compost outside and he sliced the potatoes up into cubes to dump into the water he had boiling on the stove.

I poured us both glasses of wine now that the major prep work was done, and we headed together to the garden with baskets to gather our salads.

"I feel like a pioneer," I said.

"A yuppie pioneer," he said. "But you must have had a garden in Iowa."

"It's funny, everyone thinks of Iowa as this idyllic farm landscape, but I grew up in a subdivision in a small house with a finished basement and an attached garage. We barely had grass in our little yard. My mom worked nights a lot, especially after my dad died, so that she could sleep all day. Drew and I had to feed ourselves, so it was a lot of microwave stuff."

"Oh, America," he said. "It has so many facets."

"America." I sighed. "I mean, there are nice things. My brother, who still lives there, he's in a CSA run by a farmer who is on his street. The guy just drops off any extra vegetables that he has on a daily basis. His wife is constantly trying to figure out what to do with two pounds of kohlrabi. Drew, Elise, and their kids eat amazingly fresh food. But he just has a regular subdivision yard and my mom still eats Hungry-Man dinners. I try to talk to her about it . . . but . . . I mean, she's a nurse; she knows better."

He laughed. "I'm sorry I'm laughing," he said. "But that actually sounds disgusting."

"It is," I said. "Or it was, I realized after. Moving to New York after college really helped me see the other side of things. Even in high school, going home with friends to their houses. Because you don't really know something is weird until you experience other things, right?"

"So true," he said.

"I mean, you probably thought everyone grew up in castles."

"Not really." He laughed. "Sonoma is a pretty diverse place."

"But you know what I mean."

He nodded. Our baskets were filled with vegetables. "This is probably too much for salad," I said.

"We can make a frittata for breakfast."

I tried not to think too much about breakfast. We needed to make it through dinner first.

He brought the steaks out to the grill while I made salads and mashed the potatoes.

I brought the potatoes and the salads out to the picnic table and sat there with my wine as he tested the beef. "What were your few weeks in New York like?"

"Great," he said. "I mean . . . hard. But great. My friend's apartment is small and I was staying on the couch and there was barely enough room for my suitcase. So I just spent the first two days walking. And taking notes. You hear everything everyone says. Fights and first dates and boring conversations and philosophical debates."

"I kind of miss that," I mused.

"So inspiring. For screenwriting. I mean, it's all dialogue. I filled almost an entire notebook with all the things I overheard."

"Of course they're not the things overheard in a winery."

"Some things are universal," he said. "I never heard my parents fight, but obviously they were fighting for years. I heard some good fights. A woman accusing her significant other of trying to sabotage their relationship via their pet. A woman yelling at her son for stealing money out of her purse to buy pot. I sat next to a couple breaking up at a bar, and then at the next bar, I saw a couple on a first date have their first kiss."

"Different people?"

He laughed. "Yes, different people. You're funny."

"Thanks," I said. "Sounds amazing."

"I bet people who live there for a long time get sick of that stuff, but as a first-timer, it was great. LA isn't even like that. I lived there for four years when I was in college, but the tables are farther apart and people fight in their cars. In New York, there's nowhere to hide. Even your apartment is too small to have a fight." He slid the steaks onto the plates that I'd set across from each another. "Bon appétit."

I served potatoes onto both of our plates and we dug in. After we chewed and made noises that indicated the meal was good, he said, "Did you ever talk to Ethan? After I saw him?"

"No," I said. "I meant to, but I just . . . couldn't."

"So, you're an avoider?"

"No . . . I mean, I texted him, and he wrote back. But then I didn't follow up . . ."

"You are."

We were both silent. There wasn't really anywhere to steer the conversation after that.

"I think I'm just not quite ready for what he wants," I said. "I mean, he wants things to be all serious and on a track. And he wants life to be his way. And I'm just not sure of everything yet. The further into the summer I get, the less sure I am."

"Maybe he'll be less sure after this summer."

"New York is his home. I think he gets more sure there."

"He didn't look sure when I saw him. He looked bereft."

"It makes me feel terrible," I said. "Mostly because I love it here."

That's when he got up silently, came around to my side of the table, sat next to me, and kissed me. It was a sweet kiss. Passionate, but doting. It was the nicest kiss I'd ever felt. But I didn't want a nice kiss; I wanted a great kiss, so I moved closer to him, pressed into him, and bit a little bit on his bottom lip. He bit a little bit back and slid his hand around my back and up the back of my shirt. I got even closer and returned the favor. He pulled back and looked me in the eye. "I feel like we should take this somewhere more private," he said.

"We have this whole place to ourselves," I replied.

He unhooked my bra and picked me up, somehow gracefully getting me inside the door.

Then he put me down and took my hand and we ran together up to his room, which I hadn't seen before, but to be honest, I didn't get much of a look at it because he closed the door behind us and pushed me up against the door, gently but firmly, and kissed me for real. Little bites and all. I groaned and pushed my hands all the way up his back. He lifted my shirt and bra off at the same time and knelt down in front of me. "You are so gorgeous," he whispered. I almost melted. Ethan had never said that to me. Ever. And I had never, ever wanted Ethan the way that I wanted William at that very moment. I closed my eyes and surrendered to his tongue and his fingers and the feeling that someone who wanted me for exactly who I was, was doing exactly what I wanted him to do. It was like he had always known. How was that possible? I asked as I crumpled to the floor and we crawled together to the bed, starving for each other.

Later, when we were lying in his bed, he wrapped his arms around me. "I just didn't expect this to happen so soon," he said.

"I know. I meant to break up with my boyfriend first," I said.

"No, no," he said. "I mean, I was thinking about how great this felt, but I was also thinking about my parents. I thought I had a few more good years with them. It just makes you think that you have to actually grow up and get things together. I've spent all this time being a kid . . . but I'm thirty years old . . ."

"It's all going to be all right," I said, trying to be comforting, but also knowing he was right. "What did Oscar Wilde say? Death must be so beautiful . . . something about being at peace."

"Peace. They both probably want some peace," he said. "I hope you're right."

Chapter 16

William headed to the hospital to see his father and I went down to the tasting room. It was a Tuesday, so the tourist traffic was a bit slow, but Felipe came in to hang with me, and a restaurateur from Austin came in with his wife. I poured him the special selection that we kept just for restaurants. "There are only a few places where you can drink these wines," I told him. "Here, at a few places in Sonoma County, one restaurant in Los Angeles, and one in Portland. We try to keep things very exclusive for our fine-dining clients."

He told me that his name was Alan and that he served a lot of steak, so I poured him our single-vineyard Cabernet and a plummy Zinfandel that grew on vines in a section of the farm that had originally been a fruit orchard—plums and peaches—so the Zin had a fruity quality that made it really rich.

Tannin sauntered into the tasting room and begged the wife to pick him up. He gave her kisses and sat on her lap for at least ten minutes, which was kind of a record for him. He would only sit on Everett's lap that long. Everyone else he got bored with after a few minutes. I smiled at the dog; even Tannin was in on the hard sell. And maybe was a little lonely without Everett around.

"This dog is so sweet," the wife said as her fingers massaged his head.

"I know," I said. "He's a love bug. Can I take a photo of you together for the social media? He has a really popular account."

"Sure," he said, posing with the dog while I snapped. "We just came from the coast," Alan said. "We were at a beach filled with dogs and they seemed so happy. It was called Dillon Beach. Beautiful drive. About an hour from here. You should take Tannin there."

"I have been to this beach," Felipe said. "It is very beautiful and I played with dogs who ran into the surf chasing birds."

"Wow," I said. "That sounds amazing. I haven't really explored the area at all. I've just been in Sonoma at the winery, and I went to Healdsburg for a sales call. And here, of course. Not that there's anything wrong with that."

"That's the thing about being on vacation: You explore. If you live somewhere, you kind of stick to where you need to be." Alan placed an order for a case of Cabernet and a case of the plummy Zinfandel for his restaurant and I locked the door of the tasting room behind him.

I turned to Felipe and said, "Well, I guess we need to drink this wine that's open."

"I think you are right," he said. He poured us both big glasses of the Zinfandel and we settled ourselves on barstools. "You know so much about all of us," he said, "but we know nothing about you."

"Oh," I said. "I'm an open book. I guess the thing I've just been struggling with is kind of coming to terms with myself. It seems like such a privileged problem. But I have all of this pride and I hate dealing with other people's feelings. I'm avoiding my boyfriend right now—Ethan, he's in New York, and my mother, she's in Iowa. I mean, she's a widow. Why am I so angry with her?"

"In Chile, it is different," he said. "We live with our families forever. We never want to leave them. We respect our parents; our children live so close to them. We live at home for college. It is much closer. I see here, everyone is always running away. So maybe you are just being an American."

"Maybe," I said. "But yesterday William called me an avoider, and he's right. I am avoiding."

"Why do you think you are?" he asked.

"I once had a therapist who told me that because my dad died when I was so young, some of my emotional reactions are kind of stunted. I fired that therapist after that session, but maybe he was a little right. But I don't want to blame my dad anymore. It's not his fault that he died and it's not my mom's fault that she was so sad."

"You should send all the love to your mother,"

he said. "I am sure that she sends all of her love to you, so far away."

"I should," I said. "It's just been so hard for me to forgive. But I'm going to try to work on it." Tears were running down my cheeks when William walked into the room.

"What's going on in here?" he asked. He looked like he had been crying too.

"It's a bit of a pity party," I said.

"How is Mr. Everett?" Felipe asked.

"It looks bad, Felipe," he said. "He had a bypass surgery and now he's surrounded by all these machines and tubes. And my mom just looks tiny. And she's cold all the time. She's wearing, like, three sweaters and a scarf. It's all just unbearable."

"I know," I said.

"I just want to crawl into a dark room and stay there for a long time. Maybe all of this will go away."

"What you need is a distraction," I said.

Felipe glared at me, like I was just saying I wouldn't be an avoider and here I was being one.

"I just want to wallow," William said, collapsing next to me.

"No wallowing allowed," I said. "And I promise I won't tell anyone if you have a good time. Felipe won't either. Listen, there were some people in here before and they told us about this place they went to called Dillon Beach. It's dog-friendly and a beautiful drive. We should go out there and take Tannin. Felipe went once and said it was nice, right?"

"It was very nice," he said. "And I can stay here in the tasting room. If you promise not to tweet about it."

"I won't," I said.

"Good," he said, and went into the office, but not before throwing us a knowing glance.

William looked a little bit skeptical. "I think I went there when I was in high school. It was a little rocky. But Tannin does love the beach," he said.

"It would be fun to explore a bit," I said. "Do it for me. I've barely seen anything." I wasn't much of an exploring type. Even when I lived in New York, I just went to work and back home. Sometimes on a nice day, I would venture into Central Park with a sandwich, but only far enough from the street where I couldn't smell the Fifty-Ninth Street horses anymore. Since I'd been at Bellosguardo, I'd left the property only to go for short runs around the neighborhood, to go to town for Pilates and Bar Method, plus for an occasional coffee with Celeste. And there'd been that trip to Healdsburg, as well as my local deliveries, but the deliveries were just to restaurants and people's houses and back. I did like seeing where people lived, especially the houses that were up winding roads and down long driveways. The types of houses you couldn't even see from the street. We didn't have that in Iowa.

"Okay," William said. "Let's go on an adventure. We could use a break."

I smiled, gave him a kiss, and stood up. "I'll go make a picnic!"

William stood up too, put his hands under my armpits, and swung me around. It pinched more than it was fun, but I knew he was trying to perk us both up. He exclaimed, "Let's go to the beach!"

I ran up to the cottage and packed us a lunch of cheese and bread and berries, grabbed a bottle of wine and an opener and some plastic wineglasses that I'd found under the sink. A sheet from the linen closet would make a perfect picnic blanket. Everything fit into the big picnic basket that I had found in the front closet behind flats of wineglasses. I threw a book in just in case I got bored and headed back down to the parking lot, where I found William in a vintage blue Corvette with black antique car plates, the top down, Tannin on the passenger seat.

"I pulled out one of my dad's old cars; it seemed appropriate," he said.

"It's beautiful!" I said. "I didn't know he had this! He always drives that beat-up truck."

"Yeah," he said. "He has an old Porsche, an Aston Martin, and an Alfa Romeo, but they always break down. This one is more reliable."

I threw the picnic basket in the back and leapt over the door with joy. Tannin seemed surprised, as if he'd never seen anyone do it before, but I landed with two feet on the passenger seat floor.

"Nice," William said. "It's like you've been practicing that."

"I might have had a friend who had a convertible in high school."

"A friend?" he teased.

"Okay, my brother bought a used Mazda Miata with his lawn-mowing money. It was always broken, but it looked great. And I used to practice jumping into it in the driveway. Haven't used that skill in a while."

"You're eternally surprising," William said, handing me a San Francisco 49ers cap. "You might want to cover your hair with this. Let's go see the ocean!"

I sat down and snuggled Tannin up in my lap. Put on my seat belt and made the "engage" signal from *Star Trek* with my hand.

We headed down 116, which was just windy enough, a different slope of grapes or cows or goats or vegetables at each turn. And the accompanying smells—of fruit, of manure, of jasmine—hit our noses as we went around each bend. We guessed what we would see based on the smells. Every once in a while we were right.

We passed through Petaluma and found ourselves in Tomales just when we wanted to have lunch.

"Do they have tamales in Tomales?" I asked.

"I'm sure you're not the first one to ask that question," William said. I stood outside the deli with Tannin while he went in to assess the situation.

"I'll take two," I shouted through the screen door. "Even though I packed us a perfectly good lunch."

He came back out with tacos wrapped in tin foil. "Tacos," he said. "They look amazing. And thanks for packing a lunch. I'm sure we can have a second meal later."

We sat on the sidewalk and unwrapped them greedily, partially because we were hungry and partially because Tannin was assaulting us to try to get the food out of our hands. The tacos were filled with spicy beef that made the top of my mouth tingle and made me want to both inhale them and also savor them. I felt like I couldn't get enough of this day. I took William's hand in mine when we were done eating and Tannin was done licking us. "Okay," I said. "Now we go to the beach."

It was another windy drive through hills covered in dry grass and rocks, interspersed with grazing cattle. Tannin was interested in the cows and put his paws up on the window frame to get a closer look.

"He won't jump, will he?" I asked.

William couldn't hear me because he was blasting John Coltrane and had his window down. I figured Tannin liked us too much to jump and let him continue to put his head out the window and into the breeze.

As we descended the final hill and saw the ocean peeking around the cliffs, it was enough to make us scream for joy. Everything had been so tense up until now. It felt good to just let loose. We yelled our heads off and drove all the way down to the beach, paid the entry fee, and parked the car right at the edge of the sand. We popped out of the car, let Tannin run free, and brought our picnic to the center of the beach. It was pretty empty, which was odd since it was the Tuesday after Memorial Day; maybe it wasn't the type of spot that tourists visited. Tannin had the time of his life, chasing birds, sniffing piles of kelp that had washed up on the shore. I snuggled into William, plastic cups of wine in our hands as we watched the tide.

"I love oceans," I said. "They're scary and beautiful. Kind of like being with you."

He kissed me in response.

The rest of the day was pretty much flawless—we ate the picnic, although I had forgotten a knife to cut the cheese and bread with, so we had to rip everything apart like cavemen. I almost started crying when I realized that I had forgotten such an important part of the meal, flashing back to Ethan—he would have scolded me and ruined the picnic—but William barely noticed. He smiled as he picked the cheese apart and said he liked eating with his hands and that it made the dog happier. After we gave Tannin little bits of cheese, we threw a squeaky ball for him. We held hands while he retrieved it. I took a mental picture of the scene. It was perfect. I cemented it by closing my eyes, burning the photo onto the inside of my eyelids.

"What are you thinking about?" he asked.

"Nothing," I said. "I just do this weird thing . . ."

"What is it?"

"It's hard to explain."

"I'm sure it isn't," he said.

"Okay, well, I take these mental pictures to remember good things. Beautiful things. And I want to remember this," I said.

"That's not weird," he said. "It's sweet."

"I've never told anyone that I do it," I said.

"Take one of me," he said.

I looked into his eyes, at his spiky hair made spikier by the salty air. I closed my eyes. "It came out well," I said. "Do you ever think you'll come back here?" I asked as I reclined back against him, the dog snuggled up next to us. We were savoring the last moments of sunlight after an epic sunset.

"To Dillon Beach?"

"To Bellosguardo. To Sonoma."

"I hadn't thought so," he said. "But with everything . . . I'm thinking maybe."

"Really?" I asked. A well of hope sprung up within my chest and I almost sat up taller.

"It's what my parents want. And when they get sick . . ."

"I know," I said. "It changes things."

"It made me think . . . the past few weeks have made me think that maybe it's possible."

"What is?" I asked.

"To do things differently. Not their way. To have joy in it."

"They don't have joy?"

"With them it's always a struggle," he said. "But look at what you've accomplished since you've been here and it's only been a few weeks. Sometimes when you stay in the same place your whole life, you forget that change is possible. Even within that place. You reminded me that it is possible." He kissed the top of my head. I took another mental picture of the moment. It was one I never wanted to forget.

We arrived back at Bellosguardo when it was already dark. We parked the car in front of the castle and ran inside holding hands. We were in the kitchen making sandwiches and kissing (maybe more kissing than making sandwiches) when I heard "Oh God."

Linda had walked in. We separated—almost ran to opposite sides of the room, really. I couldn't stop staring at her; my mouth must have been agape. She was pale, hair almost matted from lack of washing and brushing. She was wearing sweatpants and one of Everett's T-shirts. She looked mildly insane, or like she had been living on the streets, not in a hospital room. She was crying.

"Mom," William said.

"Honey," she said. She swiped at her face as if the crying could be erased.

"Are you okay?" he asked.

"Dad came home this afternoon. He's upstairs, in Grandma's room. There are machines and a hospital bed and a nurse. I don't know what to do."

"You should go to sleep," he said, putting his arms around her.

"I can't sleep," she said.

She looked around the room like she didn't know what to say. What to do. I felt uncomfortable and I was sure she felt more so. I looked at William, tried to telegraph to him that I didn't know what to do. He gave me a mournful look.

"You're here for him and that's what matters," I said.

"You're nice," she said.

That made me start to cry, and I didn't want William to see me crying. I nodded at him and backed toward the door. I left the kitchen via the door we'd used after our pasta primavera meal on the first night I had been at the castle. That had been a day of hope. I had thought today would be too. I had forgotten about the sadness that came with it, but I was finally starting to see that it's possible to feel joy and sadness at the same time.

Chapter 17

I spent the night alone, but the next morning, I went back up to the castle. Mostly because I was hungry and I knew how much food was in their refrigerator versus mine, which had only wine and some quince jam. As much as I liked quince jam and English muffins, I liked eggs and bacon better. I was relieved to find the kitchen empty, so I set to the task of finding the coffee and the filters, toasting some bread, scrambling some eggs. I was sitting down in the pizza booth to eat when a nurse entered the room with Tannin trotting behind her.

"Good morning," I said.

She smiled at me and opened the pantry. Tannin sat earnestly next to the door and she took out a big orange bag of dehydrated raw dog food—rabbit flavored—called Stella & Chewy's. "Mr. Everett says two patties," she said to me. "But is that enough?"

"I'm sure he knows," I said. "He really loves the dog."

"The dog loves him," she said. "He is nice."

"He is," I said. "How's he doing? Everett, I mean."

"He is very hurt. Bruised from the fall and also many stitches. But the doctor thinks it will get better. We are doing exercises, bending legs, things like that. You should go visit him. He can talk; he just shouldn't laugh." She was short and couldn't quite reach the plates in the cabinet, so I helped her. She wore pale pink scrubs and had her hair pulled back in a ponytail. Her skin was olive and her eyes almond-shaped. There was a lilt to her accent that was very calming.

"Oh," I said. "I wouldn't want to bother him."

"She is not being so helpful; she seems a little scared. He needs company."

"She?"

"Mrs. Everett."

I nodded. That wasn't really surprising since she had been running away at the time of his accident. Not that anybody knew that.

"Okay," I said. "Although he doesn't really like me."

"He needs some company. Come with me." After feeding the dog, she had put a piece of toast on a tray with raspberry jam and butter on the side. She had put the butter in the microwave for seven seconds and it looked like it was just exactly the right consistency.

I put my dish in the dishwasher and followed her through the house. I hadn't really been paying attention on the night I had spent there with William, but I did notice that when William and I got to the top of the stairs, we had walked right, and today, I walked left. I followed the nurse into the third door on the hallway and found myself in a huge sitting room with a large red brocade couch with matching chair, red oriental rugs, and heavy velvet drapes. There was a large television and a glass-fronted bookcase filled with leather-bound volumes.

The nurse, whose name I realized I hadn't asked, had set up a little medical station on top of a low bookshelf. I saw bandages and tape and towels.

"He is through here," she said, opening an inner door to a bedroom. I followed her in. The room was dark, the drapes pulled, but a bedside light was on. The room was dominated by a huge wooden four-poster bed surrounded by red velvet drapes. But a hospital bed had been set up next to it. "Mr. Everett, you have a visitor. It is . . ."

"Hannah," I said, not sure if the nurse remembered me.

"Hannah," he said.

"Your nurse found me downstairs making breakfast and said you could use some company. How are you feeling?" I approached his bed. It was dark, so it was hard to see, but his head was bandaged, I assume where he had fallen. His arm was in a sling and I could see the evidence of stitches peeking out from above his pajama top collar.

"Like shit," he said, "to be completely honest. But what am I supposed to do? The doctor says

I actually have to get up and walk around. Isn't that insane? Does he know what kind of pain I'm in? From the fall alone. No less having my chest cracked open and my leg invaded for a vein."

"I'm sorry," I said.

"Thanks for coming to talk to me." He gestured weakly toward the chair next to him. Tannin had been trotting behind me the entire time. He jumped up on the chair before I had a chance to sit in it. "Lift that dog up here. Nurse Selma doesn't like it, but he makes me feel better."

I lifted Tannin up to Everett and the dog snuggled quietly beside him, like he knew not to make too much of a fuss, that it was time to be calm. I gave Everett a smile and patted the dog on the head.

"We've always had dogs," he said. "They're better companions than humans. Loyal. Loving. Do you see my wife around here? She's the one who's supposed to love me. But the dog, he's faithful."

"She does love you," I said.

"She does," he said. "In her way. But I know she's miserable. I told her she should leave. But of course now she feels bad. And really, I do need her out there running things with me in here. Felipe can do the wine; he's probably glad I'm laid up. He's so much better at it than me. Probably you're better at business than Linda. We should just let the kids take over."

“But you know so much,” I said. “From all your years of experience. From growing up here. I’ve been dying to hear what your father was like.”

He took a deep breath, and it rattled a bit on the way out. “It was different back then. The wine was really a hobby more than anything. He sold fruit and vegetables locally. Learned about wine from some books and the neighbors. But it turned out he had a knack for it and the old vines that the count planted back in the 1800s just kind of grew without too much care. And by the time I was around ten years old, he was making more money from the wine than from the produce—selling it to a few local restaurants and the wine shop in town. He’d take it to county fairs, where it would win prizes. I used to go with him.” He stopped to cough. “It was fun, like our bonding time. And when I got a little older, he took me down in the cellar, showed me the press, the barrels; he gave me tastes of the wine in different stages of fermentation so I would know how it developed. I loved it because it was like science. But I really loved it because it was with my dad. William never really felt the same way, though . . .” He sighed. “Did you do things with your father?”

“He worked for a company called Advance, which was a trucking company. Mostly he drove the long-haul routes,” I said. “So, I didn’t see much of him. And then he passed away when I was eleven."

"That's hard," he said. "I'm sorry."

"It was," I said.

"You've come a long way."

"That's one way to look at it."

"Or you escaped?"

"Right," I said. "I kind of always felt the latter. My brother stayed."

"He drives trucks?"

"No, he's a school principal. He's a good person."

Everett coughed, winced, and relaxed back into his pillows. I wasn't sure if that was a sign that I should leave or not.

"I should go," I said.

"It's okay," he said. "You're distracting me."

I tried to think of something else to talk to him about. "Your house is really amazing," I said.

"It's too big," he said. "We barely use it."

"I know," I said. "It's a shame. William was telling me about his names for all the portraits downstairs."

"Did he tell you about the one he called Ferret Head?" He laughed a little and then winced because laughing was painful.

"He did *not,*" I said. "But now you have to tell me which one that is."

"It's the one of the woman with the huge pile of hair on top of her head. He had seen something about ferrets on TV and immediately started pointing and yelling, 'Ferret Head, Ferret Head.' I didn't know what he meant until he showed me the painting in the main hall. And then I just thought he was a comic genius."

"He did have some funny observations about those paintings," I said. "Hey, have you ever watched *Downton Abbey*?"

"I've heard of it," he said. "Not really my thing."

"I get it," I said. "But your house just reminds me . . . There's this documentary about the 'real' Downton Abbey, which is a castle called Highclere. And one of the things they did back in the day when the family wanted to keep the estate but was having some cash-flow problems was that they started renting out rooms in the mansion. And that eventually led to them filming *Downton Abbey* there. I'm not saying you should have a television show filmed in your house, but it's so big and beautiful and historic, I bet people would love to stay here. Like a bed-and-breakfast. You could sell them wine for their rooms. Linda could cook."

"Would we stay in our rooms?"

"You could, or you could live in the cottage. I know you both love it there."

"Linda loves the cottage. I grew up in this house . . . But it's not a bad idea . . ."

"You'd need a little bit of staff, but not so

much. Someone to clean and change beds, but I bet that's not too hard to find. And then someone to cook. Linda, or someone else. I have this woman named Annie who is catering the party . . . She seems nice . . ."

"It's something to think about," he said. "Let me talk about it with Linda."

"Okay," I said. "Wait. The party. What am I thinking?! We should cancel it. You should be there! We'll move it until you're well."

"Oh," he said. "Please don't. You don't need me at a party. To be honest, I wouldn't have gone anyway. It's for the winery. You don't need me. Please. Have the party. Do it for me." He kind of slumped back on his pillows.

"Have I exhausted you?"

"No," he said as he slowly petted the dog. "I enjoyed talking to you. Will you come back tomorrow?"

"Sure," I said.

I nodded at Selma and left the room. She smiled at me and mouthed the words "Thank you."

Chapter 18

I left Everett's room thinking about the inn idea. It wouldn't be hard. The place was stunning. And it was huge—I couldn't even tell how big. So, instead of going straight back to my cottage and then the office, I wandered the halls a bit, counting doors. I couldn't tell how big the rooms were inside. I didn't want to walk in on someone—Linda and William were both around somewhere—but I counted ten doors on the second floor. The room that I had been in with Everett had a kind of sitting room and bedroom, which made it a suite. I wondered how many of those there were. William had had one as well, now that I thought about it. His room had been redone in a more modern, male way. We'd have to spin that on the website. Or find out if the original brocade-covered furnishings were somewhere else in the house. At the end of the wing that housed William's room, there was also a spiral staircase that went up. Assuming that Linda's room was likely back near where Everett was staying, I figured this was an abandoned place. I followed the stairs up to two doors. I knocked quietly, listened, and opened the door on the right. What I found was a beautiful sunny room that overlooked the hills surrounding the vineyard. Rows and rows of vines, as well as the other hilltop chateaus, were visible. The room was decorated like a nursery: a small white crib, yellow decorations, framed drawings of vintage Winnie-the-Pooh and Beatrix Potter's blue-jacketed Peter Rabbit. There was a window seat surrounded by books, all vintage books for children, from *Goodnight Moon* to *Mary Poppins*. I settled myself on the window seat and opened *Mary Poppins*, remembering my favorite scene from childhood—the one where the babies are leaning against the window chattering with the birds and it is revealed that young children, before they can speak English, can communicate completely with animals.

I looked out the window and wondered about the room. Why would there be a baby nursery tucked away in the middle of this giant house? William was thirty years old and the room felt like it was a snapshot in time, but a well-cared-for one. There was no dust, and none of the furniture was covered in drop cloths like the entire downstairs. Someone maintained this room with loving care. I wondered why.

My mind wandered to the logistics of an inn. We'd put a little welcome table in the front hall, at the door that the family never used. So, we'd need a greeter, someone to check guests in, and someone to help them to their rooms. William could do that. I could be the greeter. We'd need someone to clean. It was a big house, so maybe two people. We'd offer afternoon wine and cheese in the big living room that had a piano. The one that was currently covered in white sheets. And there would be breakfast in the dining room. There would also be the option to eat outside at the picnic table. I couldn't rely on Linda because I had a feeling that once Everett was better, she would leave again, so we would need a chef.

I pulled my phone out of my pocket because I needed to call Annie anyway. The party was in two days and I hadn't properly checked in with her. She would need to start prepping in the morning.

"Annie?" I asked when she answered.

"Hannah," she said, sounding dour. But she always sounded dour when I first called her.

"Are you excited for Friday?" I asked.

"Did you do the shopping yet?" she asked.

"I think Celeste is handling it."

"Okay," she said. "The menus are finished. I sent you both the list."

"Sorry, things have been crazy. You'll start prepping tomorrow?" I asked.

"Yes," she said.

"What would you think of being a more permanent chef here?"

"For what?" she asked.

"I have an idea for a little inn. So you'd just need to cook breakfast when there are guests. It might not be every day. And put together cheese plates for the afternoon, but you wouldn't need to be here to serve them."

"That's not a bad idea," she said. "That house is so giant."

"I know," I said. "I'm sitting in a gorgeous window seat on the third floor."

"I didn't even know there was a third floor," she said.

"Exactly," I said. "It's an old nursery. But I think we could turn it into a honeymoon suite one day."

"There could be weddings . . . ," she said.

"Yes," I said.

"Yours could be the first!"

"Mine?"

"To William!" she said.

"Who told you that?" I asked.

"Just a little idea Celeste had."

"I never said anything to her . . ."

"I think it's cute," she said.

"Really?" I asked.

"I just want everyone to be happy," she said. "But I don't care either way. Your life is your life."

"Well, nothing's happening yet," I said. "I'll see you tomorrow."

I clicked the phone off but realized I finally had the courage to call Ethan. I hadn't talked to him in almost three weeks, and so much had happened. I officially felt awful for being so out of touch. I looked at my watch; it was around two o'clock in New York, and maybe he would be busy. I clicked call and he picked up on the second ring.

"Hannah!" he said. He sounded happier to hear from me than Annie had, which was a start.

"Hi," I said. I wanted to seem neutral. I didn't want to get his hopes up. Or, alternately, let him think that I was having *too* much fun.

"How's it going?" he asked.

"Good," I said. "I mean, weird; it's been intense. Linda is teaching me about the business. And Everett had an accident, so it's been crazy."

"Wow," he said.

"How's your stuff coming?"

"Coming," he said. "We have a prototype and we met with the venture capitalists today."

"Wow," I said.

"But they turned us down. There was a woman there who technically was our demographic and said that she would never use it."

"But it's a good idea," I said. "A dating app for people who don't want to write to one another sounds great to me. What does she know?"

"She said the name 'LazyDatr' was a turnoff."

"You can change the name," I said, kind of agreeing that it was a potentially polarizing name.

"It's heartbreaking," he said. "But I have to

pretend that it isn't. The guys went back to work after, but we're meeting up later."

"What are you going to tell them?"

"That we can do this without venture capital. We just need to get the thing finished and in the app store, and I'll pay for ads with my own money; maybe they can contribute some too. It's not like we need salaries or office space. We just need a server, and they already had a server that they played *World of Warcraft* on that they don't use anymore, so we're just repurposing."

"That's smart," I said. "Shoestring app development."

"It's not hip, but I guess it's what they mean when they say don't quit your day job."

"I'm sorry," I said.

"About what?" he said.

"The venture capitalists," I said.

"Oh," he said.

"You want me to be sorry about something else?"

He was silent.

"I'm looking out the window at this beautiful landscape. It's hard to be sorry," I said. "And I'm throwing a party in two days."

"Hard to be sorry? You can be so cold sometimes."

"I'm not cold," I said. "I'm just focused."

"On a party?" he asked. "That's insulting."

"At the winery," I said, instantly regretting it.

"It's like a promotional party. To get them more business and some publicity."

"Is it sold out yet?"

"I didn't really put a cap on tickets; I figured people would come and go. But we've sold a bunch and there will be food and wine and jazz."

Ugh. Nervous talking. He didn't care about any of those details. I was being callous.

"You're good at stuff like that. The party you threw for my birthday was really great. And I was even surprised."

I nodded. It was a good party. His birthday was in early February and he always said the thing he missed about New York was how it would be cold on his birthday, which was a strange thing to miss, but people are weird. So I made a deal with the local ice-skating rink that we could use the rink in the evening when it was supposed to be closed just by paying the staff overtime. I invited all of our friends from school and made spiked hot chocolate and s'mores. Everyone was skating and drinking hot chocolate when Ethan and I arrived. He was truly shocked but had so much fun—there was even an impromptu hockey game for which they got me to wear a goalie uniform that we found in the locker room.

"That *was* fun," I admitted.

"Well," he said. "I miss you a lot. I wish you were here with me. I wish you cared, but it sounds like . . ."

"This was the right decision for me," I said. "I'm sorry that it has affected you too."

"But, Hannah," I could hear the anger starting to rise in his voice. "I just still don't understand. We're right for each other. You're throwing that away."

"I don't feel that way anymore."

"You don't feel that you're throwing away our relationship? Or you don't care?"

I didn't know what to say. Should I tell him about William? The longer I was away from Ethan, the more I learned about myself during my time in Sonoma; I was coming to the conclusion that I had never come to in Iowa, New York, or Berkeley. I was enough. I didn't need a boyfriend or a fancy job to complete me. I could complete myself. It was freeing. Not needing anyone.

"I don't know what I think," I said. "But I guess I feel like we should be on a break."

"A break?! This wasn't what you said when I left California."

"Things have changed."

"It's been *two and a half* weeks. We were together for almost two *years*." He was yelling now.

"I know, I know," I said.

"I was going to *propose* to you."

I was quiet. I had had a sense, but I didn't know for sure.

"*That* was a misguided idea."

I was still silent.

"Don't be a jerk, Hannah. This is serious."

"I'm sorry," I finally said.

He paused. "Do you love me?" he asked. I could tell he was now trying to contain his rage.

"I have to go now," I said. I clenched my jaw as I hung up. I didn't want to tell him that I loved him when I just wasn't sure anymore.

I hadn't cried on the call, but the stress of it all, the rage, got to me the minute I hung up. I sat on the beautiful window seat and just let it all go. Tears about my loss of Ethan, about my loss of my past, about my uncertain future. My confused feelings. I liked William, but in order even to explore the possibilities with him, if there even were any, I needed to break Ethan's heart. What was I going to do?

When I was finished crying, I washed my face in the beautiful vintage porcelain sink that was below a window that looked out on a gorgeous mountain vista. Sometimes beauty exacerbated sadness. When I looked presentable again, I headed back downstairs, where I ran into Linda. "What are you doing here?" she asked.

I wondered if she could tell that I had been crying. "I was making breakfast, and then the nurse brought me to see Everett, and then I wanted to work on my idea."

"Oh," she said. "I'm going down to the office. Are you coming?"

"Of course," I said, following behind her.

"What was your idea?" she asked as we wended our way through the downstairs hall to the kitchen and out to the back.

I thought about telling her about the inn idea, but I realized that really, it wasn't my place. If they were going to do it, Everett and she would have to decide together.

"I'm working on some centerpieces for the tables that kind of document the history of the winery," I said. "Did you see the photo I took of Tannin licking one?"

"I didn't, but it sounds nice," she said. "Is everything else ready?"

"Jackson is coming to set up his equipment tomorrow and do a sound check."

She didn't visibly react to this fact, but I could sense that it made her excited. We settled in the office together, me calling local press to make sure they were promoting the party and she deeply engrossed in her e-mail. We didn't talk about anything serious, or really anything at all, but it felt nice to be together.

That night, Celeste came over with a whole Mercedes full of food from Costco, which would be for the party, and a bag of tacos from her favorite food truck, El Coyote, which would be for us. We put away all the fancy cheeses and greens and then settled on the patio for sparkling rosé and *al pastor* tacos. She was wearing a white jumpsuit and a pink shrug. I was wearing sweatpants and a T-shirt.

"What's happening?" she asked as she unpacked the tacos. "Are we ready for Friday?"

"I guess so," I said. "Jackson is doing a sound check tomorrow. Annie is prepping. I've sold a lot of tickets and they're going to promote it on KRCB tomorrow morning and Friday morning. What else can I do?"

"Sounds about right," she said.

We both sipped our wine and looked longingly at the remaining tacos, which we were too full to eat.

When Celeste was ready to leave, we went back inside together. I gave her a hug, and after she was gone, I collapsed on the couch. I stared at my phone for a little while and tried not to close my eyes. I was pretty much totally asleep, though, when the door opened and William came inside bearing kindling. "I was thinking I'd make a fire," he said as I looked up sleepily from the couch.

"Okay," I said. "That sounds nice."

"You're exhausted," he said, settling himself in front of the fireplace. He made a little tepee of sticks and put balled-up newspaper in a line in front of it. He pulled a lighter out of his pocket and lit the paper. The fire quickly roared to life. He examined the pile of wood that was stacked neatly next to the hearth. He picked a medium-size piece and put it on the blaze. It immediately died down. "Don't worry," he said. "It'll work."

"I believe you," I said.

"My dad told me that you came to visit him," he said. "He really appreciated it. He likes you. And he wanted me to tell you that he really does want you to have the party."

"Really?" I asked. He settled next to me and put my legs in his lap. We watched the fire together in a version of caveman TV. "I like him. We had a nice talk."

"My mom seems to be acting weird," he said.

I didn't know what to say, so I just said, "She is? I haven't noticed."

"She is," he said.

"I don't know," I said, feeling a bit deceptive about not telling William about what had happened right before the accident. It wasn't my place to say. But I also hated keeping secrets. Although I seemed to have so many these days. "Maybe they had a fight before his accident and she feels bad?"

"She made him stay in my grandma's room."

"He does have to sleep in a hospital bed and have round-the-clock care," I said.

"Good point," he said. "I think things are okay here, though, right?"

"I guess," I said.

"I mean, what I want to say is that I should go back to New York."

This made my heart fall. I tried not to look as sad as I felt, but I don't think I did a very good job. "Oh?" I managed.

"I promised myself this summer. My dad is okay. You're here."

"But . . ." I reached out and held his wrist.

"I know," he said. "But we have plenty of time."

"The party is in two days," I said.

"You'll be fine," he said.

I wilted; the idea of losing to New York made me feel sad. William scooted over and hugged me. "It's going to be okay," he said. "I promise."

Chapter 19

We were almost ready for the party. The food was staged in my giant refrigerator—the things we would need to prep last minute at the front, then the things we would serve first, and then the things we would serve later at the very back. I now understood why the cottage was arranged the way it was—Linda had planned it to be a prep station for events in the tasting room. Even though they rarely actually happened, Linda had been smart enough to plan for their eventuality. The stuff would be arriving in the morning, but for now, the cottage was empty for the first time in what felt like forever. Even though I was the only one actually living there, everyone was constantly coming and going out of the place. I was in desperate need of some time to unwind. I posted a photo of the full refrigerator on the Bellosguardo social media. "It's not too late," I wrote.

Celeste and Annie were gone for the night. William was gone for the summer. I was glad for the busy day of preparing for the party because I didn't have time to notice that William had left in the middle of it. I mean, I told myself that I didn't notice, but I did.

By the end of the day, I poured the last of

a bottle of Chablis that had been used to make a white wine sauce into a juice glass—all the wineglasses were spoken for—and collapsed into the overstuffed white couch across from the fireplace. I wished I had enough energy to light a fire because it was chilly in the cottage—a proper Northern California night in June. But I also knew I would be asleep soon and it felt like a lot of effort. So instead I swathed myself in the alpaca blankets that Linda left scattered throughout the room.

William's fire the night before had been the perfect thing. We had fallen asleep bathed in warmth and I had woken up in my bed, where he had tucked me in.

But now the day of the party was almost upon me. After a few sips of wine, I looked at my phone. I had been texting with William a bit throughout the day, but he hadn't responded to my latest missive, a photo of the packed refrigerator. But what was there to say really? I felt incredibly anxious. What was he doing? In New York, there were people everywhere, and many of them were attractive. I knew that things could change in one minute there—you could meet eyes with someone on a subway platform or in line for a sandwich and magic could happen. My first year in New York, it had felt like magic happened every day. I was sure he was experiencing the same, if he ever had time to settle in. What was funny was that I wasn't worried at all if Ethan was experiencing that magic. I even wanted him to find someone else, someone better.

Somehow I had managed not to let Celeste in on my secret romance with William, despite the fact that Celeste had been my most frequent companion the past few weeks and she was not shy about asking questions or about prying into bathrooms and even garbage cans. It was entirely possible that Celeste had talked to William and knew his side of the story—they were, after all, childhood friends—but he wasn't much of a talker, so I was pretty sure that he hadn't told her anything. It was also possible that Celeste had gleaned small details from our conversations or things she had heard from people in town. Surely someone had seen us on our trip to Dillon Beach. Celeste loved gossip, so really nothing was off-limits. And she had, as I knew, dropped a hint to Annie that she thought we were together. But she hadn't said anything to me directly, so that made me think she didn't have any concrete evidence. Not that there really was anything to know, or so I told myself so I wouldn't get too excited.

I texted William, "I miss you. xo," and a photo of the unlit fire. As I hit send, I received a text that had been sent the night before but somehow hadn't loaded into my phone.

From Ethan. "Good luck at your event," it said.

He remembered. I experienced a momentary feeling of warmth toward him, immediately followed by guilt.

I wrote back "Thanks!" but then didn't hit send. I didn't really want to encourage him.

Yet again, I fell asleep on the couch in my clothes. And woke to Celeste shaking me awake. "Hannah! It's party day! Get up!"

My first thought was to grab my phone, hoping that Celeste hadn't seen a text on it, but even if she had, it didn't matter. William still hadn't texted me back. There is nothing worse than waking up to a blank phone.

"Okay," I said, stretching as Celeste herded me toward the bathroom to take a shower. I shivered. "I'm ready. But why is it so cold?"

"You left the back door open," Celeste said. She turned on the shower and handed me my face wash. "And the heat is off because it's June. You're lucky the cottage isn't filled with snakes."

"Snakes!" I splashed my face with water and scrubbed it with grapefruit scrub.

"You haven't seen them on the patio?" Celeste asked as she handed me a towel to dry my face.

"I guess I wasn't paying attention."

"Do you want to shower now? Or wait until later? You might not have a chance . . ."

"It's five o'clock in the morning, Celeste," I said. "I have to have time later."

"Okay," she said, dropping the towel and heading back into the main room.

I picked up the towel and hung it on the hook behind the door. The cottage would be ground zero for the party staff, so this bathroom couldn't start out the day a wreck. I looked at my face in the mirror. It looked sallow and puffy, but my clavicles were more pronounced. Somehow with all the wine I was drinking, I had lost weight at Bellosguardo. Stress, maybe. Exhaustion. Love. Any of it was possible. I ran a comb through my hair, flipped my head over and back, and pinched my cheeks. I put my hands on my hips, using the "power pose" technique that I had seen on a TED talk about how just small tweaks to your body can change your entire mind-set. It was too early for a shower or makeup, but I could psych myself up. I needed all the power I could get. I counted off two minutes of Wonder Woman pose and then headed back into the front of the cottage to face the day.

In the kitchen, Celeste was wrapping forks and knives in paper napkins. "Can't we have one of the servers do that later?" I asked.

"Better to just have it done," Celeste said.

I sighed and went over to the kitchen island to help her wrap.

"Linda seems excited for tonight," I said. The sound check the day before had been kind of intense. Jackson had appeared at his appointed time with all of the band's equipment and I had been in the tasting room alone to let him in. Linda had disappeared about twenty minutes before he was supposed to arrive. We chatted about the schedule for the night (three sets: from 5:20 to 6, 6:20 to 7, and 7:20 to 8), the number of tickets I'd sold (fifty), and if he would take requests (not at the beginning, but he would consider it in the third set). I knew he wanted to ask me about Linda, but he didn't. So, instead he asked me about William.

"He's on his way back to New York," I said.

"He'll miss the party?"

"Yeah," I said. "His dad is getting better. And he's losing valuable time."

"That makes sense," he said. "And it's good to know Everett is on the mend."

As he said that Linda floated into the room. She had gone back up to the house and changed out of her normal weekday office wear—leggings and an oversize sweatshirt—and into a more fitted dress and wedge sandals. I noticed that she looked thinner, or maybe I hadn't ever seen her in fitted clothes; even on the day we went to Healdsburg, she had been wearing a blazer. She had brushed her hair and put on blush. She was smiling. She looked beautiful. And happy. Hopeful.

She came over to us, smiled at me, and hugged

Jackson. He was a lot taller than her, almost a foot, but their hug seemed natural. She whispered something to him that I couldn't hear. I should have probably walked away, but instead I kind of turned my back to them and fiddled with the placement of the music stands. I could hear snippets of their conversation.

"Glad he's okay . . ."

"Keeping busy . . ."

"Tomorrow . . ."

"New York . . ."

Finally, I figured it was rude to keep listening, so I headed back toward the office. "I'll see you tomorrow, Jackson," I said. It turned out that I didn't really want to know what was happening.

"I think she's nervous," Celeste said. "She was asking me what she should wear."

"She looks great," I said. "I mean, it's sad that she lost weight because of the Everett situation, but she does look fantastic."

"You've lost some weight yourself," Celeste said. I was secretly glad to have that confirmed by Celeste.

"I can't lose much more," I said, trying to be modest. "I can't afford to buy new clothes."

"You'll make it work," Celeste said, ribbing me in the side with a wrapped set of utensils. "Besides, I know about your secret credit card."

"I need to keep that under control," I said. "Anyway, Jackson was here yesterday doing a sound check and she came down wearing blush. She seemed really happy."

"What about you? How's your love life?" Celeste had not directly asked me about my love life in a few days, although I was sure she had been dying to.

"You know," I said. "Quiet."

"Have you heard from your boyfriend in New York?" Celeste asked. "Is he still your boyfriend?"

She was fishing. But I wasn't going to let her catch anything. "Ethan? A little. We talked once."

"He can't be all bad."

"He's not," I said. "I just don't know if he's for me."

"What's your status?" Celeste had moved on to hand-drying the wineglasses that had been washed in the industrial-size dishwasher overnight. I settled myself on one of the barstools in front of the large kitchen island and picked at a piece of croissant that Celeste had brought with her. Funny how for a person who never seemed to eat anything, she always was bringing food to other people.

"I think we're on a break. He's working on his app. I'm out here. He seems busy. Distracted."

"Do you miss him?"

"Not really," I said. "Maybe a little. I miss having someone. You know?" I did have the fantasy of William, although I still felt bad about what had happened with him. It was a betrayal of Ethan, after all.

"It's nice to have someone," Celeste said. "Although I've gotten so used to not having someone. And I met this guy named Thunder a few weeks ago at an open house I had. I mean, nothing's really happened yet, but we've been on a few dates, and of course I mentally jump to how if he's around on the weekends, I'll have to clean up after him. Feed him. It's a hassle." She poured a cup of coffee from the coffeemaker and handed it to me. I hadn't noticed her making the coffee, but I was grateful to have it.

"Thunder? Is he the head of a motorcycle gang?"

"No," she said. "His mother just loved weather. His sister is named Rain."

"California is weird," I said.

"Hey," she said. "You're one of us now."

"I don't mind taking care of someone if they take care of me, too, even if they have a crazy name."

"That's a better way to be," Celeste said. "Being too independent kind of makes you give up on life. Like, who cares if you eat that second piece of pizza or drink one more glass of wine? At least I don't have cats. Cats make you seem desperate."

"I love cats," I said. "But I will say that now that Everett is home and Tannin is back with him,

I miss the dog. He was a really nice companion." I sipped my coffee. It was strong, made my eyes open, and almost tasted like chocolate.

"He's a good dog. They've always had good dogs, Everett and Linda. Nice son too."

I nodded and took a bite of the croissant. I weighed the pros and cons of talking about my personal life with Celeste. On the one hand, I was confused and wanted a sounding board. On the other hand, it almost didn't matter what I wanted. Circumstances were what they were. And I would have to wait. To see if William wanted to stay in New York. I had agreed to a summer at Bellosguardo, but would I continue? I would have to figure out what to do with my future now that I had knocked out the possibility of working in finance, or at least at Goldman. It was easier to know what you didn't want than what you did. That was one thing I had learned this summer.

The silence got to Celeste, and somehow her desire to pry was overwhelmed by her instinct to talk.

"Back when they were in high school, Linda was with Jackson. Did I tell you that?"

"I don't think you did, but I know."

"My parents told me they were perfect for each other. True love. But her parents. It wasn't practical."

I shook my head. "Practical marriages make me sad. That was one of my problems with Ethan.

He was all about practicality. And he was angry with me for being impulsive. I think my parents married for love. But the world kind of conspired against them. They started out happy, though. Starting out miserable . . .”

“Getting married to fix your problems is never a good idea,” Celeste said. “I speak from experience.”

“Oh right,” I said. “I keep forgetting that you were married.”

“Because I’m such a successful single woman?” she asked.

“Maybe,” I said. “I just think you’re cool. But tell me about being married.”

“It was silly, really. We’d been together since high school and I wanted to get married, mostly because of bridal magazines. But once we were done with school, it turned out we had nothing in common. So, we got divorced after a year.”

“Where is he now?”

“Living with his mom, helping her with her winery.”

“So, around here?”

“None of us go very far,” she said. “My parents were relieved. Especially my mom. She said she’d never pressure me to get married again. But I will one day.”

“Your mom sounds cool.”

“Yours isn’t?”

“We’re just not that close,” I said. “I used to

talk to her more, but I feel like she doesn't really get me. The last time she left me a message all she could focus on were other people my age who have kids. I haven't talked to her since I've been here. My brother, I talk to more often."

"Why?" Celeste asked. "Everyone should talk to their mom."

"I don't have much to say to her. And she doesn't have much to say to me."

"I bet she misses you," she said.

"She's fine," I said.

"Mothers miss their daughters."

"I don't think I was the daughter my mother wanted. She wanted someone like her. Who didn't want to stray far from home. Who would marry a guy in town. Live next door. Bring over the kids on weekends to swing on a rickety swing set. Besides, she's busy with work. When she isn't working, she's recovering from work. She's a nurse."

"That's noble," Celeste said.

I had never thought of my mother as noble, but more someone who was gone for days at a time at the hospital and who was exhausted. And yet, she went back, each week her shifts slightly different, the patient load ever changing. The young doctors rotating in and out. The only constant in the hospital, it seemed to me, was my own mother. Which eventually led me to believe, after a number of years of therapy, that she was the source of her own misery. And this was even before my father died. But after, it was like she was entirely trapped, in our town, in our house, even though in retrospect she had the most portable job of all time—my mother could have been a nurse wherever she wanted. But for some reason, she couldn't get out of the house, no less out of Iowa. She felt she had to keep the same habits from before my father died, even assuming some of his habits, like watching hockey. She couldn't bring herself to change. I saw her turn inward on herself as she got older. She never was able to fully see the bright side of her life—her friends, her children, her grandchildren. All she could see was what she lost: my father.

I must have had some sort of reaction to this because all I ever wanted, from the time my father died, was to leave everything behind and never look back. And in fact, I had already reinvented myself four times. I did like Sonoma Hannah the best of all the Hannahs. She seemed to be going places.

As we finished our second cups of coffee, Annie's sous chef, Rory, entered the cottage. He was already wearing his chef jacket and had a roll of knives slung over his shoulder like a yoga mat. It was early, still not even six A.M. He started blustering around the kitchen, clanging pots together, sharpening his knives.

"Are you okay?" I asked.

“There’s no coffee,” he said, pulling the cabinets open.

“Oh,” I said. “We must have drunk it all. I’ll make you some more. There are beans next to the grinder, which is next to the coffeepot.”

“I’ll do it.” He groaned.

“Whatever makes you happy,” I said.

To keep myself out of cranky Rory’s way, I grabbed my computer and headed up to the house. Celeste followed me but headed down to her car, saying that she was going to work out and that she’d be back in a few hours. I went into the house and settled myself in the kitchen. I opened my laptop and started doing research on local wineries that also had hotels on the premises. There were a few, but none of the houses looked like Bellosguardo; at the very least, none of them were as old or as grand. By the time Nurse Selma came down to get Everett’s toast ready, I had made two pages of notes about what we would need: a staff, extra linens, great photography, a section on the website, a way to book. But people rented out rooms on Airbnb all the time; we could start that way and transition into a more official place later.

“You come up to see Mr. Everett?” Selma asked.

“Yes!” I said. “I have a lot to talk to him about.”

I followed her up the stairs and into Everett’s room. He had been moved from the hospital bed, which was now folded up in the corner, into the grand four-poster bed in the room. He smiled when I entered behind Selma and looked like he had a bit more color in his face. His arm was still in a sling, though, and I could still see the remnants of stitches. Tannin was curled up next to him. "I got an upgrade," he said. "But actually the other bed is more comfortable. This mattress must be eighty years old. It's lumpy."

"Will that be part of the charm of the inn?" I asked.

"We might need to upgrade some of the amenities," he said. "Should we put in a gym too? A business center?"

"Don't get ahead of yourself," I said. "But good mattresses and pillows might be a good investment. On the other hand, you can just bill the place as old-world charm and let them sleep on lumps."

"We'll figure it out," he said. "Big day for you, no?"

"Yes!" I exclaimed. "The party has become weirdly popular. Somehow in the last day, we've sold another twenty-five tickets. It's been covered on all the local websites and the *Napa Valley Register.*"

"Great," he said. He seemed a bit misty-eyed. "The party will be good for us. I'm so glad you're here. It's made all of this, and all of that"—he gestured toward Linda's room—"a lot easier."

"I'm sorry about everything," I said.

"What can I say? We've lived apart for some time."

"I'm still sorry," I said.

"And I'm sorry that I wasn't welcoming at the beginning. I was being . . . stubborn," he said. "I've been stubborn a lot. I've been thinking, really, that if Linda would be happier elsewhere, who am I to keep her?"

"I'm sorry," I said again.

"It's always been hard," he said. "She's always really loved him. Anyway, after we got married because our parents made us, we knew almost immediately that it was wrong. We were going to break up; my father was still alive and he could have sold the vineyard; it would have been fine. And then she got pregnant. So we thought, well, let's give this a go. At least for a little while."

"William is a great kid," I said.

"This was before William," he said.

"Oh," I said, confused.

"We had a daughter. Olivia. She was beautiful and tiny." His eyes seemed far away. "And it made us love each other more. We would just stare at her for hours. She was a great sleeper and just wanted to snuggle with us when she was awake. She was the ideal baby. She was like a doll. She lived to be six months old, and then one day, her heart just stopped. She had been perfect, no signs of anything wrong. And then, it was just over. It happened in the evening. We were putting her to bed. We were there when it happened. All of a sudden, she just stopped living. It was unbearable. And we didn't really believe it. So we spent that night with her, all three of us on the floor in the tower room. We loved her so much."

"That room is beautiful," I said. "It's very peaceful."

"We rarely go there," he said. "Just once a year, on the anniversary of her death. We loved that baby girl so much. And we grieved together for so long. We tried not to have another baby. William was . . . Well, we were very, very scared when Linda was pregnant again. We were on pins and needles. But then he started walking at around nine months and never stopped."

"He does have a lot of energy," I said, sort of trying to change the subject. I wasn't sure I was ready for this heavy conversation.

But Everett didn't want to change the subject or to talk about William. "Maybe it's time for a change," he said. "We had thought about it before. About updating the room. About updating the whole house, really. It's stuck in time, isn't it? We used to use the furniture before Olivia. All the rooms. But after . . . it was just too sad. It's just been so hard to let her go. We don't want to, but we finally have to. For us to be holding on . . ." He paused and wiped a tear from his eyes. I felt like he wouldn't go on. But he did.

"But we're just in this same cycle, all of us. She doesn't love me anymore. We're just . . . And I hate Linda seeing me like this. I think it makes everything worse. I'm weak. Sick. She should go live her life. I am ready to tell her that if being here makes her miserable, she should fly away. It'll be hard for me; I really do love her even though sometimes I don't show it that well. I know I'm stubborn and overly focused on the winery at the expense of everything else, including her feelings. And I'm hard on her, about how she runs the business, not that I could do it any better. But she's been my world for all of these years. She was always the one that I wanted. I've been chasing her my whole life. And maybe, finally, it just made my heart explode. At some point, I guess you have to stop chasing. I'm stuck in this bed. And I have Nurse Selma here to take care of me. And you can take care of the winery."

"I still have so much to learn," I said.

"It's not rocket science," he said. "Felipe does the hardest part. You seem entirely capable."

I nodded, letting it all sink in. "I mean, it's really up to her," I said. "What she wants to do." I had a feeling, though, that if Everett were to tell Linda that she was free to leave, she would go. Seeing her at the sound check the night before, the way she sparkled with Jackson, it was intense.

"True," he said. "I'll tell her about the hotel

idea before I tell her she should follow her dream. Maybe the idea would change things. Who knows?"

"Who knows," I said.

"I'm just a tired old man, though. What are you doing up here with me, getting all weepy? Get back to your party," he said. "I'll just listen from up here."

"But . . . ," I said.

"Go," he said.

"Okay," I said. I tried to pat him on the shoulder, but he grabbed my hand instead.

"Thank you," he said.

"Thank *you,*" I said, and headed back down to the cottage. "Can I take Tannin with me down to the tasting room? I need him for some social media."

"If he'll go," he said.

"I'll carry him," I said, knowing how loyal he was to Everett.

The day went along relatively smoothly: The weather warmed up, the sun came out, the office phone was ringing with people asking about the event. I hung out in the office answering calls, giving details. I regretted not charging a higher ticket price. Maybe we could have even made money. It was the first of many events, and now I was developing an e-mail list of local people I could go back to with more fun happenings. It was, after all, an investment in the future of the winery. I had a tiny suspicion that part of the popularity had to do with Everett's accident; it had made the local newspaper (there wasn't a lot of local news in Sonoma). And it was also possible that there was nosy-neighbor interest because Linda and Jackson had dated in high school, or just an honest interest in a night out drinking wine and listening to the best homegrown jazz the county had to offer. Celeste assured me that it was the latter, but the gossip in me couldn't help but think it was the two former.

I set Tannin up in the tasting room, where the wine and the band were already set up, and sent out some party-day Instagrams and tweets, hoping it looked more glamorous than it felt. I texted the photos to Everett, so that he could see what we were doing. I also texted them to Gillian and Duncan. Duncan texted back, "Cool dog," and Gillian texted back a bitmoji of herself dancing. Those two always cheered me up.

I unfurled heavy tablecloths, arranged chairs, and even pitched in to clean a bathroom that I didn't know existed behind the tasting room. It looked like it hadn't been visited in years, but at around noon on the day of the party, I had realized there was no place to go to the bathroom other than in the office. And being that the office was in complete chaos, that would be a bad idea. I decided not to post photos of the newly cleaned bathroom, but I did veer a bit into the personal by posting a photo of my sparkly dress and black heels laid out in my room. The Tadashi Shoji dress was one that I'd bought in New York at one of the many sample sales I had frequented in my budget-conscious days there. It had always been sexy, if a bit snug, so I knew it would look good after Celeste's compliment from the morning. I looked at myself in the mirror and decided to take a selfie in addition to the dress laid out. I looked good and I felt like flaunting it. All I wrote as a caption was "#livingthedream."

Chapter 20

I headed down to the tasting room to check it out before it was filled with people. I loved a party before a party. After the setup but before the onslaught of partygoers. I had to admit that Celeste and I had arranged it beautifully, and Everett agreed. He texted back to my photos, "Looks gorgeous, kid."

I had put a hand-lettered sign behind the bar that read FIRST FRIDAYS AT BELLOSGUARDO, and even though the idea about the history of the winery had been kind of spur-of-the-moment, a social media idea, really it stuck with me. I had pulled the history from the website as Linda had written it and had placed little centerpieces created from empty wine bottles around the room on the high snack tables that we had rented. Each one was surrounded by the wildflowers that grew outside the front entrance to the tasting room. Each bottle had a little sign around its neck that I had hand-lettered, detailing a moment in the winery's history—its founding, its first gold medal, the year of the founding of the wine club, the year of the first rosé. I walked the periphery of the room, straightening and resetting. Everything looked perfect. I loved the idea of the history of the winery on the little signs, and the bottles they were on (mostly) corresponded to the years that the signs indicated. They didn't have a bottle from the year that the winery was founded, but they did have one from the one-hundredth-anniversary year, so I had used that instead.

I told the servers to put the food on the bar and to hang out near the periphery until folks started to arrive. I stationed one of the servers near the door with a cashbox to sell day-of tickets and an iPad to verify the prepaid ones.

Jackson was early as well, and he and his band walked in as I was instructing the servers. He introduced me to York, the drummer, who was resetting the drums and grumbling about how Jackson had set them up the day before during the sound check. Kenny waved at me as he warmed up his trumpet.

"I think this is going to be big, Hannah," Jackson said. "I've heard people talking about it all over town."

I beamed. "You think so? I really hope so. We've sold about one hundred tickets, and the phone has been ringing all day. I hope we get a hundred and fifty people. Wouldn't that be great?"

"It would," he said.

I went back to the office and brought out bagged lunches that I had requested for the band after Rory finished prepping. "I made you some sandwiches," I said. "Not that you won't get to eat during the party, but just in case. I had the chef make them special." I put the bags on top of the low speaker.

"Thanks!" York said between drum hits.

"And of course have as much wine as you want. I also have some beer stashed somewhere if you want that."

"We're a Sonoma jazz band," Kenny said. "We drink wine."

Jackson laughed. "I'll take a beer, thank you very much."

"Well then, me too," Kenny said. York raised one drumstick and I ducked behind the bar to get them the beer I had purchased just for this purpose. They were doing me a huge favor by playing for food and tips, so I wanted to make sure they at least were fed and watered.

Behind the bar, I made sure that we had plenty of steel-cask Chardonnay chilled for the evening and put out some glasses for initial pours. The bartender, of course, hadn't arrived yet, but he didn't have to do anything except open corks and pour wine, so it's not like he needed to prep anything. I was trying not to be nervous. I tweeted a photo of the band setting up and another of the empty wineglasses. "Tix still avail for #FirstFriday at @Bellosguardo. See you there!"

• • •

Linda hadn't come down yet and guests were starting to arrive, so I pulled a bottle of sparkling rosé from the office, grabbed some glasses, and went up to her room in the house. I wanted her to see how beautiful the tasting room looked before it was overrun with people. I sheepishly knocked on her door. It took a moment, but she came to open it wearing a full-body slip and black kitten heels, her hair half-up in clips in the midst of straightening.

"I was worried that you weren't going to come," I said. "So I brought you some liquid courage." I popped open the bottle and poured her a drink. I handed it to her and she took a long sip with her eyes closed. When she finished, she looked at me and smiled.

"Thank you. That was just what I needed," she said. "I just haven't gotten dressed like this in a long time. I think I'd been wearing those leggings every day for a year."

"You look great so far," I said. She did. The slip was slimming and she'd already put on makeup. It looked like she knew how to contour. Maybe I needed to get makeup lessons from her.

"Thanks," she said.

The master bedroom was a bit more modern than the room Everett was staying in. The four-poster bed was not ornately carved, but just simple wood beams. There was a tufted settee, but it was a light linen rather than brocade. In Linda's dressing room (oh, how I would kill for a dressing room), she had a simple silver mirrored vanity and a wall of white cabinetry that made up her closet. It was relatively bare, though. She hadn't filled the shoe shelves with shoes she wouldn't wear. There were just a few pairs of ergonomic Clarks, some sneakers, a few pairs of sensible heels.

"I'm excited for the party," she said. "But also nervous. I haven't seen a lot of these people in a long time."

"You looked at the RSVPs?" I asked.

"Yes," she said. "Lots of people from the area, old friends. It's not quite like a wedding . . ."

"Well," I said. "You'll look fabulous for it."

"My dress is hanging in the bathroom," she said as she finished flatironing her hair. "Can you get it for me?"

I walked through the dressing room to the marble bath. This was entirely modern. Marble floors, walls, and countertops. A glassed-in shower with two showerheads. We could charge 500 dollars a night for this suite. Maybe even 750 dollars in peak times. Her dress hung behind the door and it was perfect. Red silk, A-line, with an empire waist and sleeves gathered at the shoulders. It would hide any flaws but be sexy nonetheless. I brought it back in to her.

"This is perfect," I said.

"I bought it a few months ago," she said. "It was going to be the dress I wore on the day I left. I called it my blaze-of-glory dress."

"I like that," I said.

"Everett called me in today," she said as she whisked a last bit of powder over her nose. She stood up and put her arms in the air, and I settled the dress over her.

"Wow," I said as it fell around her. "It's even better than perfect. You'll be the belle of the ball."

"Thanks," she said, blushing a little.

"Well, it is your winery," I said.

She nodded; her face looked a bit mournful.

"What did Everett say?" I asked.

"He told me about what it felt like to almost die. And how that had changed his outlook. On happiness and living in the moment. He apologized. For a lot of things. I apologized. He said I should leave if I wanted. But he also told me about your idea for the inn."

"And?" I asked. "What do you think?"

"It's a great idea," she said. "This old house is so wasted with just us knocking around in it. We barely even use it. And, it's been, well, too quiet. We've let it go. We should share it."

"It's such an amazing house," I said.

"Anyway," she said. "I think I am going to go away for a little while. I don't want you to be surprised when I do. I might come back, help with the inn. But I don't think I can be married to Everett anymore. Or tied to this place. I told him he could have everything. I just need a little bit of money to live on, and he agreed. And we agreed it could be temporary. Or permanent. We could decide together." There was a little tear in her eye. But I could tell she didn't want to let it flow, mostly because it would ruin her makeup.

"That sounds very mature," I said.

"It does, doesn't it?" she said. "I guess at some point along the way I accidentally became a grown-up."

I gave her a hug, trying not to muss her hair. "Well," I said, "I guess you have a date to get to, then."

"I guess I do," she said, giggling a little.

We headed down to the party, and I tried not to think about how much everything was going to change.

We entered through the office, coming into the room behind the bar. And the room was full. The music was playing, a tune that sounded like a jazzed-up version of "California Dreamin'." The bartender looked harried, opening bottles as fast as he could.

"This is amazing," Linda said, grabbing my arm. "It's never been this full."

"I love it," I said. I asked the bartender if she needed help, but she shooed me away.

So Linda and I entered the fray of the party.

The servers came up to us immediately, offering us pork sliders and salmon tartare on cucumber slices. But we weren't hungry. Instead, we wove through the party listening to snippets of conversation.

"Did you see her dress?"

". . . food is fantastic, not a hint of butter."

". . . love that song."

". . . sad what happened to Everett . . ."

"Did you know this place has been around . . ."

It felt like everyone in Sonoma had come. I looked around at the people dancing and snacking and drinking and imagined full sit-down dinners and charging people 150 dollars a seat. I envisioned bringing in top chefs from San Francisco and Los Angeles, installing them in the cottage and inviting the crème de la crème of Sonoma and Napa, even Seattle, Los Angeles, for a night of dining and dancing. Having them rave about the wines. Bringing cases back to their respective homes. Word of mouth could be a slow process. But somehow, word had spread and the tasting room was filled with energy. And for that I was thankful. I hoped Linda was too.

When the band took a break, I split off from Linda to check in with Celeste. We watched as Jackson, wearing all black and a cowboy hat, strode across the room in what looked like two steps and leaned against the bar. We inched closer, pretending to reset the bottles to hear what they were saying. It wouldn't have mattered if we had walked right up to them, though, because they didn't see anything except each other.

"You look amazing," he said, his eyes twinkling behind rimless glasses.

"Oh, this old thing?" Linda beamed.

He touched her hand and said, "This will be fun. Can I have a dance during the next break?"

"Only if you play a song that I like," she said.

"I've got it all queued up," he said.

"Wow," Celeste said when they separated. "That was intense."

"Yeah," I said. I didn't tell her what I knew about Linda. It was none of her business.

When the music started again, I faded to the back of the room, stood behind one of the snack tables, and watched the crowd. I took a mental photo of the room. I had made this happen. I wanted to keep it forever. A number of people were dancing; some were leaving; some were coming. The food seemed to be circulating in the proper amounts. I couldn't quite tell how many people were in the room, but it was at least sixty, maybe even seventy. I declared myself a success and took a sip of the sparkling wine that the bartender had poured for me earlier in the evening but that I had been absently carrying as a prop ever since. It was a little bit warmer than I wanted it to be, but I also didn't want to make my way back through the crowd to get another one. I sipped slowly and felt my brain relax. I hadn't realized how stressed I had been about the night until just this moment, as the stress lifted. I had done a good job. This was what they had hired me for, and I was doing it. I hadn't one hundred percent believed in myself at the beginning, but here was evidence that I had done something to change the winery. I was basking in my own glory when I felt a tap on my shoulder. Standing behind me was Ethan. My stomach plummeted and my hands became immediately sweaty.

"What are you doing here?" I stammered.

"Surprised?" he said.

I raised my eyebrows and tried not to clench my jaw. "Pretty much," I said.

"I tried to call and tell you I was coming," he said. I had noticed a few missed calls from him on my phone yesterday, but I had been too busy with the sound check and dog photo shoots to answer.

"It's been crazy," I said.

"It's great," he said. "I wanted to talk to you. And for once I knew where you would be."

"Can it wait until after the party?" I asked. "You can go up to the cottage if you're tired. They're using the kitchen for food prep, but you can do work in the bedroom if you need."

"I came all this way," he said, starting to get heated.

"I know, but I didn't ask you to do that."

"Hannah . . . ," he pleaded.

"I'll get you a good bottle of wine from the back." I gestured toward the office.

"That's not why I came here," he said.

I gritted my teeth and said in a loud whisper, "Ethan."

He could see that I was getting angry. "Okay, okay. I'll hang out for a while," he said, took a glass of wine off a passing tray, and disappeared into the crowd.

Celeste came over to me, drinking the sparkling rosé. "What a great party," she said.

"The food is a hit," I said, still shaken by the interaction with Ethan. I could feel my voice wavering, tears just behind my eyes. But Celeste didn't notice. She was basking in the party too.

"My pleasure," she said. "I just wanted friends I knew to go into business together."

"Is Thunder here?"

"Looking gorgeous," Celeste said.

"Show me," I said. "My maybe ex-boyfriend is here. Was here. But now he's disappeared."

Celeste pointed to an extremely tall bald man wearing a suit that looked like it was made for him. Perfect pinstripes.

"Of course that's Thunder!" I said. "Although

I was really expecting a leather jacket and a beard."

"He's a class act," Celeste said. "And he needs me."

"The question is do you need him?" I asked.

"That's always the question, isn't it?" Celeste said. "I just want someone to love."

"Don't we all," I said. "Everyone wants love."

We sipped our wine in silence.

"I think you need to ask Thunder to dance," I said, giving Celeste a little push. I just hoped Ethan wouldn't find me to ask for just that thing. His presence in the room was hanging over me like a final paper. I knew I was going to have to deal with him, but I was still procrastinating.

"Maybe I just will," Celeste said, and sauntered over toward Thunder in her slinky black dress. As she did, Jackson transitioned to "Luck Be a Lady," as if he knew exactly what Celeste was doing. Thunder went right along with it. The song seemed to play forever, and neither one of them was complaining. At the end, he whispered something in her ear and she smiled.

The band took their final break. The first song on their break mix was "Say You Love Me," and that got the crowd moving. I looked over and saw Jackson and Linda dancing. Glowing. I had never glowed that way with Ethan.

The song changed to "Black Water" by the Doobie Brothers. The whole crowd joined in when they sang, "I'd like to hear some funky Dixieland." Jackson took Linda by the hand and spun her all around the dance floor. By the end of the song, he and Linda were the only ones dancing, but everyone was clapping. Linda had tears in her eyes. I had a little bit of fear in my heart. She was finally happy. She had faced her fears and embraced her future, while I was still avoiding so much. I still didn't feel ready to face anything, but it had come on a nonstop flight to face me. Linda would be off on her next adventure and I would be here, in limbo, until I, too, dealt with what was waiting for me, both in the cottage and in my childhood home.

The room was swirling slightly, the crowd thinning a bit. I made sure that the girl who had taken tickets at the beginning gave everyone a coupon for a free tasting good through July 31 on their way out. I said thank you to as many people as I could; I shook hands, gave air-kisses, recommended wines for the next night's dinners. Lots of drunk people bought wine. It was amazing. The night had been a great success. It had hit that pitch that a party hits where there's just enough chatter and music and dancing that everything feels in equilibrium.

I took a final photo of the empty room, empty wineglasses and bottles everywhere, party decorations strewn about, a random pair of pink heels left to the side of the dance floor. I posted it to the Bellosguardo Instagram with the caption, "You know it's a great party when all the wine is empty, the band is gone, but the shoes are still ready to dance." I shared it on my personal @realhannahgreene feed with the caption "If you know anyone who has cold feet tonight, please contact me."

I followed the servers out into the parking lot. Instead of going back up to the cottage, where I knew Ethan was waiting, I headed around to the side of the tasting room. Some of the servers were smoking cigarettes and drinking wine straight from the bottle. I had never been much of a smoker, but I loved the idea of taking breaks and gossiping. I smiled at Rory, the sous chef, who should have been gone by now. He'd arrived at six o'clock in the morning. I approached and he held out his pack to me. I took one and put it in my mouth. I hadn't had a cigarette since high school, but for some reason tonight it felt like the right thing to do. He lit it and I took a deep inhale, remembering how to do it without coughing.

"Aren't you tired?" I asked as I exhaled.

"I don't get tired," he said. "Had a few glasses of wine from your stash up there after we finished cooking. Nice place you've got here."

"Tell your friends," I said.

"I've lived here for a long time and I've never come over here. I wonder why."

I sighed. There was the problem. "Well, maybe now you will?"

"Sure," he said.

"Do you like living here?" I asked.

"It's not bad. Beautiful. Good weather," he said. "And I like mountain biking and surfing."

"And you cook for a living?"

"Cook, wait tables, bartend, you know. A little of everything."

It was different than in New York or even at Haas, where people defined themselves by what they did for a living, or what they wanted to do. Here, it was about leisure time. Your hobbies, your interests—that was what you focused on. How you made money was just incidental to the other things. Iowa had been like this. People asked friends what they did on weekends as a family—in our case, we would go to Drew's soccer games, have a barbecue, or take the canoe out on Buffalo Creek (if Dad was home). If it was just my mom, we would go to Target, work in the garden, make microwave brownies, and watch a movie on Lifetime or TCM. I remembered being surprised when I first moved to New York and the first thing people asked me was, "What do you do?" And when I told them I worked at Tiffany's, they were impressed.

But what did that all add up to in the end? I

filled my lungs with smoke, noticing the head rush. There had to be something in between. That was what I wanted. I didn't want life to be monotonous or an accumulation of goals and accomplishments. I wanted it to be fun. Was that too much to ask for?

"Don't you think every day should be fun?" I asked Rory as we finished our cigarettes. If anyone would agree with me, it would be him.

"If every day was fun, you wouldn't appreciate the fun days," he said.

That wasn't the answer I was hoping for.

The servers smoking around me buzzed about where they were going after, who was driving, who was leaving, who was hooking up with whom. I listened for a little while, trying to figure out the dynamics. I was a little bit jealous of the girlfriend chatter that was happening around me. I didn't feel comfortable enough with Celeste yet to really talk with her, although she had been a good friend to me; same with William and Linda. Weirdly, the person I felt closest to at this very moment was Everett.

I had already finished my cigarette, so there really was no more reason for me to stand out there other than procrastination. So I headed back toward the tasting room. I passed a couple making out next to the front door. At first I tried to look away, give them their privacy, but

I couldn't help but wonder if I knew who they were. I looked more closely to discover it was Linda and Jackson. I smiled. In a way Linda was embracing the life she had always wanted. I hoped nobody had seen them, so they had time to figure out what it meant, so that others (like Celeste) didn't decide for them. Or maybe they didn't care. I passed through the tasting room, which could have used a good cleanup, but I decided to leave it until the morning. I trudged slowly toward the cottage to what I expected would be a major fight.

Miraculously, though, Ethan was asleep on the couch in the living room when I returned, so I tiptoed by into the bedroom. The kitchen had been cleaned up and there was a note from Annie, the chef, thanking me for the chocolate-covered espresso beans I had left for her and the staff. My body ached and my head hurt, so I just took off my clothes and slipped under the weight of the down comforter.

Chapter 21

I didn't sleep well that night despite being exhausted from the party. While I was lying awake, I tried to make a list of the things that I missed about Ethan. He was supportive and smart, bought the best plane tickets, got the best hotels for the best prices. He was nice to my brother and my niece and nephew; he had been kind to my mother the one time he had met her. And he was rich, which made life just a tiny bit easier. It also made life more complicated because . . . I stopped myself. I had to stop thinking about negatives. He was here. To support me on a big day, and I had shunted him to the side. The real thing was that Ethan loved me a lot. He thought I was destined for great things and was willing to support me. But he also wanted me to stay home and teach French to our babies. *Argh,* I said to myself. *It's hard to avoid the negatives, isn't it?*

Rory did have a point: If every day was fun, how would you appreciate it? But I saw how miserable Linda was with Everett and I saw what tragedy did to my family. And I looked at couples I knew in grad school, folks who had been together for five or six or ten years, and there were only a few who seemed to really enjoy life together and looked forward to seeing the other person, no matter what.

That was one thing that I was realizing more and more as I got older, that you can change lots of cosmetic things about your life. You can get a graduate degree and have your pick of cities to live in and careers to pursue. You can move from coast to coast, from apartment to house to apartment to cottage and back again. But at the end of the day, you're still yourself. I was still the slightly shy book-reading girl who wanted more. The one who would sit on the front steps of our small house on an unremarkable street in Winthrop and wish I lived in the bigger house with the nicer yard one block over. Was I always going to be that way? Was there ever a point when it would be enough? I didn't want to always be striving, but I also didn't want to be bored. And it wasn't about who my partner was; it was about me. How to figure out my own internal rhythm so that I was satisfied. Not because of anything that anyone else did for me, but because of what I did for myself. And wasn't that what this whole summer was about? Figuring out what I wanted for myself? I was trying. That was what I needed to tell Ethan, I decided as I fell asleep.

I woke up a few hours later, not feeling rested at all, to the smell of toast. Wonder Bread toast. A smell I could never forget and would forever love. I rolled out of bed and groaned because my back still hurt from the long day of standing and lifting and hostessing. And my sleepless night didn't help things. I splashed water on my face, ran my hands through my hair, and put on jeans and a University of Iowa sweatshirt. Loungewear felt too intimate. And it was a chilly Northern California morning. I chose Iowa over Berkeley to show my independence. I was myself, even though I was still, at age thirty, trying to figure out who that person was.

I emerged from the bedroom and he was indeed in the kitchen, wearing a T-shirt that read WEWORK on it and his hideous yellow-and-blue Cal shorts. He knew those shorts drove me crazy. But there was a plate of Wonder Bread balls, and a second plate of toast slathered with peanut butter and raspberry jam and a French press full of coffee.

"Good morning," he said.

"Good morning," I said. "Fancy meeting you here."

"Weird, I know," he said. "Wonder Bread?"

"You know me so well," I said. I settled myself at the island on a stool and he poured me coffee and pushed the plate of peanut butter toast toward me.

"Good party," he said.

"Did you hang around for a while?"

"For a minute. I talked to your friend Celeste. She's a character."

I grimaced. What had she said to him? "I know," I said.

"She grilled me about you. She really likes you. Thinks you're a bit hard to read."

"She just says that because I won't give her any details about my personal life. I'm an open book, really."

"Personal life?"

"You know, she wants to know what's going on with us," I said.

"I want to know that too," he said.

"Stop," I said.

"Fine," he said. "It was a good party. The wine was good. And so was the music."

"Thanks," I said.

"But did I see the band leader dancing with the woman who hired you? Isn't she . . ."

"Yeah," I said. "It's a long story."

"So, it's been a crazy summer so far," he said.

"It has," I said. "What about you?"

"Okay, I guess. We're just trying to figure out what to do next since we didn't get that funding. Graham and Jesse are bummed because they really wanted to quit Google and now they have to suck it up and stay there."

"I'm sure you'll figure it out. Sounds like we're in the same boat all of a sudden," I said. "Start-up mode."

"Yeah," he said. "That's why I'm here . . ."

"So boring," I teased. It was actually nice

being with him. That was what I had forgotten when I was trying to think of positives. The positive was that we had known each other for a long time at this point and we were friends. We felt comfortable around each other. I felt more relaxed than I had in a long time. That said, we were obviously both avoiding the topic that he had come here to talk about: our relationship.

"I've learned a lot in New York," he said finally, after a longish silence.

"Oh yeah?" I asked.

"I mean, living with my friends, with Graham and Jesse, and working with them, but also being disappointed about what happened between us. It's just taught me that friends and community are really important. And that it's really more about the process than the end goal."

"That seems mature of you," I said. I knew it was hard for him; he was a black-and-white thinker—he had spent so many years with the opinion that either things worked or they didn't—and gray areas were difficult for him.

"I'm all about flexibility these days," he said. "Now that we didn't get the funding, we're figuring out other ways to make it work."

"I think we both needed to step outside of our comfort zones for a little while," I said.

"But can't we do that together?" he asked. "Why do we need to be apart?"

"It's only been a month," I said. "You've been

alive for whatever twelve times thirty is. And that's a lot more months than one."

"Three hundred and sixty," he said.

"Exactly," I said. "You know I'm not good at math, so what percentage of three hundred and sixty is one?"

"Point two percent," he said.

"Right, so I think you could wait until point four percent or point six, no?"

He inhaled deeply. "But this isn't a math problem, Hannah. I love you. And I want to be with you. I don't care what you're doing with your life anymore. If you want to run a winery, go for it. I just want us to be together. I looked for you for a long time . . ."

I didn't know what to say in response. I was scrambling for words when Celeste burst through the front door. I was accustomed to this by now, so I wasn't even surprised, although I was annoyed, as I *was* having an important conversation.

"Linda is gone!" Celeste said. She was frantic, waving her phone around, her purse falling off her shoulder, her hair slightly less perfect than usual. "The nurse just called me. She didn't come to check on Everett this morning and so Selma and I searched the house and we can't find her. Selma kept saying it was okay, but clearly she doesn't know what she's talking about."

"Oh no," I said, feigning surprise. "Are her things gone?"

"I don't think so," Celeste said.

"So . . . maybe she's just sleeping off her hangover," I said.

"Has anyone checked that saxophone guy's house?" Ethan asked. "They were kind of hot and heavy."

I shot Ethan a look of death.

"Oh . . . ," he said. "Was I not . . . ?"

Celeste either didn't hear Ethan or chose not to. She was frantically typing into her phone.

"Do you want some coffee?" I asked.

"I don't need coffee!" Celeste said. It was true—she was pretty amped up. "Text me if you see her! Or hear anything!"

Celeste ran out of the cottage and I sat down on the couch. "God," I said.

"I don't understand," Ethan said.

"Understand what?" I asked.

"Why I can't say that I saw her with the saxophone guy."

"That's obviously where she is," I said. "But I just don't want them to be discovered yet."

"You people are all crazy," he said. "I'm going to take a shower."

While Ethan was in the shower, Celeste came back into the cottage. She looked around and, not seeing him, said, "Do you want to take a break from here to go look for Linda? I was thinking about it and I think if you found her at Jackson's it would be easier. You're a neutral party."

"I'm not entirely neutral," I said.

"But you won't judge her—you're not married; you're having relationship issues; you're a good sounding board for her."

"I feel weird about it," I said. "I mean, I just want her to be happy . . ."

"Perfect," Celeste said. "You remember how to get to Jackson's?"

"I think so," I said.

Celeste drew me a map on the back of Annie and Rory's thank-you note and patted me on the back. "You're doing a good thing," she said.

I didn't really want to go and confront Linda, because I knew exactly where she was and I knew why. But I did like the excuse to get out of the cottage that contained my crazy friend and the boyfriend I had no idea what to say to. I knew that I was being evasive regarding Ethan. And I knew that what was going on between Jackson and Linda wasn't my fault: She'd been feeling unfulfilled before I got to Bellosguardo. And she had already technically left once. *And* Everett had told her not to feel badly about going. But it was possible that my throwing the party and introducing Jackson back into her life had been a catalyst. Even though she had suggested him,

I was the one who enabled it to happen. I could have said no. I felt a tiny bit responsible.

I also wanted to talk to her. And I was officially in the middle of a crisis. Of course, part of the crisis involved having a crush on her son and having a possible soon-to-be-ex-boyfriend in my cottage. And my own deep indecision and fear. What would she tell me to do if she was around? What would my own mother advise? I just didn't know.

As I drove, I passed the cows and the goats. One of the goats was standing on the back of a cow and that made me smile. I turned onto the long dirt road that led to Jackson's cabin, with forks off it for a variety of properties, all surrounded by high fences and set off by electric gates. Mini compounds. So different from the streets of Iowa or the apartment buildings of New York and Berkeley. The dirt flew up around me as I drove; the road was dry, reminding me of the never-ending drought. I approached the closed but unlocked gate, got out of my car to open it, and passed through. I drove up toward the cabin, making sure to look out for the dog now that I knew there was one, not that the dog had been very interested in my approach the last time. I stopped the car in the same place I had last time, but Jackson did not emerge to greet me. His truck was parked by the side of the house, though, so I suspected he was home.

I got out of the car, approached the door, and knocked. No answer. "Hello? Jackson? It's Hannah."

The door was open, but I felt afraid to step inside. In case there was something intimate happening I didn't want to see. I waited and knocked again. Then I took out my phone and called Jackson. The landline rang. Then, finally, he answered. But I still didn't see him. He must have been in the back, the bedroom, perhaps.

"Jackson? It's Hannah. I'm at your front door . . . I'm looking for . . ."

"She's here," he said. "But she doesn't want to be found."

"Can I just talk to her?" I asked.

He mumbled for a moment and then I heard some static and fumbling. Linda got on the phone. "Hello?" She sounded a little groggy.

"Linda! It's Hannah. Celeste sent me out here to check on you."

"I'm fine, you know that. I told you what I was going to do."

"I know," I said. "I just wanted to make sure you were okay. As a friend."

"Please keep this just between us, my conversation with Everett, why I'm here."

"Okay," I said. "But I need some help in what I should say."

"Just say I'm traveling for a little while. Tell them I'm fine. I'll be in touch when I'm ready.

Tell them I trusted you with the winery, with the business. Everything will be fine."

I was quiet. I didn't know how to respond. I wanted Linda to be happy. I also knew this would hurt her family.

"What should I tell William?"

"He doesn't have to know for now. He's back in New York already, as you well know. If you can just keep it to yourself for a little while, I'll tell him when I'm ready."

"What if he asks?"

"My advice is that he should do whatever makes him happy," she said. "And he shouldn't wait until he's old. He should do it now. Those are my words of wisdom for him. There's no reason to wait or to settle. Taste everything," she said. "Don't just buy the first bottle that comes along."

I nodded, still unsure how I would relay all that advice. "Thanks, Linda. I wish you the best," I said.

"You're a good person," Linda said. "You really seem to care about the winery, and I appreciate that. And if you and my son like each other, you should work on that, but if you love that other boyfriend more, or someone else, you should follow your heart. Don't do things because you think you should. Do them because you want to."

"What if I don't know what I want?"

"You do," Linda said. "You just need to be

quiet long enough to listen to what your heart is telling you."

I nodded. There were tears in my eyes. It was the truest thing anyone had ever said to me. And the last thing I ever allowed myself to think. I clicked my phone off, threw it in my bag, and returned to the car, wiping away the tears. I got back in the car, turned on the air-conditioning, and just sat there for a while, in silence. I resisted the urge to turn on the radio. To even think about anything. I tried to empty my mind the way they told you to in yoga. I considered attacking my cuticles and then resisted. I whispered to myself, "It's going to be okay."

I just had to figure out what my heart was telling me. I didn't want to blame my mother, but of course, I could. It wasn't like our house growing up was a feelings-rich place. My only solace had been going to the library, where Mary Ellen gave me *Eloise* to read, and that helped me generate a vision of myself as a grown-up Hannah in a convertible driving down Fifth Avenue in front of the Plaza. A vision that took me to Tiffany's. I had accidentally envisioned my future, as off as it was in terms of specific details.

And now I found myself in a place that I did care about. And with people who also cared about the same thing that I cared about: making this winery work. It wasn't just about the wine or the scenery or the beautiful cottage or the castle, although all of those things were amazing. It was finding something that needed help and having the ability to help it grow and change.

As I sat in front of Jackson's house, I dug my phone out of my bag, put it on speaker, and called Drew. He was the only one who knew what my past was like. He had paved the way for me by going to college, figuring out the network of scholarships that one could get from a small place like Winthrop with parents who lived paycheck to paycheck.

"Hannah," he said after the third ring.

"Drew," I said.

"Did he come back?"

"Who?"

"Ethan. For the party. To tell you he loved you."

"Sort of," I said. "How did you know he would do that?"

"He called me."

"I don't know what to do," I said. "Is your life boring?"

"I wish it was a little more boring," he said.

"Are you happy?" I asked.

"Mostly," he said. "As happy as you can be, I think. Without being crazy."

"Is Elise?"

"I'll ask her. We're driving to Target."

Drew and Elise did have a pretty great relationship. I should have put them on my list of couples to aspire to emulate. Drew was the principal of the middle/high school in Winthrop and Elise taught high school biology in nearby Independence.

"She says yes."

"You guys get the summers off, so that's why. You should come visit me here. Bring the kids!"

"Elise still has to grade final exams," Drew said. "And I have to have field day. A bunch of kindergarteners throwing water balloons at one another."

"Sounds fun," I said. "But how do you know? When it's right?"

"Something just clicks."

"Nothing is clicking for me," I said.

"It will," Drew said.

"But Mom didn't . . ."

"It's not her fault anymore, Hannah. You're a grown woman. You can do it yourself."

I sighed. It was true. I had found this place and I had made a choice. "Okay," I said.

"You're an attractive, smart, and capable person, and any man would be lucky to have you."

That put tears in my eyes, so all I could say was, "Thanks."

Still confused, I clicked the phone off, turned the radio on, and drove back to Bellosguardo.

As I drove, the NPR host delivered a soothing report on a recently published study that reported there are some people who are head people and some people who are heart people. Head people think "rationally" when making moral decisions and heart people think "emotionally." I diagnosed myself as a head person; Ethan was one too. William was more of a heart person, I thought. I wondered if it was possible to change—to become a heart person after being a head person for so long. Maybe I was transitioning and I wasn't sure which way I was going to go yet. Maybe I had always been a heart person but had been masquerading as a head person. Or maybe it was just a problem if two head people were together. Maybe you need a mix. All I knew was that I was going to keep following my heart for a little while longer and see where it got me.

When I got back to the winery, I assumed that Ethan was still in the cottage, so I decided to go up to the main house instead to see how Everett was doing. So for the first time, instead of pulling into my usual parking spot, I drove up to the house, around the grand entranceway, and along the circular drive that led to the huge carved wooden door flanked by columns and ivy. It was going to make an amazing hotel. I couldn't wait to get started.

Chapter 22

I went inside, and even though I knew Ethan was in the cottage, I headed straight up to Everett's room and knocked on the door. There was no answer, but I assumed that maybe he couldn't hear me since he was all the way inside, through the sitting room. I cracked the door open. The lights were on, which they hadn't been the other times I'd come by, and I took that as a sign that he was feeling better. I went through the empty sitting room toward the open bedroom door. I peeked in, but he wasn't there. The bed was made and the hospital bed was completely gone. There was still a little tray of medicines on his nightstand, but the curtains were open. Maybe he had gone out for a walk or down to the kitchen.

There were only a few places that he could possibly be, so I headed back down to the winery. I went down the main stairs of the house, gazed upon William's great-great-grandfather's giant portrait, and headed to the kitchen. There I found the nurse standing on her little stepstool.

"Hi, Selma," I said. She jumped a little and I rushed toward her to keep her from falling off the stool, but she righted herself in time.

"Hello, miss," she said.

"Where's Mr. Everett?" I asked. "I just tried to visit him."

"He insisted on going to the cellar with Felipe," she said.

"Oh," I said. "Where's that?" I couldn't believe I'd never been to the cellar.

"Under the big room," she said.

"The tasting room?"

"I think so," she said. "Big room with big brown couches."

"Yes," I said. "Okay. So he's feeling better?"

"I think he should rest more, but he is feeling better," she said. "He needs to walk. So this is good. Plus, Mrs. Everett leave and I think that help his spirits."

I nodded. Strange. But possible.

"Thanks, Selma," I said.

I walked out the kitchen door and headed down to the tasting room. In the office, a door was open that I hadn't noticed before. I followed a circular metal staircase down to the basement to find the wine cellar. I had wondered where the wine was made, and here was the answer, literally right under my feet for weeks. The cellar was cool; the floor was packed dirt and the walls were stone. The first room I entered was lined with floor-to-ceiling stainless steel tanks, each labeled with grape names and dates. All the tanks had thermostats on them set at different temperatures. In the next room were the barrels, and in the final room, the bottling machine. This was where I found Everett and Felipe.

"Hi, kid," Everett said.

"You're a hard man to find," I said. "Are you feeling better?"

"Much," he said. He did seem brighter. He was standing up, which was one difference from the last few times I'd seen him. He had a cane, but he was standing. And smiling. His cheeks were flushed red.

"You shouldn't be stressing," I said.

"I'm relaxing," he said. "And I'm supposed to be walking. And Selma is here. I'll be fine. Besides, Felipe is bottling our 2014 Cabernet today and I wanted to try it."

"How is it?" I asked. And then: "Should you be drinking wine?"

"I'm clearing my arteries! It's our best yet, don't you think, Felipe?"

Felipe nodded.

"What did you do different?" I asked.

"I stomped the grapes first," he said.

"Really?" I said. "Like in *I Love Lucy*?"

"Yes," he said. "It is a little out of fashion, but it releases some of the juice before you start fermenting. It brings up the color and the fruit."

"It's brilliant," Everett said. "We're so lucky to have him. Here, try some." He took a long contraption that looked like a giant syringe and dipped it into the barrel. He squirted wine into two glasses that he had sitting in front of him.

"That's for Felipe," I said. "I couldn't."

"I insist," Felipe said.

"Let me run upstairs and get you another glass," I said.

"There are more around here somewhere," Everett said.

"Are you sure you should even be down here?" I asked again.

"This is healing me," he said. Felipe unearthed another glass from behind a barrel. He squirted wine into his glass from the syringe and we all clinked glasses and tasted very seriously. It smelled like leather and tasted like plums and pepper and a tiny hint of dirt.

"Amazing," I said.

"I think it will get ninety-two points," Felipe said. "We will mix it one last time in the tank and bottle this week."

"Sold," Everett said.

"I've never been down here," I said.

"We keep it secret," Everett said. "Do you want me to give you a tour?"

"Of course," I said.

"This is the kind of end of our process. Many wineries outsource their bottling, but my father bought this machine ages ago. It's not the fastest or the highest tech, but it works and keeps us from having to pay bottling fees."

"You should rent it out," I said. "Let other

wineries use it when you're not busy," I said.

"You're so smart," Everett said. "That's a great idea." We then walked through the barrel room. I had seen only the first part of it, but instead of going straight into the tank room, Everett turned left and we walked through rows and rows of barrels. "These are all in various stages of aging," he said. "Felipe decides when we bottle. I like to age a Cabernet for a few years, but some kinds like the Pinots we bottle pretty quickly. Really depends. I use oak barrels from France for the reds. And I have started aging the whites just in stainless steel because people seem to like them better."

He kept walking through the rows of barrels, tapping his cane on them, and I followed him. It started to feel like a maze and I wondered how big this underground cellar was. "Has this cellar always been here?" I asked.

"We're about to go into the oldest part," he said. "We're actually under the house now. We were in the tasting room. But the count, when he built the place, dug a storage cellar under the house. Then over the course of the next generations, the cellar was expanded into a wine-making place." We got to a huge, round, barrel-shaped door with iron fittings. Everett raised the iron bar and I followed him into a cool dark room. He flipped the light on to reveal a gorgeous wine cellar. Racks of bottles organized by vintage. Reds on top, whites on the bottom. A soft light emerged from behind the bottles and faintly from a chandelier overhead, making the room feel cozy even though it was quite chilly.

"It's naturally sixty degrees in here, year-round. Maybe fifty-eight in the winter. It's a perfect place for storing wine," Everett said.

"What's the oldest wine you have?" I asked.

"Well, I have a few bottles of the count's first vintages, but those are likely vinegar by now. It's more just to have something to see." He pulled out the bottles, which did look quite aged, and the labels were handwritten: *The Count's Cab Franc. The Count's Riesling.*

"Is that his handwriting?"

"Maybe," Everett said.

"Amazing. Do you have anything you've been meaning to drink?"

"I have a bottle of 1973 Stag's Leap, which was one of the first bottles that put California wine on the map. In the 1976 Judgment of Paris, they did a blind taste test and one of the wines they tasted was the 1973 Stag. It was deemed the best wine in the world. And that revolutionized wine making here. My father was already making wine then, but it was a side business. The 1973 Stag's Leap changed everything. But I've only tasted it once."

"Wow," I said.

"I have a few 1985 Bordeaux that I've been

saving for the right moment," he said. "I bought them for very little back then, knowing I would age them. I buy Bordeaux every year and age it . . . and then I wait and see. Nineteen eighty-five was really the best. Linda and I opened one bottle on our anniversary last year, but it was spoiled by a fight. I can't even remember what we were fighting about."

He pulled a bottle of 1985 Château Margaux from the middle of the rack. He held it up to the light, turned the bottle. "This will be amazing," he said. "With a steak. Potatoes. Something simple but flavorful. I probably shouldn't eat red meat yet, but one day, soon."

I smiled. "I hope I get to try that wine one day," I said.

"It's at its peak right now," he said. "It would be a crime not to drink it after aging it for all these years."

"Well, then we absolutely have to! Speaking of which, I should probably be in the tasting room now. After yesterday, people might want to come."

Everett looked momentarily sad as he remembered that Linda was gone. "Yeah," he said. "If you need help . . . you can hire someone temporary. It's not the same without her, is it?"

"It isn't," I said. "I think I can do it. But I am going to line up a distributor to come in and meet with you and Felipe so that they can go out there and sell your wines more widely. Do you have any favorites?"

"I'll meet with whoever you like," he said. "I'm so glad you're here."

"I'll do some research," I said.

"Good," he said.

I helped him toward the stairs in the cellar and he slowly ascended back into the house. We found ourselves right in the dining room. The door to the cellar was hidden in the wall, covered in wallpaper and moldings.

"I never would have known this was there," I said. "How cool."

"This house has lots of secrets," he said.

"I'll be sure to put that in the advertisement for the hotel," I said.

"No ghosts, though," he said.

"Selma!" I yelled. "We're back." She came quickly from the kitchen.

She said immediately, "You must rest, Mr. Everett."

"I find that hard to believe," I said.

"What?" he asked.

"No ghosts," I said.

"Maybe one or two," he said. "But they're benevolent."

I nodded. Who didn't want to sleep and eat in a house filled with benevolent ghosts?

Chapter 23

I finally got back to the tasting room, which had mercifully been cleaned and reset by someone. It must have been a cleaning service. I had to thank Celeste for that. She did an incredible job managing all of those details so that I didn't have to think about them. I unlocked the front door and found Ethan sitting with his back to the door, book on his knees.

"Hi," I said.

"Where have you been?" he asked.

"It's been a long morning," I said.

"I'll say," he said, looking at his watch. "It's almost one and I think I have a sunburn."

I touched his forehead and pulled my finger away. It was a little pink, but not so bad.

"I think you'll survive," I said. "Want to come in and have a glass of wine?"

He nodded and pushed himself up from the ground.

"Did anyone else come by while you were waiting?"

"A few cars. I told them I was waiting for you to open—you were cleaning up after the party—so they said they'd come back."

"I hope they do," I said. "I should have been

here to open earlier . . . but we're a little short staffed."

He shrugged and followed me into the cool darkness of the tasting room. "It is nice here," he said.

"I know," I said.

"And you have a great shower," he said.

"Amazing, right? Someone here has remarkable taste in bathroom fixtures. You should see the ones in the house."

"You've been in the bathrooms of the house?"

"I was evaluating the rooms for their next business venture."

"And that is?"

"An inn! Isn't that brilliant?"

"What do you know about running a hotel?" he asked. He sat at the bar and I went behind it and opened a bottle of Cabernet Franc.

"You'll like this," I said. "It's light and spicy."

He swirled it around in his glass and tasted. "Nice," he said.

"I resent that you don't think I can learn how to run a hotel," I said. "You don't believe in me. You never have. You say you do, but what you really want is for me to fit into your vision of who you want me to be, not who I actually am."

"I do believe in you," he said.

"Well, you don't show it very well."

"I'm sorry," he said. "I tried." There were tears in his eyes.

"Me too," I said. "I'm sorry I'm not the person you want."

"You are . . . ," he started to say.

I put my hand on his arm. "I'm not," I said. "I might resemble her somewhat, and maybe when we met, I was closer to being her. But I just don't think I am anymore. But I'm sure she's out there somewhere."

He sighed. I could see tears forming in his eyes. But if he really disagreed, he would be fighting more. "When will I see you again?"

"I'm not sure," I said. "I think I'm going to stay up here. See how it goes. Or something." I hadn't actually thought of this idea until it came out of my mouth, but as I said it, it seemed perfect. This was where I belonged right now.

"What about our stuff that's in storage?"

"I don't really have a lot," I said. "I guess some clothes. Some books. I can get them whenever. Or never. I don't know. We can abandon the storage unit and send the key to *Storage Wars*."

"I don't think they'd really find anything of value," he said.

"Will you ever come back to California?"

"I don't know," he said. "Everything I know is back in New York. Except you."

"You better go back, then," I said.

"Right," he said.

I didn't really know what to say, because this

really did feel like an ending. "It's all going to be okay," I said.

"I know," he said. "I do love you, Hannah, even now."

I came around the bar and gave him a long hug that did actually bring a few tears to my eyes. He had, after all, cared about me. He had come all the way back here to come to my party. But it wasn't enough.

"I'm sorry," I said.

"Me too," he said.

I think we were probably sorry for different things, but after that, he turned and walked away. He didn't look back to check if I was watching him leave. But I was.

Later that day, he called me from the airport. He clearly was hiding in a bathroom stall. I could hear the waver in his voice. "Are you sure?" he asked.

"I don't know," I said.

"Me either," he said.

"I know I really am sorry, though," I said. "I wish I felt differently."

"Me too," he said. "What do we do next?"

"I don't know that either," I said, but I was getting more sure that my next step was to stay right here.

Part III

DESSERT

Warm chocolate brownie, served with sea salt caramel ice cream and cacao chips

PAIRING

Buena Vista, Syrah Port, 2008
(Sonoma, California)
Deep berry and chocolate flavors

Chapter 24

The summer had flown by, and by the September harvest we had gotten five of the ten bedrooms of the house ready to rent. We'd updated the mattresses and the Wi-Fi, and Celeste had found us a photographer. I'd put together a website and also figured out how to post the rooms on Airbnb. I got Rory, the sous chef from the party, to agree to come and cook breakfast on the days that we had guests. I had originally asked Annie, but she said she was too busy. Rory, naturally, was grumpy about it and complained that it would cut into his surfing, but I told him life was long and if it turned into a real job he'd be able to have all his afternoons and evenings off, which was unheard of for a chef. He agreed.

While we were getting the house ready, lots of business things had happened too. At Everett's request and really because I was kind of in over my head, I hired a distributor. Our team was doing too good of a job and the demand for our wines was higher than we could fulfill. It turned out that having a distributor was a blessing and a curse. I spent the evenings with Everett at the kitchen table looking at the orders, managing inventory, looking at our database of what we had bottled and stored (another thing I had had to create after we signed the distribution papers) and figuring out what we reasonably could give them to sell. It was also important for us to keep the tasting room open, although I had had to hire someone to staff it because getting the hotel ready meant that my days were erratic at best.

Things were growing and thus becoming totally overwhelming. I regularly posted pictures of piles of paper on Instagram with captions that read, "Who knew running a winery required so much paper?" and pictures of boxes of wine captioned, "More wine out the door today! Order your Sancerre before we run out." Poor Tannin's feed was severely neglected. I barely talked to William. He would call, I would show him what was going on in the hotel and the winery via FaceTime, and then we would generally run out of topics. A silence would fall over the call and we would find an excuse to hang up. I tried not to overanalyze it, but it did weigh on me.

And then it happened. In late September, I got a little ping on my phone. "Request to Book from Sean." It was late in the afternoon. I had spent the entire day in the wine cellar reconciling my database with what was actually there—for some reason I couldn't keep it accurate. I wondered how Linda did it. I was sitting by myself in the cottage, reading *A Thousand Acres* by Jane Smiley—she was whom I read when I wanted both to feel nostalgic for home and also to be kindly reminded that I didn't belong there—and Sean's request popped up. I grabbed my phone and opened it. Sean and his wife, Meg, wanted to book the master suite for the Harvest Festival in early October. Sean described them as wine enthusiasts from Denver who had always dreamt of attending the festival and they found the suite on Airbnb and were interested in it. I squealed, dropped my book, and ran up to the main house. Everett was sitting on one of the brocade settees in the living room working on a crossword puzzle. I had forced him to hire a housekeeper and remove the white sheets from all of the beautiful living room furnishings. It turned out that they were surprisingly comfortable and now Everett spent more time downstairs than in his sitting room upstairs.

"Everett, Everett!" I yelled. I knew I wasn't supposed to get him excited, but I couldn't help it.

"What is it?" he asked. He was used to my excitement at this point and generally didn't react to it.

"We have our first booking!" I exclaimed, brandishing my phone in his direction.

"What am I looking at?" he asked.

"It's a message from people named Sean and Meg. They want to stay here during the Harvest Festival!"

“Well then,” he said. “That’s something.”

“It’s everything!” I said. “I’ll call Rory and Celeste and Marta the house cleaner, and get everything ready!”

Everett nodded and went back to his crossword.

“Everett,” I said. “Are you okay? Isn’t this exciting?”

“It is,” he said. “But it’s a bit strange. People coming to live in my house.”

I sank down into the chair next to him. “Oh,” I said. “Do you want me to tell them not to come?”

“There’s just been a lot of change around here,” he said.

“Are you okay?” I asked.

“I’m just a little blue,” he said. “It used to be a mom-and-pop operation, but now mom is gone and pop is kind of sidelined. And William . . .”

“Do you want me to call him and see if he can come back?” I asked.

“I don’t know,” he said. “I don’t want to bother anyone.”

“You’re the most important part of all of this,” I said. “You’re the brains behind everything!”

“I’m just an old man,” he said.

I was so sad that Everett was feeling out of the loop. I’d really come to love him in the months after his accident and since Linda left. We’d spent a lot of quality time together and he was wrong that he wasn’t important. He was the linchpin for everything. He knew everything about the winery and I consulted him daily on all the questions and problems that came up. He always knew the answers.

"You are the only reason that any of this can happen," I said. "You're just not comfortable with your new role as CEO. You sit in the corner office, or the corner living room in this scenario, and tell all of us peons what to do."

"CEO?" he asked.

"Yes," I said. "That's exactly who you are. I mean, you only have, like, three employees, but that *is* what you're doing here now."

"Well, really I just do the crossword and taste wine."

"That's an understatement," I said.

"Well then," he said. "If that's true, we should celebrate. Let's make some steaks for dinner, and remember that 1985 Bordeaux? Tonight is the night we should drink it. And we should call William together and tell him all the good news."

Hearing William's name was like a shot of adrenaline. I had been too busy to think about him too much, although I did occasionally check his Instagram and his most recent Facebook friend adds (late at night only) for clues to any girlfriends he might have. Our conversations had been stilted and we hadn't talked much, other than sending a few friendly texts back and forth. I would occasionally send him a photo of Tannin. It seemed right to call him to tell him this news.

"I love that idea," I said. "I'll go talk to Selma. You stay here and act like the boss that you are."

Two hours later, we were sitting outside at the picnic table, with steaks and mashed potatoes in front of us. Everett had gone down to the cellar to get the bottle. He'd opened it an hour earlier to let it breathe, and then we decanted it into a glass pitcher, just to open it up a little. He ceremoniously put the pitcher and the bottle between us on the table.

"This wine is from the past, but we're drinking it to celebrate the future," Everett said as he poured it into our glasses. We clinked and he closed his eyes and sniffed. "Honeysuckle. Smoke. Cedar. Cassis." He tasted, thought. "Blackberries. Wow."

I sniffed and tasted. I could also taste blackberries, but it also tasted a little like freshly cut grass. Not in a bad way. And not that I had ever had grass. I didn't know if I should say that. Then I decided that I didn't care. "I kind of taste grass, but clippings."

"That might be a scent, but yes." He sniffed again. "Grass. Maybe moss. And there's an herbal taste. Thyme, I think. It's very good." He cut a piece of steak, chewed, and then tasted the wine again. "Even better," he said. "It's definitely a food wine. And on the palette, it exceeds the nose, which is so rare."

"Thank you for sharing this with me," I said. "It is really incredible."

"Oh! We should call William." He pulled his phone from the belt clip he kept it on and handed it to me. "Do the thing where we can see him."

I looked at Everett's contacts; all he had were Linda, William, Felipe, me, and Nurse Selma. I wondered if she had programmed in her number herself. I felt badly for him, that he didn't have a wider network. But then I realized that I didn't really either. The hotel would be good for both of us. I dialed William and went around the table to sit next to Everett. I propped the phone against the bottle of Châteaux Margaux. William answered.

"Hi, son!" Everett said.

"Hi, guys," William said. He had about two days of stubble and his hair was too long. It was kind of flying around his head because he was outside, but it was hard to tell where he was because it was dark. A streetlight above him illuminated his face in a halo.

"Where are you?" I asked.

"Battery Park," he said. "It's so gorgeous down here. I come down to watch the sun set."

"Looks like you missed it," Everett said jokingly.

"I guess I just kept sitting here after," he said. "I've just been listening to people talk and writing down their dialogue."

"How's it going?" Everett asked. "Have you started the new semester yet?"

"Yes," William said. "So far, so good."

"We have our first hotel booking," I said.

"Wow," William said.

"Early October," I said.

He looked a little bit sad at that news.

"Are you okay?" I asked.

"It'll just be weird," he said. "Having people stay in the house. And with Mom not being there . . ."

"I know, I know. But we're putting them in the rooms we don't use," Everett said.

"Still," William said.

"And we uncovered the living room furniture and you wouldn't believe how comfortable it is!" Everett said.

"Oh, I know that," William said. "I used to try to take naps there when I was a kid, but Mom would always find me under the white sheets."

"That's cute," I said. Then I looked over at Everett to see if that story made him nostalgic. But he didn't betray any emotion.

"I know it's asking a lot," Everett said. "But I'd love it if you came back for the first guests. Just so you see that it's okay."

"I'll think about it," William said.

"Thanks," Everett said.

"It would be nice to see you," I said.

"Yeah," he said. "It would." And then: "Well, I better go."

I held up my glass to the phone and clinked it onto the phone so that William could see. "Think of it as a glass half-full, rather than a glass half-empty," I said.

"I'll try," William said.

"Bye," we said together. William clicked off his phone and I set Everett's down on the table.

"I hope he comes," he said after a long silence. "It's quiet around here."

"It won't be quiet for long," I said.

"I know," he said. "But, you know . . ."

I did. Everett was allowed only one glass of wine, so when Nurse Selma helped him up to his room to go to sleep, he insisted that I take the rest of the Bordeaux back to the cottage with me. "And finish it tonight!" he said.

"I've never had a boss insist that I get drunk before," I said.

"It'll be good for you," he said.

Back in the cottage, I made a fire. Even though it was September it was starting to be cool at night and I just loved the look and feel of the fire. It was so relaxing, the best feature of a well-appointed cottage. As I sat in front of the fire, warmed by the wine and the flames, I was struck with the sudden need to call my own mother. It was not a need I had felt often, but ever since Ethan and

I had broken up and I had decided to stay in Sonoma, I had been thinking about her. Just a few days earlier she had left me her shortest message ever: “Hannah, I love you, darling. I hope you’re okay. Please call your mother.”

That message had broken me. She didn’t want anything other than to know where I was. How I was doing. So I broke down and called her. She answered on the second ring. “Mom?” I said. “It’s Hannah.”

“Hannah Greene. As I live and breathe. How are you?”

“I’m good.”

“Are you still at that wine place?”

“I am,” I said.

“How’s that going?”

“Good,” I said. “I’ve helped them grow their business and now we’re starting a hotel.”

“Good for you, honey. I always knew you would make it.”

“Thanks, Mom.”

“I was just telling Wendy Iverson the other day at the hospital how good you were doing.”

This was a new tactic for her, to tell me I was doing a good job.

“It means a lot to hear that,” I said.

“I mean, before you were a secretary, but now you make things that people buy.” This was more the mother I remembered.

“And Mrs. Anderson, she thinks it’s just great.

She's been buying wine at the grocery store to see what you're doing. She likes the one with the little Penguin on it."

"That's good," I said.

"And Gillian and Duncan are both getting As in school. A few Bs. Oh, and that one C. But mostly As."

The girls at the hospital. Wine with animal logos. Grandchildren. It brought tears to my eyes. I had been running away so fast from that place, from that life. From her. But she was just someone who wanted to be happy. Who didn't need a lot to be happy. She was inspiring. She was real. People like Ethan, and I was guilty of it too—we were just making up structures to make ourselves happy, chasing the extraordinary when the perfect ordinary is put right in front of us.

"I love you so much," I said. "You're the best."

"You're my daughter," my mom said. "I don't always know what you're doing, but I love you anyway. And I know whatever it is, you're good at it. And I admire you."

I was silent for a minute because that was the one thing that I didn't have here in California. I had a job and a passion. But I didn't have love. The love was back in Iowa, where it had always been. Where I had been running from it. But it was always back there waiting for me. And that, for now, had to be enough.

"Thanks for being my mom," I said finally, when I had composed myself a little bit.

"Thanks for being my daughter," she said. "I'm sending you a kiss through the phone."

I smiled. I knew that she was.

Chapter 25

The morning of the day of our first guests' arrival, I headed up to the house to work on the final touches. I opened the kitchen door with my usual flourish. I had been at Bellosguardo long enough to learn that running a business and starting a new one were way more satisfying than strategizing about how to keep a relationship going. I was having way more fun being Business Hannah than being Relationship Hannah.

I was gleeful and ready to share my excitement about our first guest with Everett, only to find myself retreating back out of the room. He was sitting with Linda at the orange pizza table in the kitchen. They were holding hands and they leaned across the table so that their foreheads touched in the middle. I softly closed the door, but there was no way they hadn't heard me. I stood outside, waiting for a moment until I heard, "Hannah! Is that you?"

I reluctantly went back in. I felt like I had walked in on an intimate moment of my own parents. Worse than finding them naked, really, but finding them in a true moment of quiet connection. "Hi," I said.

"Hi," Linda said. She got up to give me a hug. "It's good to see you."

I smiled at Everett, who was still at the table. He was grinning.

"It's great to see you," I said. "What a surprise."

"I know," she said.

"Well," I said. "Can someone tell me what's going on?"

"I should make some eggs first," she said.

"Okay . . ." I said, and settled myself with a cup of coffee at the table, although I wasn't sure I was going to be able to stand the suspense through the entire process of breakfast being cooked. But there was a newspaper on the table, so I shuffled through that, reading nothing but turning pages nonetheless. Everett focused on the crossword puzzle. Linda hummed a little as she scrambled eggs.

Finally, the eggs were done; the toast was buttered. Linda settled down with us, placing plates in front of us. There was a sprig of rosemary on our eggs, which had the perfect amount of herbed goat cheese folded into them. I had missed her cooking. "Amazing," I said, eating too quickly. "Now tell me."

"It's not really a complicated story," Linda said. "After the party, I felt like I needed to go. And I did. And Evvy left me alone for a while . . ."

"Granted, I was on my deathbed," he said, laughing a little.

"Okay, point taken." She laughed and patted him on the arm. "I'm glad you survived. Anyway,

I was happy, but I was also lonely. And I didn't really have anything to do. I started inventing projects for myself—painting, knitting, making elaborate soufflés. I did start taking long walks in the mountains, which I liked a lot. I might keep doing that. Anyway, Everett called me and told me that the hotel was really happening. He told me all the work that you had done to make it real. And I thought about it a lot and I knew it was a good idea, but I didn't say anything. And he just kept calling and telling me about the progress and how you had hired Celeste and Rory, and I think the Rory thing kind of just sent me over the edge . . . Why should Rory be cooking breakfast for guests in my home when I can do it better than he can? So, when Everett told me that our first guest was coming today . . . I came back."

"Wow," I said. "Well, I'm so glad to have you. I mean, I wanted you to be cooking for the guests. You were my first choice."

"Thanks," she said. "I like doing it."

"The only problem," I said, "is that I moved all of your things out of your room, because it has the best bathroom, so we can rent it out for the most."

"It's okay," she said. "I understand."

"You can pick any other one," I said.

"I'll probably just bunk with this one for a while," she said, taking Everett's hands.

My face must have turned bright red. "Okay,

okay," I said. "Whatever you want. You just talk to Celeste about it. She's handling the staff. They'll put your things wherever you need them."

"Great," Everett said.

"At the end of the day, this is where I belong," Linda said. "The other life, it was a fantasy. A fantasy that took a lot of years to get out of my system. But it's gone now. And I have a purpose here. And I have love here. I'm needed here. More than anything, I need to be needed. It's what I've learned about myself. It took long enough, but I finally know."

"Well," I said. "I guess I need to go check on our hotel and leave you lovebirds to it." I stood up from the table. "I really am glad you're back, Linda. And it should be easier for you here now too. I had to streamline things because I was the only one, and . . ."

"Whatever you did is great, dear," Linda said. "I'm just glad to be home."

"Me too," I said.

I left the room and went into the main foyer to check on our "front desk," which was just an iPad on a side table. I was rearranging the flowers that Celeste had left on the entryway side table when she walked in the front door.

"Welcome to Bellosguardo," I said teasingly. "How can I help you?"

"It looks so good here," she said. She ran in and gave me a hug. "I'm so excited for this to take off. Did you see that we have two more bookings for next weekend?"

"We do?" I asked. I hadn't looked at my phone in more than an hour.

"Yes!" she said. She was almost jumping up and down.

"I'm really glad," I said. "And guess what: Linda is back to cook for us! You can let Rory off the hook."

"She's back? Wow," she said. "Almost all is right in the world. Now all we need is to find you a boyfriend. I've kind of moved in with Thunder. What's taking you so long?"

I bristled a little. "I just want to focus on all this."

"What's this if you don't have someone to share it with?" she asked.

"It's just me," I said. "Accomplishing things. That's better than anything. I'd rather say that I did it all myself."

"Sometimes your midwestern independence is irritating," she said, but I could tell that she was joking.

"I'm sorry," I said. "I can't help it."

"Fine," she said. "We have a lot of work to do. Let's go upstairs."

I nodded and followed her up the stairs.

Later that day, we welcomed our first guests, Sean and Meg, with a glass of sparkling wine and mints on their pillows. Linda also decided to cook a big dinner for everyone, free of charge. "I am going to try and not make a habit of this," she said as she showed Sean and Meg to their room, formerly her room. "But I'm so excited that you are our first guests. Will you join us for a barbecue?"

"Of course," Sean said. "How could we turn that down?"

So, later that night, I found myself out at the family picnic table, eating homemade fried chicken with Sean and Meg and Everett and Linda and Celeste and Felipe and his wife, Maria José, who had come to join Felipe after many months of separation. The only people missing were William, and Felipe's children, Alejandro and Lucia, who were back at the house with a babysitter. Tannin was lounging under the table, waiting patiently for someone to drop something or give in to his big brown eyes. Sean and Meg had bought some wine at the festival that afternoon and insisted that we open it since we had generously invited them to dinner. I was fine with that because the Bellosguardo wines were so precious at the moment, we were rationing them for the guests, the tasting room, the wine club, and the distributor requests. I had told Felipe that he needed to up production for the next year. The 2012 Dutton-Goldfield Pinot Noir was perfectly balanced and paired impeccably with the crispy panko-encrusted chicken.

Meg was telling us about her post-retirement tourism company, which she had started in Denver—she offered personalized tours for small groups to the best restaurants and breweries in the area. She drove them around in her own SUV for half- or full-day tasting menus. She loved doing it, since she was the ultimate extrovert, as she described herself. "And it keeps Sean and me out of each other's hair. I don't know how you two do it, running a business together," she said to Linda. Everyone at the table bit their tongues.

"It's not always easy," Linda said magnanimously. "But at the end of the day, it's the most important thing. Family."

As if on cue, the kitchen door was thrown open and William strode out into the yard. I almost started crying, I was so happy to see him. Linda *did* start crying. And Everett stood up to hug him.

"Looking good, Dad," William said. "And, Mom! It's good to see you here!"

"William!" I said. "Wow!"

"I wouldn't miss this," he said. He walked around the table and gave his mom a hug and then stood behind me and massaged my shoulders. I let him do it for a second before I slid over and invited him to sit. It was good to be near him again.

"Have some chicken," Linda said, passing the

plate down. “It’s a little cold . . . but it’ll still be good.”

“Don’t mind if I do,” he said.

As William heaped his plate with chicken and salad, Everett stood up and raised his glass. “I want to make a toast,” he said. “To family, old and new. If you had told me six months ago that we would all be sitting here together right now, I would not have believed you. But I’m so glad that we are. Sometimes change is stressful and bonds can get stretched and life is not the straight road that we think it is going to be, that we see in the movies . . .” He winked at William. “But whatever form it comes in, we have to celebrate it. To health and love,” he said, raising his glass.

“To health and love,” we all said, and raised our glasses with him.

“And a glass half-full,” William said, looking at me.

“May they always be,” I said.

Tannin let out a little bark when our glasses clinked, and we all laughed.

Chapter 26

After dinner, I went back to my cottage alone, but William knocked on the door a few minutes later. I was in the process of making a fire, so he sat on the couch and watched me. "You've gotten so good at this," he said as I balled up newspaper.

"I wasn't just going to sit around waiting for you to come back and make me a fire," I teased. "Besides, I like knowing I can do it myself."

"But you missed me just a little?" he asked.

"I guess," I admitted. "It's been a day full of surprises."

I settled back on the couch, but not next to him.

"Everything you've done here is great," he said. "And you somehow got my mom to come home."

"Your dad did that," I said. "And it sounds like she missed us."

"Well, it seems like things are all as they should be," he said. "Except one . . ."

I didn't really know what I wanted from William now. If he had asked me back in the summer, on our day at the beach, if I wanted to be in a relationship with him, I would have said yes. But after everything that had happened since then, my new friendship with his dad, Linda's leaving and returning, all the things that I had accomplished with the hotel, it felt different. I wanted to see if I could make things work on my own. I had been that way in New York before graduate school. I felt proud to have escaped Iowa and I felt proud of what I had accomplished in finding my own place and getting a job at Tiffany's and then in studying for the GMAT and getting into grad school. Those were all things that I did on my own. Nobody helped me. In school, maybe because I met Ethan on the first day and we were inseparable after that, I started to feel like it was "us" who were in school, not "me." And I wasn't ready for "us" again; I still wanted to be me. I wasn't exactly sure how to explain that out loud, though.

William scooted toward me on the couch and I scooted back.

"What if I were to tell you that I wanted to come back here permanently?" he asked, backing away a bit.

"I'd say that your parents would probably really appreciate that," I said. "But what about your screenwriting dream?"

"I can do that from here. It doesn't really make sense for me to be in New York when everything that I love is here."

Tears welled up a bit in my eyes.

"We could really be together," he said. "And really make this place great. We could move into town to one of those little colorful bungalows that you like so much. We could get a dog of our own."

"Oh, William," I said. "I love the idea of that. It's perfect really. But I'm just not ready for it yet. I need to be myself for a while before I can be a girlfriend again. I need to figure out what I want. Who I am. The past few months have been exactly what I needed. But I need more time."

He cast his eyes down and fidgeted his hands, making little circles with his thumbs. "Oh," he said.

"And you should stay in New York; this is your only chance. When you have no responsibilities and I'm here taking care of things."

"But I'm lonely there," he said.

"Everyone is," I said. "You'll find your place. We all will. And it's entirely likely that that place is here. For both of us. It just might not exactly be today."

I then stood up to give him a hug and usher him toward the door.

I got in bed alone that night, completely happy. I chose my life; I chose my career; I chose my friends, as unexpected as they might be. I didn't need to post a contented photo on my Instagram with the hashtag #Ichooseme. I just could feel it myself without seeing how many likes I would get on the post.

None of what happened to me this summer was

what I expected when I walked into the tasting room of Bellosguardo on that beautiful May morning, but everything that happened as a result seemed right.

Will I one day live in a brightly colored bungalow with William and a Cavalier King Charles spaniel with a wine-inspired name? I hope so. But for now, I spend my nights alone in the cottage, my days in the tasting room office and managing the hotel. I learn something every day and I get to work with two best middle-aged friends who don't understand the Internet. What a life.

I woke the next morning to sunlight streaming through my window. In my happy exhaustion, I had forgotten to close the blinds. There was a lot to do at the inn, but I took a moment to appreciate the sun and the beautiful place where I found myself. As I looked out the window, our inn guests, Sean and Meg, walked by carrying a basket overflowing with flowers and pastries, a thermos of coffee, and two mugs that I recognized from the castle kitchen. They each had an arm hooked through the basket and they carried it together, smiles on their faces. As they tried to walk carefully down the hill, a croissant fell out of the basket and Tannin darted into the scene, ready to pounce. That dog did love carbs. They put down the basket and tried to get the pastry away from the dog, but he defeated them. Laughing, Sean put his arm around Meg and kissed the top of her head. She looked up into his eyes, and without speaking about it, they broke into a waltz. It was clearly one they had done before. He put his arms around her and they twirled together. He dipped her and she put her leg up in the air. They stayed frozen in the dip just long enough for a virtual photo to be snapped. Then he brought her back up, spun her one last time. A kiss. They separated, bowed to each other, laughed, and then picked up the basket again, swinging it between them. They must have been going toward the picnic area we'd set up among the grapevines. The dog trotted after them, in hope of another pastry. I smiled, stretched, and jumped out of bed, ready to face the day in my new home.

Acknowledgments

If you've been writing and trying to publish a book for more than ten years, there are a lot of people to thank. To say it takes a village to publish a book is an understatement. For me, it's taken almost an entire country. I feel so lucky to have encountered so many talented and supportive people along the way.

To Lauren Grodstein and everyone in our little writing class all those years ago in Brooklyn. Those times in the early days were when I really started feeling like a writer.

To my friends from "writing camp," Helen Wan and Kera Yonker, and to Soren Palmer, who pointed me toward UNCW. I will be forever grateful for you.

To the amazing group of writers and friends I made in North Carolina at UNCW—first to Clyde Edgerton, who took me under his wing and read so many of my failed attempts at novels but was supportive and didn't mock me too much. To Robert Siegel, Karen Bender, Wendy Brenner, Rebecca Lee, David Gessner, Megan Hubbard, Lisa Bertini, you are my heroes. Thank you for everything. To Joel Moore, Bill Carty, Kat Anderson, Melissa Robon, Ashley Hudson, Ashley Talley, Sumanth Prabhaker, Hannah

Abrams, and Emily Smith. God, we had fun. Can we all live together again one day?

To the inimitable Haven Kimmel, who gave me *eleven pages* of single-spaced notes on one of those failed novels. I did everything that you said, Haven, and it made me a better writer. You are so generous and wise.

To Kate Lee, who believed in me first. You gave me hope. Thank you.

To Peter Steinberg, who made it all happen.

To Allison Hunter, you have swooped in and made me better in every way. And thanks to Clare Mao for being such a careful and sensitive reader.

To Elin Hilderbrand, who is just the most amazing Grand Dame of all time. I adore you.

To Rumaan Alam, for your generosity and for always making me laugh when I log on to Twitter.

To Cynthia d'Aprix Sweeney, you are a genius, thank you for your generosity, friendship, and for liking my book.

To Lexi Beach and Quincy Wags, all my love to you and the Astoria Bookshop. You're changing the world one book and dog kiss at a time.

To my colleagues at Ecco, the best backseat drivers in the game. Thank you to Megan Lynch, Zack Wagman, Denise Oswald, Allison Saltzman, and Sara Wood. And to Dan Halpern, I learn something amazing about writing, publishing, food, or just life from you every day. I feel so honored to work with you. To my amazing marketing and publicity team: Meghan Deans, Sonya Cheuse, Ashley Garland, Martin Wilson, James Faccinto, Bridget Read, and Ashlyn Edwards.

To everyone at Dutton, but especially Maya Ziv for believing in me and my book. You made my dreams come true and I will never stop appreciating it. To Maddy Newquist, who helped with so many things. To my incredible publicity team, Jamie Knapp, Becky Odell, and Amanda Walker. To my divine marketer Kayleigh George, your highlighted lists bring me so much joy.

To Christine Ball, John Parsley, LeeAnn Pemberton, Susan Schwartz, Carrie Swetonic, Cassie Garruzzo, and Hannah Dragone. To Eileen Chetti, who caught all the mistakes I made. I also must acknowledge the editorial input of Nina Tavani, an excellent editor and artist.

So many other people have helped along the way as well, talking writing, publishing, books, and sometimes (shockingly) about other things too: Heather Fain, Josh Kendall, Judy Clain, Lee Boudreaux, Tracy Behar, Reagan Arthur, Renee Daley, Roy Gabay, Marcia Rooney, Kathleen Perkins, Michele Karas, Susan Wanklyn, Sabrina Callahan, Lisa Erickson, Pam Brown, Brian Grogan, Andy LeCount, Juliette Shapland, Jen Doll, and Alex Rice, who boosted my confidence when it was very low!

To M. J. Rose, who has talked me through this crazy ride for so many years. Thank you for all of your support and all of the lunches!

My dearest book mavens, Maris Kreizman and Rachel Fershleiser: you are geniuses at spreading the love about books and I so admire you and feel lucky to call you my friends.

My best friend, Megan Heuer, we have been through so much together. Thank you for always being there for me and listening to me complain. To Alafair Burke for being my soul twin and for providing me with a beautiful place to write in and the wine to drink while we did it. To Natalie Sandoval, I'm so glad our dogs brought us together. There's nothing better than a neighborhood friend, even though now our neighborhoods are a country apart. To Melissa Kuzma, longtime book-sharer and friend. To my dear sister, Beth Parker, and Luke Epplin, you've taken care of me (and Leo!) in so many ways. I love our little trips and now our writing retreats. You make me think and get me to explore. Thank you! To my uncle Jake, who has always been there for me. To Ben Olson, you make life better every day. To my parents, Elaine and David Parker, who raised me to love reading and writing and have tolerated me through all of my writing phases. And even though my dog, Leopold Bloom, can't really read, he's good at pretending. He's helped me write this book in so many ways—from couch companion to travel companion—the quote "Outside of a dog, a book is man's best friend, inside of a dog it's too dark to read" couldn't be more true.

And to you, dear reader! If you are reading this, you have read my book all the way to the end. How can I even begin to thank you? As a reader and a publisher, my whole life has been devoted to bringing books into the world and none of it would happen without you. Thank you for reading and sharing books and loving words.

About the Author

Miriam Parker is the associate publisher of Ecco. She has an MFA from UNC Wilmington and a BA from Columbia University. She lives in Brooklyn with her dog, Leopold Bloom.

Books are produced in the United States using U.S.-based materials

Books are printed using a revolutionary new process called THINKtech™ that lowers energy usage by 70% and increases overall quality

Books are durable and flexible because of Smyth-sewing

Paper is sourced using environmentally responsible foresting methods and the paper is acid-free

Center Point Large Print
600 Brooks Road / PO Box 1
Thorndike, ME 04986-0001 USA

(207) 568-3717

US & Canada:
1 800 929-9108
www.centerpointlargeprint.com